Wretched Corruption

Ruthless Desires 4

Elira Firethorn

Copyright © 2023 by Elira Firethorn

All rights reserved.

No portion of this book may be reproduced in any form without written permission from the publisher or author, except as permitted by U.S. copyright law.

This is a work of fiction. Any resemblance to real-life people, events, etc. is coincidence.

To the brave ones who've been called cowards.
I see your hearts.

Playlist & Storyboard

Playlist:
Falling in Love – Cigarettes After Sex
Demons on the Side of My Bed – Teflon Sega
Vendetta – UNSECRET, Krigarè
Let You Go – ILLENIUM, Ember Island
Butterfly – UMI
everything i wanted – Billie Eilish
You Belong to Me – Cat Pierce
Electric – Alina Baraz, Khalid
Helium – Sia
Put On Repeat – Sabrina Claudio
Talking Body (The Young Professionals Remix) – Tove Lo, The Young Professionals
Die For You – VALORANT, Grabbitz

Storyboard:
You can find Wretched Corruption's storyboard by going to pinterest.com/elirafirethorn.

Before You Read

Important: Some minor changes were made to the first three Ruthless Desires books in February 2023. If you read those books before then, you can find a list of all the changes at elirafirethorn.com/ruthless-desires-changes

Wretched Corruption is a dark romance book intended for people over the age of eighteen. Please read over this content list to make sure there's nothing inside this book that could affect you negatively. Put your mental health first please!

Emotional: anxiety attack/flashback, reliving childhood trauma (emotional abuse and neglect, death of a young sibling, police corruption) and dealing with the aftereffects, suicidal thoughts in the past, internalized misogyny, fear of water, running anxious thoughts, aversion to vulnerability, skipping meals (due to anxiety/lack of appetite), feelings of unworthiness, and infidelity (not between the MCs, in backstory).

Physical: insomnia, threats of torture, violence (with guns and knives), and a threat to a child's safety.

Sexual: degradation, bondage, impact play, spitting, semi-public sex (no one sees), domination and submission, and roughness.

Wretched Corruption ends on a mild cliffhanger with an implication for what will happen in book five. As is the case with all the books in this series, you won't find many physical descriptions of the main characters (and most of the side characters) so you can imagine them however you'd like.

The scenes in this book aren't meant to be a guide to kink or BDSM. This is a work of *fiction* and should be read as such.

wretched CORRUPTION

Chapter One

Wren

Note: This book contains darker themes. Please flip back and read the Before You Read section if you haven't already.

It's just water.
It's just water.
It's just water.
I can't get in enough air. My chest feels constricted, like some invisible force is trying to crush me until I'm nothing but dust.
Not enough air.
Need to breathe.
Let me up, please just let me up.
My lungs are aching. My body is screaming for air. My head is pounding, my mind is going fuzzy. Is this what it feels like to die? How close *was* I to death? How close am I now?
My name. Someone's saying my name.
But I can't make it out—the word is a blur, and there's no distinguishable voice. Hell, I can't even see the water in the sink anymore.
"Wren? *Wren.*"

Hands are on my waist, arms encircling me. I'm pulled away from the stability of the counter, but I don't lose my balance. No, something—someone—is holding me up. Someone familiar. Warm.

"Wren, look at me. I've got you. No one's going to hurt you here."

Something soft presses against my cheek. A sweater, I think. It smells nice. Like safety and sandalwood and oranges.

Ell.

"Love, please." He takes one of my hands and presses it to his chest. "Focus on my heartbeat."

A sound leaves my throat. Not a sob—I don't think I'm crying. It's more like a hum, startled and confused and the only acknowledgment of his presence I can manage.

"Take a breath through your nose," he says soothingly. "Just like that, Wren. Now let it out slowly. Good, good. Again." He does it with me once, twice, three times.

As I follow his instructions, I begin to regain my senses. I'm in the kitchen. Late afternoon light is streaming in from the windows. Elliot has one arm tightly around my waist, and the other is pressing my hand into his sweater. His heartbeat is steady as he searches my face, his eyebrows furrowed.

"There you are," he murmurs, his voice weighed down with relief and terror at the same time.

"What..." I glance around, catching the still-full sink in my peripheral vision. My body goes rigid at the sight.

"Hey, it's okay. I've got it." Elliot loosens his hold on me, reaching into the sink to pull the plug. The water level immediately starts going down.

Fuck. What was I thinking?

Probably that I'm about to go on a trip to the fucking ocean and that I need to get it together.

After drying off his hands, Elliot turns toward me. He keeps himself in between me and the sink as he runs a hand over my hair.

Guilt twinges in my chest. Did I scare him? I'm not exactly sure what he just walked into, but I know it was probably concerning.

"Can you tell me what just happened?" He keeps his voice even and gentle despite the panicked gleam in his eyes.

"I . . ." My gaze drifts back to the sink and the receding water. How *did* this start?

After following my line of sight, Elliot pulls me out of the kitchen. The more distance there is between me and the water, the more clearly I can think. It's like I can literally *feel* the tension leaving my body.

In the living room, he sits on the love seat and draws me onto his lap. "Talk to me, love."

My idea comes back to me, and I cringe. It's stupid—god, it's so stupid. But it was the only thing I could think of.

"Being around water has been difficult since . . . well, you know."

Elliot nods slowly, watching me intently, but he doesn't say anything.

"I'm trying to get over it," I say. "I figured the sink is a good place to start. It still scares me, but I can step away from it if I need to."

He frowns. "You didn't look like you were able to do *anything.*"

"I wasn't anticipating it to go that poorly," I mutter. "The first time I did it, it was horrible. But I tried it again yesterday, and it went all right. But today . . ." I shake my head. "I couldn't control my thoughts."

When I meet Elliot's eyes, my stomach sinks. He looks so worried.

"You weren't breathing."

Holding his gaze feels too intense, so I look down, trailing my fingers along the ridges of his sweater. "I felt like I was drowning."

With a sigh, Elliot pulls me closer to him. I rest my head on his shoulder, focusing on taking deep breaths.

"I didn't mean to scare you," I mumble.

"I know, love." His lips feather over my hairline. "But you don't have to do this on your own. You know that, right?"

I nod.

"It's up to you," he says softly. "I don't want to push you into anything you're not comfortable with. Just promise me you won't do anything dangerous."

"I promise." It's not like I can't swim, either. But I'm also planning on avoiding pools and large bodies of water while we're in Florida. The thought of being surrounded by that much water makes me shudder.

"That's why you had Rhett drown Jordan, isn't it?"

"Yeah," I whisper.

It's been three days since we killed Jordan in the basement. I'm glad we got it over with, but I've had a couple moments of regret. Not for killing him, but for ending his life too soon.

Now is one of those moments.

Why am I the one who has to live with the aftereffects of his actions? He's not in pain anymore. He's not *anything* anymore. But I am. I'm tired and angry and trapped in my own thoughts and terrified I'll never find a way out.

In a way, death was mercy for Jordan. And I hate that we gave it to him. At the same time, regretting that we didn't torture him more is such an unexpected thought for me to have. It's unsettling.

"Are you still okay to . . ." Elliot trails off, grimacing, and I understand why. He was about to give me the opportunity to ask for something he can't really follow through on.

"I'm good, Ell. Promise."

We leave tomorrow for the job Ludo Holloway hired the guys for. It's entirely too late to back out now, and we both know it. The guys need to get as close to Ludo as possible, and this is the best opportunity they've ever been presented with.

After a long breath, Elliot nods. "You'll always have one of us with you. And if you ever find yourself alone, no one will know where we'll be. You'll be safe. I swear, Wren, I'm never letting anyone hurt you again."

"I know," I whisper.

I don't.

It's not that I doubt how much they'll try to keep me safe. But everyone's human. Everyone makes mistakes. In a life so full of danger and violence, of secrets and lies, how can anyone guarantee their own safety, let alone someone else's? The guys are good at what they do, but no one can be *that* good, right?

Still . . .

"I trust you."

And I mean it.

The three of them have done nothing but care for me ever since we came together. And based on the way they've all been looking at me the past couple days, they're about to get ten times more protective.

As if they weren't before.

Last weekend is the perfect example. When Jordan kidnapped me, I was barely even in that house for twenty-four hours. The guys did everything they could to get to me. *That's* what matters. As for future dangers, we'll deal with them as they come. As long as I'm not taken from them again, I'll be okay.

Rhett and Oliver come into the living room, hands clasped together.

"Hey, I was thinking we could head to the museum a little early to—" Oliver stops abruptly when he gets a better look at us. I must look like shit, because his smile fades. "You guys okay?"

"Yeah. I just had a flashback, that's all."

Rhett's expression hardens, like I shouldn't be brushing this off. He doesn't say anything, though.

The remnants of Oliver's smile morph into a full-on frown. "Did something trigger it? Or did it just happen out of the blue?"

My stomach twists. Why do I have to be such a mess? What if we get to Florida and the mere sight of the ocean makes me panic? What the hell am I going to do? "It . . ."

Instantly, Oliver is on his knees in front of me. Taking my hands in his, he gazes up at me and says, "It's okay, Wren. You can tell us."

I squeeze my eyes shut. "I can't look at water without thinking about drowning. I was trying to work through it, so I filled the kitchen sink with water, but it backfired and I froze up. It felt . . . awful."

"She wasn't breathing when I found her," Elliot adds in, tightening his arm around me.

"Princess," Oliver murmurs, and I hate the concern mixed with disappointment in his voice. "Why didn't you tell us?"

"I was hoping it'd go away," I mumble, squirming in Elliot's lap.

"Wren. Look at me."

Grudgingly, I open my eyes, terrified that Oliver will be looking up at me with hurt and more disappointment. Instead, I find a gentle compassion shimmering in his eyes that makes my throat ache.

"It's okay," he whispers. "We'll take it one day at a time. We're here with you no matter what, got it?"

All I can manage is a relieved nod. They've had to deal with so many emotions and problems from me. How they haven't run out of patience and understanding yet is beyond me.

"Got it," I say, squeezing his hands.

"What were you going to suggest, Ol?" Elliot says.

"That we head out a little early," he says, not taking his sad eyes off of me. "So we could get back for ice cream with enough time for our stomachs to settle before bed."

"That sounds good to me." Elliot glances between me and Rhett, and we nod in agreement.

Oliver tugs me to my feet. "You wanna get ready with me?"

"That sounds nice."

"Perfect." He kisses both Rhett and Elliot. "You two won't know what to do with yourselves when we come back down."

The thought puts a smile on my face. When Oliver dressed me to go to Evolve, Rhett and Elliot's eyes practically bugged out of their heads when they saw us. I thought they looked hot as well, I was just too focused on the fact that I was going to *the* Evolve to show it.

Upstairs, Oliver stops the second his door is closed. "Princess. Are you really okay? If you'd prefer, we can stay in and watch movies and cuddle and—"

Placing my hands on his shoulders, I cut him off with a kiss. "I'm good, I promise." With the best smile I can manage, I say, "Now, tell me what you're wearing so I can figure out what I should put on."

Eyeing me, Oliver says, "I actually have a sweater that I think will fit you perfectly. It's a little small on me, but I've kept it around for . . . reasons."

He doesn't elaborate, instead pulling me into his closet. I smile at the array of colors and variety of styles as he goes through a dresser at the back.

My gaze drifts to a dress that's separate from all the other clothes. It's small, a child's dress, and it looks vintage. The blue fabric is faded, and there's a faint stain on the skirt.

"Aha! Here it is." Oliver whips around, holding a forest green sweater in his hands. His eyes flick to the dress, and I realize I'm holding the material between my fingers.

I drop my arm. "Sorry."

With a halfhearted shrug, he says, "You're allowed to touch it."

I don't. I just look at it. "Whose was it?"

"My mom's," he says softly. "And then it was my sister's, and then she gave it to Sammy when she grew out of it." Oliver pauses, and I don't miss the heartbroken look he tries to hide by running a hand over his face. "Rhett's dad was going to throw it out after Sammy died, so we stole it back."

"Oh," I say quietly. *How awful.* "I'm glad you got it."

He nods, placing the sweater in my hands. "Here. I can—uh. I'll just stay in here so you can get changed."

"Thanks."

After earlier, I'm definitely not in the right headspace to take my clothes off in front of another person. It's silly, the idea that a couple layers of fabric feel like armor, but I can't help it. So I step out of the closet to take my T-shirt off.

The sweater is soft against my skin, and it fits almost perfectly. The sleeves are a bit too long, but I don't mind. It just makes me feel cozier. Paired with my jeans, I bet I look cute.

"I'm done," I call, stepping in front of Oliver's mirror. I was right—it's a simple look, but it does look cute.

He comes up behind me, his hands on my waist. I can just see the dark shirt he has on. He left the top buttons undone, and it makes my mouth water.

Fuck, he even has his sleeves rolled up.

"Oh, that's hot."

It takes me a second to realize the words slipped from my mouth. I groan from embarrassment, but Oliver snickers, kissing my neck.

"Can I do your makeup, too?"

"Sure."

With a grin, Oliver grabs my hand and pulls me into the bathroom. He lifts me onto the counter next to the sink before stepping in between my legs. "God, I love you, princess."

"I love you, too."

He looks like he's about to reach into a drawer, but he stops and embraces me instead. My body is pressed to his in as many places as possible as he captures my mouth in a kiss. His lips move against mine so softly, so tenderly, like he needs to be gentle with me or I'll break.

Maybe that's the case. Or maybe not. One minute, I feel like I'm the strongest woman in the world. But the next, I feel like I *will* break if someone even looks at me wrong. It's a tumultuous roller coaster I can't seem to get off of.

When Oliver pulls away, I sigh, resting my forehead against his. I've grown a lot as a person over the past couple years. I've found strength in times when I thought I'd wither away. And being with these three men has given me more determination, more resolve. I feel like I can *keep* growing with them.

"I'm excited to go on a date with you all," I say.

Oliver smiles. "Group dates are fun. So are one-on-one dates, but I think I'll quite like having all four of us together."

All four of us. The phrase has warmth cascading down my body from my head to my toes.

"Have you ever been to the museum?"

"Me? Nah. Rhett's gone before, though."

"I've never been either," I say as Oliver starts applying makeup to my cheeks. "Ava went a couple months ago. She thinks I'll like it."

"Rhett thinks you will too. Was his idea."

Oliver continues with the makeup, tilting my chin up with one hand and working with the other. He looks happy, a faint smile never fully leaving his face.

"You like doing this?"

Oliver nods. "I do, yeah. Because I love it and because it reminds me of happy memories."

"Oh?"

"I loved playing dress up as a kid. Used to do it with my little sister all the time. Sometimes Sammy would join in too, but she was a little younger than Maria, so they didn't have play dates together often. My mom has a whole scrapbook of the different looks we came up with. Maybe I'll show you sometime."

My stomach does a little backflip at the thought of meeting his family. Then it melts at the thought of young Oliver playing with his little sister. "I always wanted a sibling."

"Mmm, you get a built-in sister by being with me, so I guess it's a dream come true." He winks, probably because he knows *he's* a dream come true all by himself. "Maria will love you."

Hope flares in my chest, and I sit up straighter. "Really?"

"Oh, she already does. Ever since she saw us together at the ball, she's been bugging me to let you guys meet. Maybe we'll take you to our next Friday lunch."

My shoulders sag. "Ah. I don't think that'll work, O. I have to go back to the coffee shop after this week. My boss is already annoyed enough."

For a second, it looks like Oliver is about to protest. But then he sighs and shakes his head. "Then we'll find another time for you and Maria to meet. As long as you're ready, that is. If you want more time before meeting the family, that's understandable."

"I'd like to meet her. And your mom."

He boops me on the nose with a brush. "Then we'll make it happen, princess. Now close your eyes. It's time for your eyeshadow."

"What color are you using?"

"Same as your sweater. This stuff is super pigmented," he says, swiping the brush over my eyelids. "I love it. Don't use it a lot, though."

"Why not?"

He laughs, a tired and almost bitter sound. "Work-life balance is almost nonexistent when you're trying to avenge your little sister's death. Most of the time, our jobs require blending in, staying in the background. Not exactly conducive to wearing colorful makeup."

"I guess not."

"But," he says brightly, "it just makes it more fun when I get to. The red is my favorite."

"That makes sense."

"Does it now?"

I grin. Even with my eyes closed, I can imagine the smirk on Oliver's face. "It's your favorite color? Dark red?"

"Someone's observant." After a couple more strokes with the brush, he says, "You can open your eyes now."

"So why forest green today?"

He shrugs, not answering, but his smirk widens.

"Oliver!"

"You'll see," he says in a singsong voice.

Once he finishes with my makeup, he moves onto his. I watch as he applies it confidently, adding a little red eyeliner underneath his lower lash line. When he finishes, he puts everything away and helps me off the counter. His hands linger on my waist.

"Princess?"

"Hmm?"

"I'm really glad we have you."

I smile, kissing him. "I'm really glad I have you, too."

Chapter Two

Elliot

We did this to her.

I've been trying to keep that thought at bay. But seeing Wren in the kitchen like that? *Fuck.*

She was gripping the edge of the sink so hard her arms were shaking. She wasn't breathing either, like she was so deep in a flashback she actually thought she was underwater.

This is exactly what I was afraid of.

It doesn't matter, though. Wren is one of us now. And even if we could break things off, I wouldn't want to. We belong together.

I just wish we'd been more careful.

Trust is such a hard thing to earn and such an easy thing to break. It's even harder to build it back, I'd say. We didn't intentionally betray Wren, but we promised we'd keep her safe, and then we failed.

And now? Now we have to prove to her that we'll never let something like that happen again. I think the worst thing is that the only way to do that is with time.

As I watch her and Oliver head upstairs, I wonder if it would be a bad idea to suggest that Wren start going to therapy. I know a psychologist who could help her—he's helped me, Rhett, and Oliver a lot over the years. The problem is how Wren will take it. Some people view needing therapy as a sign that they're broken. Unfixable. That's the last thing I want Wren to feel.

"You look like you have a lot on your mind." Rhett perches on the arm of the love seat, towering over me. "Talk."

"We need to help her." Rubbing my face, I work through the different ways we could bring it up to her. Or maybe she's already thought of it? Or maybe I should mind my own business and let her handle it the way she wants to.

With a hum of agreement, Rhett slides onto the cushion. It's a tight fit, so our bodies are pressed up against each other. Normally, it's something Rhett would avoid, but it doesn't seem to be bugging him.

"Relax," he murmurs, tilting my chin up with two fingers so I have to look into his eyes. The smell of cedar and sage acts as a soothing balm to my stress. "You've been tense all week."

"I'm worried. About Wren. And Ol. Fuck, I'm worried about all three of you."

He sighs, a knowing smile flitting across his features. "Get on the floor. Face away from me and sit in between my legs."

I don't question him. At this point, I'm too tired to think an independent thought. As I move to the floor, he adjusts himself so his legs are spread.

"Deep breaths," he says. As I lean against the love seat, his hands find my shoulders, massaging lightly.

"You don't have to do this."

"I'll do it every night if I have to. Now relax."

I try. After a couple deep breaths, some of the tension leaves my body, and Rhett starts massaging deeper into my muscles. I groan, and my eyes slide shut.

"I'd fuck the stress out of you if we had time," he mutters. "Maybe tomorrow."

"We're gonna be on a plane tomorrow."

"Only for a few hours. Not that that's ever stopped us."

As a smile spreads across my face, I say, "True."

There's silence for a few minutes. Then Rhett says, "Tell me what you're planning."

"For Florida?"

"No. I don't want to think about that tonight. What are you planning to do to help Wren?"

"I don't know," I say defeatedly. "And I don't want to tell her what to do, either."

"Sometimes just being there is enough," Rhett says quietly. "Especially when it comes to healing. You can't make someone do that."

I sigh. "Yeah."

"She needs to take things at her own pace."

"And what if she tries to push herself too much?"

"Then we'll step in." He kisses the top of my head. "We aren't going to stand by and let her hurt herself, I can tell you that much."

For the next couple minutes, Rhett continues working through the knots in my shoulders. Then he tugs my head back so I'm looking up at the ceiling. He leans over me, gripping my chin to hold my head in place, and kisses me.

"We'll be okay," he says. "Just six more months."

And then we're free.

Guilt pangs in my chest for thinking of it that way. Sammy deserves justice, and we decided she'll get it within the next six months. It means we have to change our current plans for Ludo, which is a pain in the ass, but it also means we can see the light at the end of the tunnel.

We've been working toward revenge for so long that I've forgotten how to exist outside of it. I'm tired—we all are. And while I can't wait to take Ludo down, I also can't wait for all of this to be behind us.

"I should get changed," Rhett says, releasing my chin. "Pretty sure whatever Wren and O end up wearing will be nothing like this." He gestures to his current outfit—sweatpants and a black T-shirt.

"Since when do you care about what you wear?"

"I don't. But Oliver does. And I'll always care about him."

Well, can't argue with him there.

"Wait, you already know what he's planning on wearing?"

"Maybe." With another kiss to the side of my head, Rhett carefully disentangles himself from me and stands. "You'll see."

I'd try to convince him to tell me, but I know better than that. When Rhett doesn't want to admit something, there's almost nothing that'll get him to open up. So I watch him go, because how could I not? It doesn't matter what Rhett is wearing—his ass always looks good.

With a sigh, I get up from the floor and head to the kitchen. I definitely haven't had enough water today, so I pour myself a glass. Not the smartest thing to do before a long drive into the city, but I'll survive.

It was Rhett's idea to do something nice for Wren. She's been through hell the past week or so, and I think we all want to give her the best distraction we can. She deserves more than the absolute terror that was in her eyes earlier.

So we planned a small date. Nothing too extravagant, especially since we leave for Florida tomorrow. But hopefully it'll help all of us to de-stress.

"Ell?" Oliver calls after a couple minutes. "Where are you?"

"Kitchen," I yell back, taking a swig of water.

Just then, Wren steps into my view with Oliver behind her. I freeze. Apparently, I also forget how to function as a human being, because I swallow my water wrong and drive myself into a coughing fit.

"You," I wheeze in between gasping breaths, "little *shit.*"

Wren pauses, doubt flickering over her features. But then Oliver throws an arm around her shoulders and chuckles.

"No worries, princess. He's not talking to you."

That fucking color.

Once I stop coughing, I say, "Wren. Come here. Now."

Her eyes widen in surprise at my demanding tone, but she doesn't hesitate. The second she's within my grasp, I pull her into me and waste no time fusing her mouth to mine.

He even did her eyeshadow with it.

Grabbing onto my sides, Wren rises onto her tiptoes to deepen the kiss. My thumb brushes over her cheek as I groan into her mouth.

"You look perfect," I say against her lips. "So fucking beautiful. I'm never letting you out of this sweater."

"What—" Wren pulls away slightly, looking between me and the sweater, and then she laughs. "O! Why didn't you tell me?!"

Oliver grins. "Because this was funnier."

"Fuck," I hear Rhett say behind me. "Did I miss his reaction?"

"Yeah, sorry," Oliver replies. "I didn't realize you were gonna go get changed." His gaze travels up and down Rhett's body before he slowly licks his lips. "You look nice."

I can't stop ogling all three of them. But Rhett is frowning at Oliver, his arms crossed over his chest.

"Well," Oliver says, seemingly oblivious to the way Rhett is looking at him, "are we ready to go?"

"I don't think so." The words don't come out harshly or angrily. On the contrary, Rhett's tone is firm but not intimidating. I doubt his calm demeanor will last long, though.

"What?" Oliver asks.

"Go finish getting ready."

With a nervous glance at Wren, Oliver says, "I am ready."

"We talked about this," Rhett replies darkly.

"Look, it's fine—"

"Go. get. ready."

"I *am*. Let's—"

"No." Marching up to Oliver, Rhett grabs him and throws him over his shoulder.

"Hey! You can't just—"

"We'll be back," Rhett says roughly, keeping a firm grip on Oliver as he stalks out of the kitchen.

Wren watches the encounter with wide eyes before turning to me. "What was that about?"

"You'll see."

Oliver has worked a lot on his insecurities over the years. I suppose it makes sense that adding Wren to our group is unearthing some of them. We *did* talk about this, but one conversation is rarely enough to solve a problem.

When Rhett and Oliver come back, Oliver is wearing some of his favorite pieces of jewelry. A couple rings, a bracelet, and then two necklaces. One is a silver chain and the other is a necklace that has a coin hanging from it. It's from the first international trip the three of us ever took together.

"*Now* we're ready," Rhett says, giving Oliver a pointed look. Then he moves his gaze to Wren, like he's waiting for her to say something, but she's so fixated on Oliver that she doesn't notice.

For a second, it looks like she wants to talk, but she doesn't.

"Let's go." I reach for my keys, but Rhett grabs my arm.

"I'll drive. You need to relax."

In Rhett's truck, I take the passenger seat, and Wren and Oliver get in the back. Once we're on the road, I settle against the seat and close my eyes. *Damn.* Rhett is right—I didn't realize how tired I was until he pointed it out.

"I love you for who you are," Wren says quietly enough that she probably thinks Rhett and I don't hear.

Oliver stays silent for a minute. Then, "I'm just..."

"*You.* You're you, Oliver. You're not Elliot. You're not Rhett. And I don't expect you to be, just like I don't expect them to be you. You're charming and funny and cool and sweet and caring and *you*. And every time I discover a new part of you, I fall *more* in love with you."

Oliver sighs. "I guess I just figured that since you were attracted to Ell first, he was more your type."

"Kindness is my type, and you fit that perfectly," she says, and I can hear the smile in her voice. "And I was actually attracted to all three of you the first time I saw you. Ell didn't come first."

"Oh," Oliver mumbles.

"Come here," she says, taking his face in her hands and kissing him lightly. "Don't ever feel like you have to hide yourself from me. Okay?"

"Okay."

Hearing Wren's reassurances takes a huge weight off my chest. And when Rhett's large, warm hand rests on my thigh, I'm lulled even deeper into a state of peacefulness.

The last thought I remember before nodding off is that Rhett has been touching me more lately, and that I hope it's because he's doing better.

...

Walking into an art museum's brightly-lit lobby isn't the most appealing thing to do after waking up from a nap. My head feels foggy, and my eyelids are still too heavy. But Rhett heads to the museum's cafe as soon as we arrive and grabs me a coffee.

As we wander through the museum, I sip it, welcoming the energy the caffeine gives me. The four of us have a lot of fun, going from exhibit to exhibit and exploring together. By the time I've finished my coffee, I'm fully awake and happier than ever.

Rhett was right to suggest this. We all need space to reconnect. Getting out and doing something with them instead of holing up at home and prepping for Florida is a nice change of pace.

"I like this one," Wren says, gazing at a large European painting high up on the wall.

With a snort, Oliver points to one of the people in the background of the painting. "He looks like he's taking a really bad shit."

"OLIVER!"

"What? Tell me I'm wrong, princess."

I hide my smile by pretending to take a sip out of my empty coffee cup. That's *exactly* what the guy in the painting looks like.

Grumbling out an admission that Oliver is right, Wren grabs his hand and pulls him to the next painting. Even with a grudging frown on her face, I can't peel my eyes off of her.

Of course, Rhett notices. What *doesn't* he notice? He chuckles as I follow after Wren.

"What?" I say. "It's not my fault she looks like a goddamned dream in forest green."

"As I've said before, you think she looks like a goddamned dream in anything," Oliver calls over his shoulder. Then he winks at Wren. "Or nothing."

I can't even pretend he's wrong. Wren shoots me an amused smile, swaying her hips slightly as she walks.

"Fuck," I mutter.

The next room is a series of painted American landscapes. Some are more muted while others are more colorful, but you can tell with all of them that the artist has taken a lot of time to hone their skills.

"These are all so pretty," Wren says, turning to get a three-sixty of the whole room. When she sees that my eyes have already made their way back to her, she hides a giggle behind her hand.

"It's rude to stare, Ell," Oliver says playfully.

"Shut up. This is your fault anyway."

With a snicker, Oliver comes up beside me and whispers in my ear, "Maybe next time, we'll *both* wear forest green."

I groan.

"Oliver!" Wren exclaims. "Stop teasing him."

"Not a chance." Oliver kisses me, not bothering to keep it sweet and chaste even though we're in a public place. He grabs my head and kisses me so hard I almost forget that I'm about two seconds away from dragging him into a closet and spanking some sense into him.

Almost.

When Oliver finally lets me go, he's grinning. "I love when I make you forget how to think."

Tilting her head, Wren watches me with an amused expression. She's quickly distracted by something behind me, though. "Oh, that one's extra pretty."

I turn to check out the painting she's talking about, almost missing the way Rhett ducks down and whispers in Oliver's ear. They both look at me mischievously before Rhett walks over and plucks my cup from my hand.

"We're gonna run to the bathroom. Have... *fun*."

"Rhett," I hiss. "We're in public."

"What?" He shrugs innocently. "I just said to have fun."

I roll my eyes. "Don't pretend—"

"No, *you* don't pretend." The smirk growing on Rhett's face makes me wish we had the luxury of privacy that home provides. "You're not going to pass up this opportunity, pretty boy. Drop the propriety act."

I bite my tongue. *Why is he always right, dammit?*

"That's better." He drops a kiss to my cheek before grabbing Oliver's hand. They saunter out of view until I'm left with Wren.

Holding my arm out to her, I say, "C'mere, love."

I love the way she doesn't hesitate. She enters my reach, and I sweep her up into my arms, twirling her around. With a gasp, she grabs onto my shoulders, still holding on as I set her down gently.

"You really think I look that pretty in green?" she asks, brows furrowed.

I laugh. "*Pretty?* You're a piece of art all on your own, love. But seeing you in my favorite color? It does something to me I can't even describe. All I can think about is fucking devouring you. Touching you." My head dips down, and I kiss her neck before saying lowly in her ear, "Making you scream for the whole museum to hear."

She whimpers, squeezing her thighs together.

"Am I turning you on?"

She slides her hands down my body. "You know you are."

Running my thumb over my lip, I say, "You want me to do something about it?"

She groans, nodding.

I trace a finger across her jawbone, down her neck and chest, and in between her breasts. "Use your words, Wren."

"Please," she whispers. "Do whatever you want to me."

That's all it takes. Grabbing her, I spin her around and press her back to my front. We're standing so we're right in front of the painting she pointed out earlier, which is exactly how I want her.

"Oh god, oh god, *right here?*" she squeaks out. "But the security cam—cameras—oh, *oohhhh* never mind." Wren's head falls back onto my shoulder as I brush my fingertips over her nipples.

"Look at the painting, love. Tell me what you see." As I say it, I undo her jeans. The texture of her panties isn't the soft cotton I was expecting. She's wearing something lacy, and the thought makes me groan.

"It's . . . beautiful," she gasps as I run a finger over the fabric.

"Go on." I dip my fingers into her panties.

Her body melts from the lightest stroke against her clit. "Ell, god."

"What do you see, Wren?"

"The sky is so colorful," she manages. "Pinks and purples and blues."

"A little orange, too," I add.

"Y-yeah."

As I circle her clit, I nip at her neck. "What else do you see?"

"There's—fuck. What if someone comes in?"

"I'm watching." I pause my finger. "Unless you want me to stop?"

She lets out a tortured whine and shakes her head. "Please keep going."

"Then keep describing the painting to me."

I can see it for myself—of course I can. But exploring the minds of Oliver and Rhett has always been one of my favorite pastimes. The same is true for Wren. There's so much to learn about her—about all three of them—and it's my lifelong goal to never stop diving deeper into who they are.

"You can do it, love." I want to see the painting through her eyes. I want to know what parts stand out to her, what she appreciates the most.

Inhaling deeply, she continues. "The artist added in some purples and pinks to the snow on the mountaintop. Like it's—" Her breath hitches as I start moving my finger again, "—like it's reflecting the sky. It makes the whole thing so much fuller."

Gazing at the painting, I realize she's right. "I hadn't noticed that."

"They did the same thing with the water. Just in parts of it." The last sentence comes out as a whisper. Her breaths are heavier than they were a minute ago, and it makes me smile.

Trailing kisses down her neck, I ask, "What's your favorite part?"

She whimpers. "The . . . the angle, I think."

"Oh?" I circle my finger faster, making her jerk against me.

"Most paintings of lakes and mountains are from below, at eye level," she explains. "But this one is from above, like we're looking at it from another mountain. I like the different perspective."

"Interesting."

She tenses. "Is that not what you were expecting me to say?"

"I was expecting you to say whatever you thought, love. Is that what you did?"

"Yes."

"Good girl," I say lowly in her ear.

She whimpers again, arching into me. Fuck, I love the sounds she makes.

"Give me your hands."

"What?"

"Put them behind your back." It's not like I can tie her up in the middle of the museum, but that doesn't mean I can't restrain her. I love seeing her squirm and wiggle helplessly as she comes.

After she obeys, I grab her wrists, holding them in place. Her fingers brush against my dick, and I groan. If I knew we could get away with it, I'd bend her over and fuck her right here. But I know I won't be able to keep an eye out for anyone else wandering through.

"Ell," she moans. Her body is so riddled with tension that she's beginning to tremble.

"Are you close, love?"

"So close." She tries to turn her head to look at me.

"Uh uh. You know what you should be focusing on." My finger slows.

"Ell, please. I want to kiss you."

"And I want you to be a good girl and do as I say so I can let you come."

The helpless sound she makes has me hiding a smirk in her hair. She tries to free her arms, but I keep my grip on her wrists firm.

"Look at the painting, love."

She acquiesces, staring at it.

"That's it," I murmur, picking up the pace of my finger again. When she shudders against me, I pepper her neck with kisses. And then she comes apart silently in my arms, throwing her head back until it hits my shoulder. "Look. at. the. painting."

With a quiet sob, she does. I'm still stroking her clit with a feather-light touch, not letting her come down all the way.

"Tell me what else you see."

"Ell, I can't—*ahhh*—" Her knees go weak momentarily, but she's able to catch herself.

"Lean against me and do as I say, Wren."

"*Shit.* The—the brushstrokes. They added a lot of details to the pine trees, with all those tiny lines. The artist didn't have to, but they did anyway."

"See? That wasn't so hard." I pull my hand out of her pants and lick my fingers clean. "Delectable."

She whimpers, squirming, but I still have her wrists pinned behind her. Gently, I let go and spin her around. Her eyes instantly flit to my mouth, and they flare slightly when I lick my lips, savoring the taste of her.

"Ell, please." She rises onto her tiptoes, clutching my sweater.

With my clean hand, I cup her chin and kiss her softly. I eat up her moans, moving my lips more hungrily when she wraps her arms around my neck.

She sighs against my mouth. "I love tasting myself on you."

Pulling away, I gaze into her eyes. The forest green eyeshadow is almost exactly the same shade as the sweater, and it does wonders for her. Maybe I'm biased, but I don't care. "If I could, I'd never let any of you wear another color."

She laughs. "No wonder Oliver kept this."

I kiss her again—can't fucking help it. And then my hand is sliding into her panties like it has no other purpose but to please her. "Come for me again," I whisper.

She moans, her nails digging into my shoulders through my clothes. As I swipe a finger over her clit, she bites her lip to keep herself quiet. Normally I'd tell her to be loud, but this isn't the place for that, no matter what I said earlier.

I hear footsteps to my right. When I turn to look, it's just Ol and Rhett. Oliver's eyes are lit up with amusement.

"Told you," I hear Rhett mutter to him.

Oliver snickers, shoving his hands into the pockets of those black skinny jeans that make him look sexy as hell. At the sound, Wren turns her head to look at him.

"Eyes on me, love," I say, gripping her chin with my free hand and forcing her to meet my gaze. "And don't look away."

She's still so wound up, I'm sure it won't take her long to come again. Especially since Oliver and Rhett are watching. Our girl has some exhibitionist tendencies, and I'm happy to fulfill them. We all are.

"Do you like that they're watching you?" I ask quietly enough that only she can hear. "That they want to touch you, too?"

She nods. Her eyes are wide and full of desperation.

Just the way I like her.

I slip a finger inside of her, playing with her clit with my thumb. Wren tries to hold in her squeak of surprise, but she does a poor job of it.

I click my tongue. "Someone's going to hear you."

"I can't—I can't help it."

Rhett ducks closer to Oliver, watching us intently. "Ten bucks says she'll scream loud enough that we get kicked out."

"Nah," Oliver says. "Ell is too practical for that. He'll keep her quiet."

"Oh god," Wren gasps, and Oliver is right. I clap a hand over her mouth as she cries out and comes all over my fingers.

I move my thumb from her clit, focusing on curling my fingers deeper into her. It does the trick, because her eyes roll into the back of her head. She groans, the sound muffled by my hand.

"Fuck," I say lowly, watching her. All I want is to pull her somewhere with a little more privacy, strip her down, and wrench that reaction from her as many times as I can.

As I ease my hand out of her panties, Wren practically withers. I lick my fingers clean and wrap my other arm around her while she catches her breath. Her eyes are half-closed, and a sated smile graces her features.

Rhett hands Oliver ten dollars, grumbling something about how Wren *would've* screamed loudly enough if I hadn't silenced her. Just then, we hear a couple voices. Wren's eyes blow wide as she quickly zips and buttons her pants. I help adjust her sweater, kissing the tip of her nose.

"Too close?" I ask when she still looks nervous.

She bites her lip before grabbing my hand and grinning. "Maybe just close enough."

Chapter Three

Rhett

Ever since Wren stepped into the kitchen back home, Elliot has practically been drooling over her. He loves when we wear his favorite color, so I'm not even surprised. Hell, I practically expected this, which is why I made plans to drag Oliver off to the bathroom. Elliot tries to protest, and I act annoyed even though I'm not. He's cute when he's flustered.

This is supposed to be a date with all four of us, yes. But I don't mind giving Elliot and Wren a quick moment alone. We won't be gone for long.

In the bathroom, I stalk toward Oliver. He gives me a quizzical look, but it's quickly replaced with realization when I back him into the sink. I place my hands on the counter on either side of him, effectively caging him in.

"I swear you wore these jeans just to tease me," I mutter.

"It crossed my mind."

We stare at each other for a second. A challenge sparks in Oliver's eyes, a silent *Are you going to do anything about it?*

And fuck.

Yeah, I think I will.

Our mouths crash together as I press my body against his. His dick is already hard, just from me cornering him in the bathroom. I'd say I'm surprised, but I'm not.

When Oliver licks across my bottom lip, I open my mouth just enough for him to get a taste of me. Then I slide my tongue inside his mouth, reminding him who's in charge. He groans, rolling his hips into mine.

"You never did have any patience, did you, O?"

Pulling away, I spin Oliver around so he's facing away from me. I undo his pants and shove them down with his boxers. Not all the way—just enough that his cock springs free.

"Spit on my hand."

He does, and I do too before reaching around him and spreading the saliva on his dick. With an expert grip, I stroke up and down, watching Oliver's reaction in the mirror. He's trying not to make any noise, holding onto the counter for balance.

"Rhett, anyone could walk in," he protests halfheartedly.

"Mmm, and they'd find you in such a compromising position, wouldn't they?" I squeeze gently at his tip before making my way back down.

"Shit," he hisses, gripping the counter more tightly.

He knows I'm right. He's the one with his dick out in a public bathroom, not me. Not that I'd care either way—I stopped caring about other people's opinions years ago. Oliver has come a long way in doing the same, but apparently he needs another lesson.

"Look at me," I murmur softly.

He meets my gaze in the mirror.

"You don't have to hide parts of yourself from her."

He grunts as I lightly squeeze the head of his cock again before moving back down, falling into a pattern. "Are we really having this conversation right now?"

"There's no better time." My lips brush up his neck until they're right next to his ear. "You're always more obedient when you want to come."

Oliver lets out a low whine, and it's one of the most delicious sounds I've ever heard. He moves his hips in time with my hand, and I can't help but smirk at him.

"So desperate, aren't you?"

"Rhett—*fuck*."

"Are you going to listen to me?"

Oliver is giving me a look that's half lust and half irritation. But he pants out, "Fine. Yes. I'll listen."

"Good boy," I say lowly.

He melts. Fucking putty in my hands.

"She's not going to judge you."

"I—I know."

"And self-expression is nothing to be ashamed of."

It takes him a second to catch his breath before he says, "I know, I promise."

"Then why? Why did I have to haul you back upstairs?"

"Because—fuck, god, Rhett. Shit." He breaks our gaze, staring at my hand as I work his cock.

"Spit on my hand again."

He does immediately.

"See? So obedient."

"Damn you, Rhett."

"Pretty sure you'd rather fuck me."

He groans in response, pumping his hips forward. "Why do you always do this to me?"

My smirk widens. "Because I love you."

Oliver's eyes snap upward again, locking with mine, an almost panicked look on his face. I've been saying it more lately—at least I think I have been. It's not enough, but it's what I can give.

I'm trying.

"Rhett," he pants.

I promise I'm trying.

"Why are you hiding parts of yourself if you know you don't have to?" I say, switching the subject before the intimacy of the moment makes me feel like my skin is on fire.

"I'm just in my head," he forces out. "I know we can trust her."

With a sigh, I press my face into his neck. That's not something I can help with. All I can do is be here and try to be supportive. And dammit, I hate it. If I could take all his problems away and bear the weight of them by myself, I would.

"I love you, too," he says quietly.

"I know," I murmur against his hot skin.

After that, I continue moving my hand up and down his dick until he's nothing more than goo. When he finishes, he's barely able to keep quiet. His cum covers my hand, and I make him lick it all off. He does so with no protest.

"Such a good boy," I say, shoving my fingers into his mouth.

He sucks them greedily. I love when he's like this. Compliant and cum happy. He'd probably do anything I asked him to. Not that I have anything in mind—we need to get back.

I know from multiple fuck-ups that Oliver needs affection after sex. When we were younger, I left him alone right after because it's what I needed, so I assumed it's what he needed, too. Instead, it made him feel used and unloved, which was the exact opposite of what I was trying to accomplish.

We had to find different types of aftercare that worked for both of us. Cuddling after that much intimacy is hard on me, so we found other things that work. Lazy conversations, showering together, touches here and there or with enough distractions, et cetera. We make it work.

But now, my attention is about to be divided between him, Elliot, and Wren, and I don't want him feeling un-prioritized. So after I wash my hands, I keep an arm around him as we walk back. It doesn't have the best effect on me, but I can manage.

Or so I think. But my father's voice invades my thoughts much more quickly than I anticipated.

You don't deserve my forgiveness.

Nothing good in you.

Oliver slides my arm off his shoulders. "Stop."

"I want to."

Say it back, boy.

"No." Oliver shies away when I try to pull him close again. "I don't like where you go when you force yourself into it like this. It's like I lose you for a few minutes."

Now get up and give me a hug.

My chest tightens.

That's better. No more bullshit, all right? You're old enough to know better.

Fuck. I'm slipping. I shouldn't've tried. I shouldn't've—

"Hey." Oliver's voice keeps me tethered to the present. Out of habit, he moves to grab my hand, but he pulls back at the last moment.

The action cracks my heart in two. I crave his touch and the comfort it brings, but I know it'll be anything but soothing. It'll throw me farther into moments where I had no control. My body will seize up, my heart will beat too fast, and I'll end up shoving him away.

"Look at me." Oliver's voice is soft, like he's talking to a scared kitten. He hovers close without touching me. "Stay with me."

With a gulp, I focus on his eyes. I used to dream about getting lost in them when we were younger. There's so much to them. Like how they soften and somehow pull me in whenever he looks at me, or how they sparkle when he gets that stupid grin on his face. There's so much depth, so much care, just in this one part of him.

Fuck. This man can put me in a goddamn chokehold just by looking at me. No touch required.

"I'm here," I whisper, and I am. My father's voice always fades when I can focus on something else.

"Good. And I feel fine, okay? Promise." He smiles at me.

"I just didn't want you to think I don't care," I mumble. "I didn't want you to feel used."

"I know you care. And I know your limits."

"But—"

"Uh uh, no. I'm not asking you to give me something when I know doing so will hurt you." His smile is gone, replaced with a seriousness that makes my heart skip a beat.

I blow out a short, frustrated breath.

How is he so understanding?

"You always do your best," Oliver continues. *"That's* what matters, Rhett."

"Okay," I mutter.

He still looks worried, but he doesn't address it any further. Instead he nods in the direction of where we left Wren and Elliot. "Let's get back. I want you focused on something else."

The tightness in my chest loosens as he gives me a reassuring smile. It's the kind that makes his eyes crinkle, which means it's real.

"C'mon," he says, and I realize he's taken a few steps while I haven't moved.

"Right. Yeah, coming."

He smells good—that vanilla and woodiness that's always had a calming effect on me. It's like hugging him without touching him, which is the best I can give myself right now.

Inhaling deeply, I follow him, hoping he's right. My childhood has haunted me for all my life, but Elliot and Oliver—and now Wren—have always been able to chase away my ghosts.

I just have to let them.

...

After I lose my bet to Oliver, the four of us look through a couple more exhibits. We stop to admire the museum's collection of Chinese architecture, as well as a Japanese ceremonial teahouse. Before we know it, it's been multiple hours, and we need to start heading home.

On our way in, we immediately started with a side room, so we missed the large one most people walk into first. I was hoping to avoid it, but Wren is heading in that direction, following signs for the Archway of Love installment.

The problem is, Wren seeing it is a horrible, horrible idea.

"Sweetheart, I don't think we should go that way."

"But the Archway sounds so cool," she says, spinning around to look at me and walking backward. "I want to know what could've possibly inspired a name like that."

"Wren..."

Fuck.

We enter the room, and the piece comes into view.

"Shit," Elliot mutters.

"What?" Wren finally turns around, only to stop dead in her tracks. Her body goes rigid as Oliver exchanges a worried glance with me.

"Oh." Her voice is high-pitched and squeaky. She lets out a nervous laugh. "That's . . . that's a lot of water."

The ceiling in here is high—three stories, if not more. And in the center of the room is a massive copper heart archway. With water falling from it. Directly into a large, square pool.

"Right," Wren whispers. She takes a step back, bumping into me. "It's a water sculpture."

"We can go around it," Elliot says, eyebrows furrowed with concern. "There are other ways to get back to the main lobby."

Slowly, Wren nods. But she doesn't move. Then, finally, "No. I want to go closer."

Elliot's frown deepens. "Love, after earlier—"

"I have to get over the fear," she says firmly. Well, as firmly as someone who's so terrified she's beginning to shake can say anything.

The three of us glance at each other before we look back to Wren. She's pushing herself too hard. It's barely been a week. But none of us want to get in the way of her healing, either.

Elliot looks like he's about to say no, but Oliver speaks first.

"Fine. But if you start to panic, we're pulling you out of here. No protesting, princess. Got it?"

She nods, her eyes glued to the falling water.

Taking her hand, Oliver pulls her forward. She rolls her shoulders back, walking toward the fountain with as much courage as she can muster. They stop a couple of feet away with me and Ell right behind them.

"It's pretty," Wren says, gazing at the skylight above the fountain. "I wonder if it creates rainbows on sunny days."

"I bet it does." Oliver squeezes Wren's hand, watching her carefully. When she tries to take another step toward the water, he tugs her back. "No. This is close enough."

"I'm fi-"

"You're *not* fine. Stop lying to us and stop lying to yourself."

I raise my eyebrows. I know that tone—the one Oliver is doing his best to hide. There's a hint of impatience that he's stowed away just enough that Wren doesn't notice, but I do. Of course I do. I bet Ell picked up on it, too.

The past couple days, we've watched as Wren has tested her limits and gone too far with herself. Elliot finding her in the kitchen earlier is a perfect example. She's refusing to give herself space to not be okay.

I used to do it all the time—a side effect of my childhood, I suppose. It took a lot of relearning and a lot of self-acceptance to let myself feel things I always thought I wasn't allowed to feel. While I struggled through it, Elliot and Oliver had to as well. They had to watch me pretend to be okay when all I wanted to do was die, even though they assured me repeatedly that I didn't have to perform around them.

So it's no surprise that Oliver is trying to get Wren to pace herself. He doesn't want to see her put herself through what I did.

Oliver slides an arm around Wren's waist, anchoring her in place. For the next couple minutes, we gaze at the fountain, watching the water fall and splash into the pool. Wren doesn't try to get closer, and her hands stop trembling at some point. Elliot notices at the same time I do, and we share a look of relief.

"I think I'm good," Wren says after a while. She hasn't taken her eyes off the water at all, almost like she's afraid it'll rise up and attack her if she looks away.

Oliver plants a kiss on her temple. "Then let's get you home."

Chapter Four

Oliver

Our ice cream tradition isn't as fun and lighthearted as it usually is. Elliot is pacing around the living room, barely even eating his as it melts in his bowl. Rhett is tense as well, and I don't think it's because of our earlier interaction.

I suppose I should've expected as much. This job is stressing the hell out of all of us. But going to the museum and spending time with these three has filled me with so much happiness, so I was hoping it'd bleed into the rest of the night.

From across the room, Wren shoots me a worried look. She's sitting on the love seat with Rhett while I'm on the couch by myself. Elliot is *supposed* to be sitting with me, but I understand that he needs to move around.

Eventually, Elliot turns to face the three of us. "We need to maximize this opportunity. We have a chance to get inside Ludo's temporary home. Inside his operations. We need to make the most of it."

Rhett freezes with a spoonful of ice cream halfway to his mouth. "Are you saying we should bug Ludo's condo?"

For a few seconds, they stare at each other. Then Elliot sighs. "I'm not sure we could pull it off. No doubt, he'll have security cameras positioned all over the place. There's no way we could plant something without getting caught."

For the first three days of this trip, Ludo is going to be gone in the mornings and early afternoons. That's when we're supposed to be with his fiancée, Aubrey. But during the rest of that time, being able to hear Ludo's conversations could give us essential knowledge into his life.

I'm pretty sure all of us have thought about bugging the resort condo he's renting out. None of us have voiced it because it'd never work. But maybe...

"Do you have an idea of how we could pull it off?" I ask.

With a big sigh, Elliot sets his ice cream on a side table and plops onto the couch next to me. He leans forward, resting his elbows on his knees and clasping his hands together tightly—too tightly. "If we break Ludo's trust, we'll never get it back again. We can't afford to make mistakes here."

I glance between Elliot and Rhett. There's no way we're losing everything we've spent the past decade working toward. But we have to move forward, and there's no way to do that without some risk. It's just a matter of determining what's too far.

"You can hide a bug in anything these days. Clocks, fire detectors, electrical outlets, sunglasses. But if Ludo finds out we did..." Elliot shakes his head.

"So you don't think it's worth the risk?" I ask.

Instead of answering, Elliot presses his lips into a thin line. When his eyes flit to Rhett, I wonder if he's worried to say it's too far. We're already compromising on multiple aspects of our grand plan, and we feel like that's enough of a disservice to Sammy. But at the same time, we need to be careful. We have Wren to think about now.

"What about me?" she asks. She's fidgeting in her seat, her eyes bouncing from me to Elliot to Rhett.

"We'll keep you safe, love. I promise."

Shaking her head, Wren says, "That's not what I mean. You guys can't bug the condo because there's a chance you'll get caught on camera. But no one would ever expect me to do something like that, so no one would be watching me. Right?"

Elliot narrows his eyes. "I don't like where you're going with this."

"Just hear me out," she says. "You can teach me how to plant something discreetly. We're going over to the condo tomorrow night, right? So Aubrey can meet you guys? What if I do it then?"

"No," Elliot says. "Not in a million years. You're a horrible liar, Wren. I have faith that you could pull it off, but not without training and practice. And we don't have time for that."

"But—"

"Sweetheart, no." Rhett covers his hand with hers. "We're not risking it. You've been through enough."

"I agree with Elliot," I say, which earns me a halfhearted glare from Wren. *"But* I think we could make it work."

Now Elliot and Rhett give me glares from hell. Wren, however, perks up. I give her the most reassuring smile I can.

"What if," I start, ignoring the look on Elliot's face that means he's going to shut me down no matter what, "Wren doesn't plant anything?"

"That's what we're saying," Elliot says, gesturing between him and Rhett. "She can't be a part of this."

Wren crosses her arms. "I already *am* a part of this."

Elliot lets out an exasperated sigh, but I cut him off before he can say anything.

"She won't plant anything. But what if she 'forgets' something at the condo? Something that could easily be mistaken as Aubrey's, like sunglasses?"

"It won't—" Elliot stops himself, and his expression turns almost surprised. "That could . . ." His eyes kind of glaze over as he thinks, and I smile when he runs his thumb over his bottom lip. It's an old habit I've always found cute. "That could work. Rhett? What do you think?"

He's staring at Wren, his features clouded over. I can practically see the battle in his eyes. He wants to keep her safe—we all do. But she committed to this, and we could really use her help.

She's right. She *is* a part of this.

"Please?" she whispers. She takes one of Rhett's hands in hers, squeezing gently. "I want to help. I want Ludo to get what he deserves."

Her willingness has Rhett's expression softening. "You're sure?"

"I'm positive."

Slowly, he nods. Then, with his eyes still locked with hers, he says, "Could we get sunglasses in time?"

"I bet Finn could whip something up quick." Elliot checks his watch before explaining to Wren, "He's always been obsessed with tech and gadgets and whatnot. I'll give him a call."

Wren's eyes are lit up with excitement as she throws her arms around Rhett's neck.

It makes me a little nervous—she's committed to this, to us, but I'm not sure how I feel about her actually getting involved. At the same time, seeing her planning and coming up with ideas has pride flaring in my heart. She wants this, and she's trying her best.

Fuck, I love her so much.

Elliot leaves to call Finn, and when he returns, he says, "Finn can get us what we need before we leave. One of us will just have to stop by his place early tomorrow before our flight."

"I'll do it," I say quickly. Rhett has slept like shit the past couple nights, so if there's a chance he'll be able to get rest tonight, I'm not cutting it short. As for Elliot, he looks just as exhausted. I can handle an early-morning errand no problem.

"Thank you," Elliot murmurs, leaning over and kissing my temple.

"Of course." Intertwining our fingers, I rest my head against his shoulder. He smells good, sandalwood and sweet citrus, and I inhale deeply. I barely even realize I say the words out loud until I hear my own voice. "I'll do anything for you, Ell."

. . .

When my alarm goes off in the morning, I shut it off and settle back into bed.

Just a couple more minutes.

Wrapping my arms around Wren, I pull her into me. She barely stirs, but her arm still comes around my waist. Gently, I kiss her forehead. Her body fits so perfectly against mine, and I never want to leave our cocoon of warmth.

The past couple days have been hard on me. I can't convince the anxious side of my brain that Wren is safe now. It's like it thinks she's going to vanish into thin air, and that eventually I'm going to end up tied to that chair, watching her teeter on the edge of life and death.

"You're safe," I whisper to her sleeping form, more for my own benefit than hers.

My eyes close of their own volition, and just as I'm drifting off again, my second alarm goes off. The sound makes me jerk awake, and the sudden movement disturbs Wren.

Groaning, she removes her arm so I can roll over and turn off my alarm again. She tries to push herself up, but then she collapses onto the mattress. "Too sleepy."

"You don't have to get up, princess. I'll wake you when I get back."

Groggily, she reaches for me. Her fingertips brush against my skin, and she sighs at the physical contact. "I love you."

My stomach does a giddy flip as I smile down at her in the darkness. Hearing those words from her lips feels too unreal, and I wonder if that'll ever change. It still makes me melt when Elliot and Rhett tell me.

Leaning down, I press a kiss to her jawline. "I love you, too, Wren. Always will."

She makes a small noise, one that has me smiling. She sounds tired enough that I'm not sure she'll even remember this when she wakes up fully. That's okay, though. What matters is that it happened.

"I'll see you later," I whisper.

In the bathroom, I don't turn on the light until the door is fully closed. I get ready for the day as quietly as I can so Wren can stay asleep. Then I slip out of the bedroom, but not before kissing her cheek again.

I don't bother turning on any lights since we have all the night lights we set up for Wren. I walk through the dimly lit house, pausing in the kitchen to grab a snack before heading out to the garage. Finn stayed up late getting a pair of sunglasses ready for us to use. Now we just have to hope everything else works out.

Finn's house is thirty minutes away, and I spend the drive worrying about the job. We don't normally offer protection services like this, and

Ludo knows it. It sparked suspicion in me when he first asked until I thought it through.

There are plenty of good reasons for him to think of us. First, we delivered on the Williams job. It was stressful and scary for us, but Ludo got exactly the end results he was looking for.

Second, considering we're going to be watching over his fiancée, he trusts us at least somewhat.

And lastly, we bring something the average bodyguard doesn't bring to the table: experience trailing and killing people. It doesn't sound relevant until I realized we'll look at every situation more thoroughly.

We're hitmen first. At this point it's part of our DNA. So every room, every scenario, every event we go to will be analyzed from a different perspective. We know what we'd do if we were hired to do the opposite of protecting Aubrey, which gives us a leg up in keeping her safe. Extra vigilance and foresight are valuable to Ludo.

Once I get to Finn's, he's waiting for me at the front door. His dark hair is tousled and messy, like he's been running his hands through it absentmindedly all night. Hell, now that I'm looking at him, he looks paler than normal as well.

"You good?" I ask as I step inside.

"Just tired." His voice is rough and scratchy. When I give him a look of disbelief, he rolls his eyes. "Maybe a touch sick, too. Probably best to keep your distance."

"Sorry to keep you up all night." Hovering near the door, I grimace. He really does look like shit.

"Probably wouldn't've slept anyway. Too much on my mind." He tosses me the sunglasses. "Wanna explain why you're doing things this way? You know, instead of doing it yourself, since you guys are the fucking professionals?"

I catch the sunglasses with ease, eyeing him carefully. "Are you worried?"

"How the hell could I *not* be worried? You're going up against one of the most powerful men in the city, and Wren isn't ready to protect herself if something goes wrong."

"That's what we're for. We're not letting anything else happen to her."

"Right." Finn crosses his arms, cocking an eyebrow. "And if Ludo decides to use all his resources against you? What then?"

"That won't happen. We're being careful. He won't know what hit him until it's too late."

"Going to the man I'm trying to get close to and accusing him of knowing where my kidnapped girlfriend is, is far from *careful,* Moore. Jesus. What were you thinking?"

"What? How did you find out about that?"

"A little bird told me." With a shake of his head, Finn says, "Don't you think the timing is odd? You storm into his club and accuse him of keeping tabs on Wren, and not even a week later he's offering you guys a job."

That makes my blood run cold. "I hadn't thought of that."

My admission seems to make something break inside Finn. He laughs, throwing his hands up, like he's dealing with a petulant child. "You guys are losing your touch. I don't know if it's Wren or if it's that you've been playing the game for too long. But if you don't get your shit in order, you're going to lose her. You're going to lose *more* than her."

"Fuck," I mutter.

"Seriously. How did Elliot not put this together?"

The snack in my stomach sours. "I never told him."

"What?" Finn yells.

"I . . . shit." Scrubbing a hand over my face, I say, "I forgot to mention it. There was so much happening, and I was so focused on getting Wren back. And then she's been—fuck. That isn't relevant. I have to go. We need to figure this out."

"Damn right you do," Finn growls. "And you need to do something about Wren. She couldn't even protect herself in her own apartment."

"We're doing our best," I grit out.

"Are you?" he snaps. "Are you doing your best? Or are you *hoping* to do your best?" He taps his head while his glare bores into me. "It all starts up here, Oliver. Don't leave room for mistakes in your head, or you'll find yourself making them. Get your heads straight."

I'd be angry about the way he's talking to me, but it's well-warranted. If I hadn't been so distracted, my earlier suspicion of Ludo would've made a lot more sense.

Finn sighs when I don't give him an answer. "I know you know what it's like to lose someone," he says, much more softly this time. "But Sammy's murder wasn't your fault, not even remotely. And being the reason behind the death of someone you love . . ." He doesn't continue.

He doesn't have to. I know his past.

"You're right. Thank you."

He nods. "Let me know if you guys need anything. I'll try to help in whatever way I can." With that, he claps me on the back. "I'm glad you're safe. And I'm glad you guys got Wren back. Now let's keep you all together, okay?"

"Yeah. Yeah, I'd like that."

And then I'm off, trying to figure out how to break it to Elliot, Rhett, and Wren that I've fucked up royally.

Chapter Five

Wren

Oliver wakes me up with cuddles and kisses. It's hard to keep my eyes open, but the promise of coffee and more kisses gets me out of bed after a minute.

It's not until I'm brushing my teeth that I'm awake enough to realize how nervous Oliver looks. He's pacing his bedroom, wringing his hands while he mutters to himself.

Once I'm done, I hover at the threshold between the bathroom and the bedroom. "Oliver? Are you okay?"

"Hmm?" He looks up, stopping in the middle of the room. "Yeah, yeah. Just gotta . . . talk to everyone. Something came up."

"Came up?"

"I'm not sure if it's a problem or not. We may have to approach things differently." When he notices my concerned look, he grabs my hand and squeezes. "We'll be okay. The sunglasses were always a good idea, but now I think they're definitely our safest bet."

"Safest bet?"

"I'll explain over breakfast. C'mon." He tugs me out of the room and downstairs.

Elliot and Rhett are already sipping coffee at the kitchen table, and I smile at the sight of them. I'm not sure what'll happen after this week.

It feels too soon to move in permanently, but I never want to miss a morning with them. My only issue is that it feels too fast. I need to maintain some sense of individuality, otherwise I'll end up repeating all the same mistakes I made with Adam.

"Morning." As Elliot says it, he leans back in his chair and watches us. He looks much more relaxed than he did last night.

"Morning," Oliver says, pulling out a chair and pushing me into it. Then he blurts, "We have a problem. When we got back from Wyoming, I went to Evolve to talk to Ludo."

"What?" Rhett spits out, turning in his chair to stare at Oliver. "Why the hell would you do that?"

"Because of the way Ludo was looking at Wren when we took her to Evolve."

Now I'm the one turning in my chair. "Looking at me? What are you talking about?"

Elliot stands and immediately starts pacing. All of the tension that bled out of him overnight is back. "What did he say?"

Oliver doesn't answer my question, only gives me an apologetic glance. "She's his type, we all know it. I figured Ludo was keeping tabs on her. With the way he couldn't keep his eyes off her, it was at least a decent hunch. He claimed he wasn't and that he didn't know where she was, but I'm not sure I believe him."

I shiver. At Evolve, I was so focused on Oliver and on having fun that I didn't even notice Ludo was watching me. It leaves me with a vulnerable and icky feeling, like I need to take a shower and scrub my skin clean.

Elliot stops behind Rhett's chair, gripping the back of it. "Tell me everything Ludo said. Word for word if you remember."

Oliver does, going into as much detail as he can. Apparently Ludo is the one who gave Oliver the idea of getting himself kidnapped. As Oliver explains, I start putting together a timeline. My stomach drops to the floor as everything falls into place.

If Oliver went to Ludo the afternoon he got kidnapped, that means Ludo had already stopped by Jordan's house and seen me. Ludo knew exactly where I was, and he chose to keep that piece of information to himself.

Why? Why would he do that?

I need to tell the guys.

"I'm going to kill him," Rhett growls. "How *dare* he suggest something so—"

"Let's not dwell on it," Elliot cuts in, resting a hand on Rhett's shoulder. "He'll get what's coming to him."

Rhett clamps his mouth shut, but the deadly anger in his eyes only grows. It has me biting my tongue. The last thing we need is Rhett snapping and acting on his emotions. If he knows Ludo could've helped me, he'll flip his shit. I can't be the reason their revenge plans go awry.

I'll tell them. Just not right now.

"One thing is sticking out to me," Elliot says. "He said that he likes having us as allies, right?"

Oliver nods.

"Ludo doesn't extend that kind of grace very often. One sign of disloyalty is usually enough for him to cut someone out entirely, yet he did the opposite. He hired us." Elliot is staring at me, but he's not really *seeing* me. He's deep in his mind, working on some grand, invisible puzzle.

"That's bad, right?" I ask.

"I don't think so," Elliot replies. His hand is still on Rhett's shoulder, and he's tapping his fingers absentmindedly. "No, I think that's a good thing."

"How?" I ask.

"It means he needs us." As Elliot says it, his gaze finally sharpens on me. A hint of worry fills his eyes, but it's pushed to the side by a hard determination. "And we need to figure out why."

"It also means this could be a test," Rhett says. Gently, he removes Elliot's hand from his shoulder, and I wonder what's happening in his head. "And while a test doesn't mean active malice, we need to proceed with caution."

"Exactly," Elliot replies, shoving his hands in his pockets.

I slouch in my chair. All of this is so *complicated.* We can't read Ludo's mind, but we need to know what he's thinking. "I really hope these sunglasses work."

"Me too, princess," Oliver mumbles.

Tension is high as we get ready to go. My stomach is too queasy, so I skip breakfast, even though the guys try to get me to eat something. It's sweet of them, but I'm not sure I'll be able to keep food down right now.

Once we've boarded the plane, Elliot leads us to a sitting area. There are two leather seats that are close together, and then two more that are facing them. I immediately claim one of the ones next to a window. It feels as nice as it looks. Really, the whole thing is much fancier than I expected. I've only been on a plane once, and it definitely wasn't a private one.

I spend the entire flight staring out the window, watching as cars turn into tiny dots and then disappear entirely. It's probably childish, looking out the window the whole time, but I can't stop myself. It's fascinating.

Oliver is seated next to me. "Have you never been on a plane before, princess?"

"Once," I reply without looking at him. "I didn't get the window seat though."

He hums. "If you'd like, you can always have it when you fly with me."

That finally gets me to pull my focus away from the world below. I bristle when I realize all three men are watching me. "What?"

Rhett averts his gaze immediately. Elliot doesn't answer—just smiles.

After kissing my cheek, Oliver says, "Nothing. It's just nice to see you happy."

I don't realize I was expecting them to make fun of me until they don't. A warm feeling creeps through my body. It's like eating a chocolate chip cookie fresh out of the oven, or like coming home and cuddling in front of a crackling fire. Except, somehow, it's more.

"You make me happy," I say softly, looking between the three of them.

When Rhett looks up again, I make sure to lock eyes with him. He doesn't smile, doesn't say anything, but that's okay. I know it means something to him.

Oliver tips my chin toward him and kisses me. He tastes like the orange juice the flight attendant got him and smells of vanilla, and it makes me want to crawl into his lap and kiss him for the rest of the flight.

"Fuck, princess," he murmurs into my mouth. It's almost like he can read my mind, because he slips his hands under me, grabs my ass, and pulls me until I'm sitting sideways in his lap.

I have to turn my torso to keep kissing him, and when I do so, he grips my waist. My hands cradle his face as he leans back in his seat, taking me with him. With my body pressed against his, I feel his cock harden underneath my thigh.

"Not to be a downer," Elliot says as Oliver slips a hand under my shirt, "but we're going to be landing soon."

With a groan, Oliver breaks off our kiss. His hand slides down my back until it rests on the curve of my ass. "Poor timing on my part. You're just too pretty not to kiss."

I seal my lips to Oliver's once more before he sets me back in my seat. His hands linger on my body as he buckles my seatbelt. He pulls it tight, burying his face into my hair and inhaling deeply.

"So sweet," he whispers. "And too damn sexy."

Landing is possibly the most anxiety-inducing part of the flight for me. When the wheels hit the ground, we're still going so fast, and it feels like we'll spin out of control at any second.

"Hey," Oliver says, "we're okay."

It's not until he says it that I realize I have a death grip on his arm. Releasing him, I say, "Sorry."

Grabbing my hand, he squeezes gently. "I don't mind."

The plane starts slowing down so quickly I can't help but tense up again. But in under a minute, we're rolling along in a much more controlled manner. Breathing out a sigh of relief, I slump into my seat.

"You'll get used to it eventually," Elliot says.

"Took me a while too," Rhett adds in. "First time I flew, I puked."

With a chuckle, Oliver says, "And I had a panic attack my first time."

"Both of those happened simultaneously, by the way," Elliot chimes in. "God, that was chaotic."

I'd laugh if I didn't feel so nauseated. "I think I might've hurled if I'd eaten breakfast."

"Which reminds me," Elliot says, glancing at his phone. "The first thing we're doing after we check in at the resort is getting you some food. Assuming you're up for it?"

"Um. Let's see how I feel once this thing isn't moving anymore."

The corners of his mouth lift up. "Of course, love."

Turns out, the resort isn't terribly far from the airport. My stomach settles pretty quickly, and by the time we're piling out of our rental, I'm finally ready to eat something.

We head right past the elevators, which confuses me until we turn down a hallway to another area. Here, there are only a few elevators, and they're labeled for the higher-up suites and penthouses. Elliot has to swipe our room's key card to use it.

As we step into it, I can't help but smile to myself. Of course they didn't book a normal room. Why am I even surprised?

We head up to the highest floor, which opens up into a large hallway with huge windows at either end. There are two doors aside from the elevators, each across from each other.

"Two different suites?"

"Two different *penthouses,* love." Elliot swipes a keycard in front of one of the doors, and we hear the telltale *click* of it unlocking before he pushes it open.

My jaw drops. Never in my life did I think I'd ever step foot into a penthouse. And from the peek I'm getting through the open door, it's a really, really, *really nice* one.

"Let's go, sweetheart." Rhett's hand comes to rest on the small of my back, pressing gently.

"Oh, sweet," Oliver exclaims as he walks inside. "You booked one with a piano."

"Figured you'd appreciate that," Elliot says, following him.

Rhett catches the door before it closes, pushing me forward until I'm inside. "It's just an apartment, Wren. It won't bite."

The place is luxurious. Like, tall ceilings, huge windows, sparkling surfaces, billionaire's-home-away-from-home type luxurious.

There's a balcony. No, scratch that, *two*. Or maybe it's just one big one. There's also a hot tub outside, a magnificent view of the ocean, a sprawling living area, and a TV that's as big as the grand piano that's in front of the windows.

"Um," I squeak out. "How much money does being a hitman pay, exactly?"

"Depends on the hitman," Rhett replies, adjusting my bag over his shoulder.

"And the target," Elliot adds.

"And who's hiring," Oliver says, flopping onto one of the pristine white couches.

"Okay, but . . ." I wave my hand around, still trying to take in the space. *"This* much money?"

"Ah, no," Elliot says. "The money we make helps, of course, but most of this came from my trust fund and managing it well. My parents are loaded."

"It meant Rhett and I got to go on the sweetest vacations in high school," Oliver says, looking up from where he's been admiring the piano. "Took some convincing, but eventually his parents said yes."

"A *lot* of convincing," Rhett mutters, his tone tinged with bitterness. Before I can dwell on it, he's glancing at his watch and saying, "We need to get moving. We have a lot of ground to cover today, and it's already noon."

"Shit, right." Elliot turns to me. "And we need to get you food."

"I've got it handled," Rhett says. "Why don't you and O start exploring, and the two of us can check out the first-floor restaurant?"

"Works for me," Oliver says with a sly smile.

"I get to help?" I ask.

"You get to learn," Rhett tells me. "Now come with me."

The penthouse has two bedrooms, and we take the one that's decorated in silver and light blue. It's a cooler color scheme than I would've picked for a bedroom, but the balcony—the *third* balcony, so far—makes up for it.

"Wow," I breathe, moving to the sliding glass door. "That's a beautiful view."

The resort overlooks the ocean, and the sky is so clear today that the water is a deep, vibrant blue. Relief washes over me when I realize it's not causing me to panic. It must be far enough away.

"So I get to stay with you?"

"We'll probably switch at some point, but Elliot and Oliver need some time together. And I—you . . ." He clears his throat. "Never mind."

I'd pry, but based on the way he's fiddling with the lilac strap of my bag, it'd just make him more uncomfortable. "That's thoughtful of you."

He doesn't seem to know what to do with the compliment. He shifts from foot to foot and awkwardly clears his throat. "Uh, thanks."

Rounding the bed, I take my bag from him. "I just want to get changed before we eat. I'm not dressed for summer weather."

Rhett nods. "Right. That makes sense."

After cleaning up in the bathroom, I slide a light and flowy dress on. It's black with a sunflower print on it. The back and the straps are crocheted black lace that I fell in love with the moment I laid eyes on it.

I put my hair up so it's off my neck and check in the mirror to make sure I look okay. The woman staring back at me makes me smile. I look like a main character in a sweet romance novel. Maybe even a romcom. Or maybe I look like the fun, supportive best friend. But hey, that's okay too. I love a good side character.

Back in the bedroom, Rhett takes a long look at me. He's changed into a black T-shirt, but he's still wearing pants, and he has his hands in his pockets while he leans against the dresser. Slowly, almost lazily, his eyes travel up and down my body.

Okay, definitely a main character outfit.

"Ready to get food?"

He nods, but he doesn't move. His gaze hasn't left me, and it's a really long stare. Like, really long.

Okay, maybe it's not *a main character outfit.*

"Do you not like the dress?"

"What?"

"You haven't stopped looking at me."

He raises an eyebrow. "And you're automatically assuming it's because I think you look bad?"

"I—well, no, but you're not the easiest to read, and—"

All it takes is a couple long, sure strides, and he's towering over me. "Do *you* like it?"

That's very much *not* the answer I was hoping for, so I sigh. "I just want to know if you think it's too girlish, or if you think I look silly, or anything like that."

"Would you change if I told you I didn't like it?"

"That's not what I'm—it's not—I . . ."

"I love the dress," he says. "I was staring *because* it looks good."

I relax. "Thank you. That's what I wanted to know. Okay, we can go get food—"

"Mm mm, no." He shakes his head. "Would you have changed if I told you I didn't like the dress?"

I can feel my whole body heating. My heart starts beating too fast, and I can't hold Rhett's gaze, so I look away.

"Answer me, sweetheart," he says gently.

"I probably would've changed," I mumble.

"And do you, just possibly, find that a touch ironic?"

"Um . . . ?" I risk a glance at him, hoping his expression will hold some answers, but all I find is a hint of a smile.

God, why is he so damn *attractive*.

"Last night," he prods. "Oliver."

"What? Oh. *Oh.*"

"What exactly did you tell him? *Don't ever feel like you have to hide yourself from me.* Something like that."

"You heard?" I whisper.

His smile widens the tiniest bit. "Yeah. And I think you need to apply what you said to him to *yourself*. We like you just the way you are, sweetheart."

I squirm, twisting my fingers into the skirt of my dress. "That's easier said than done."

"Yeah," he says with a shrug. "Oliver's been working on it since we were kids."

"That's a long time," I mumble.

"The important thing is that you don't have to change yourself to earn our affections. Got it?"

It's a concept I'm not entirely familiar with, but I'm getting more used to it by the day. Honestly, I should be relieved. In this instance, the guys are the total opposites of Adam and my family. Instead of shaping me to be who they want me to be, they're giving me room to be myself.

"Thank you."

Rhett shakes his head. "Never thank me for doing the bare minimum, sweetheart."

I take his hand when he holds it out to me. "I think you and I have different definitions of the bare minimum."

"I agree," he says, and I can't help but notice the darkness that tinges his tone. "And I'm going to try my damndest to show you just how high your standards should be."

Chapter Six

Rhett

As we head down to the restaurant, I do my best to shake off my anger. With every passing day, it becomes more and more apparent just how much of a number Wren's ex and her parents did on her. Encouraging her to be herself is such a basic thing a loved one would do, so it took me a moment to realize *that's* what she was thanking me for.

It's a relief that I'm so used to it now. I used to thank Oliver and Elliot for that type of stuff all the time. It's taken fourteen damn years, but my mind is starting to default to their affection being the standard instead of my asshole of a father.

Truly, I don't think I would've survived to twenty-eight if it hadn't been for those two. They taught me what love actually looked like. Now, we're always trying to make sure we're caring for and supporting each other.

It's why I decided to have Wren sleep with me tonight. I doubt I'll sleep, so who better to wake Wren from her nightmares than the one who'll be affected by it the least? Now all I have to do is make sure I'm in a good enough mental state to comfort her.

Almost out of habit, I start doing one of my breathing exercises. It's not like doing it now will help me later, but maybe it'll calm me down for the time being.

Once we're at the restaurant, the host leads us to a table on the deck, right by the railing. From here, there's a decent view of the beach and the water. Off to one side, you can see the luxury condos, shrouded with meticulously-kept gardens.

"There are a lot of palm trees down here," Wren says once we're seated, tugging me from my thoughts. She's staring past the railing toward the beach. "Like, a lot. And they're taller than I thought they'd be."

"Never seen one in real life before?"

She laughs. "Oh, definitely not. My mom and I barely scraped by for years—my biological dad was never in the picture. We lived with my grandma, and my mom took care of the house and me while my grandma worked. Once my mom married Thomas, our money situation changed drastically. He had a good job—a *really* good job. But I usually avoided going on trips with them whenever I could, and neither of them protested much. I spent a lot of nights alone."

"I bet you were one of those teenagers who threw absolute ragers when they were gone."

She gives me a baffled look. "What? No, I spent most of my free time reading. Wait, do I give that impression?"

With a snort, I reach over the table and squeeze her wrist. "No, sweetheart. It was a joke."

For a second, she stares at me with her head tilted, but then she laughs. "I don't know how I didn't pick up on that." Her smile fades, and her gaze drops. "Thomas would say it's because I spent too much time reading and not enough time making friends."

Leaning across the table, I tilt her chin up with a bent knuckle. "Ell would say there's no such thing as reading too much."

"And you?" she whispers.

"I'd say what you do with your free time is no one's business but your own, and if you ever don't understand a joke, I'll happily explain it to you."

At that, she relaxes. Hell, she even smiles, but this one is void of embarrassment. It's a relief, seeing some of the spark in her eyes that's been missing ever since Jordan kidnapped her.

After we order, I continue taking the place in. I got a decent look at the inside portion of the restaurant earlier, but I want to double check things like entry points, exits, potential blind spots, all that.

"So what exactly are you looking for?" Wren asks.

Right. I want to include her in all this. We were only able to fit in one more self-defense lesson since getting her back, and while this is different, situational awareness is important.

"There's a lot to consider. First, you have to watch the people around you and look for anything that might be slightly off. But in a spot like this, you also have to keep an eye on things outside of the deck. See how the resort is curved?" I nod to the part of the building we can see. We're on one end, and since it's curved in on itself, the other end is perfectly visible from the edge of the patio.

"Mmhmm."

"From one of the balconies, a good shot could take you out right where you're sitting," I say. "From there, things could get messy. Would the shooter be able to get out of the resort in time before the authorities show up? How many security cameras and resort staff would they have to dodge? But it's plausible."

Wren's eyes widen. "Then how are you supposed to keep Aubrey safe? It's not like you can keep her from *all* open areas."

"In a situation like this? Either I'd have us inside the restaurant, or we'd sit farther inside the deck. The roof would hide us from most of the balconies. That table right there would be decent. It's close enough to the doors leading inside that it provides a quick escape, and if we can't get her that far, we can shove her behind the bar until we fight off her potential attacker."

"Wow," Wren murmurs. "I never would've thought of any of that."

I shrug. "Odds are, no one would try an up-close attack here. Too many people around. In a restaurant, you're more likely to have to deal with poisons. But as long as—"

"Poisons?" she squeaks out, her eyes widening. "How could you possibly know if her food is poisoned? I mean, I know there are ways to test your drinks for drugs, but what about other stuff?"

"Most poisons take more than one dose to kill," I say, sipping on my water. "Most. As for checking, the better option is to not announce where she'll be. That type of attack takes premeditation. Any potential threats can't think ahead if they don't know where—or what—she'll be eating."

"Oh," she says, relaxing. "You guys have really thought all this through."

"That's why Holloway hired us, I suppose."

After we finish up at the restaurant, we spend the afternoon exploring more of the resort. Elliot and Oliver head to the spa, probably because they know the last thing I want is a massage from a stranger. Wren and I check out the rest of the grounds, mostly just walking around to get familiar with the place.

"We should probably walk the beach by the condos," I say, glancing at my watch. "I'd leave it for Ell and O, but it's getting late. We have to figure out dinner still, and I definitely want to shower before drinks."

Wren chews on her bottom lip as her gaze travels toward the water. Just as I'm about to suggest that she can hang out in the penthouse while I check it out, she nods.

We take our time, following a paved pathway for as long as we can before stepping onto the beach. Wren takes her sandals off, but then she immediately puts them back on because the sand is burning hot.

As we walk along the beach, Wren keeps glancing toward the water. Her grip on my hand has gotten progressively tighter as the strip of sand narrows, forcing us closer to the waves.

"Why don't you stand on the other side of me," I say, tugging her so I'm the one closer to the water.

She resists. "No, please. There's plenty of distance between us and the ocean, and this is . . . it's good. If I start struggling to control my thoughts, then we can switch."

"You're sure?"

"Yes. If I put it off, the thought of being around water will get scarier and scarier until I never face my fears. I know you guys think I'm pushing myself too hard, but I have to."

She doesn't, but obviously she disagrees with me. As we walk, I divert some of my attention from our surroundings to her. It's too easy to get lost in horrifying thoughts without realizing it. I want her to be able to pull herself out if she goes too far, but I'll be watching in case she can't.

She purposefully looks away from the water. "The condos look really nice." There's a row of them, all with their own slice of beach.

"I believe Ludo booked that one," I say, pointing to one of them. It has its own pool and hot tub, along with a small yard, an outdoor bar, and a large fire pit. "He mentioned getting an end one."

"Wow," she breathes, staring at it. "These are all so *nice*."

"Not terribly private, but yeah."

"Is that why we're in a penthouse? For privacy?"

I nod. It's also because the thought of staying so close to Ludo would've driven me up a wall. Both of us living in the same city is already hard enough as it is.

As we walk, I take in as much as I can. I already got a decent look at the beach due to the aerial photos on the resort's website, but I wanted to check it out in person anyway. You notice different things from different angles.

"Rhett?"

"Yes, sweetheart?"

"Can we go up to the water?"

"Sure."

The water is mostly calm. After taking off our shoes, Wren hesitates right at the point that the waves wash up to. She digs her toes into the sand. Then, carefully, she steps forward. The waves lap lazily up the shore, covering her toes. She doesn't jump, doesn't back away, just takes a long, shuddering breath.

After a minute of watching the water, she turns to me, wrapping her arms around my neck. "You wouldn't let me drown, would you?"

I'd be offended that she thinks she even has to ask, but that's not what's going on here. Oliver asks things like that often. It's less him questioning my character and love for him, and more him asking for reassurance to help get past his anxiety. I'm unsurprised that Wren is doing something similar.

"Absolutely not."

She sighs, resting her head against my chest. It's too hot to stay like this for long, especially with the sun beating down on us, but I let her lean against me for a minute before easing some space in between us. Her arms are still looped around my neck, but we're not touching anywhere else.

"It's really pretty out here," she murmurs. "I've only seen the ocean once. I think I'm glad we're staying farther from the water, though."

"Same here."

Her eyes meet mine. "Does it bug you? Knowing we'll be this close to him?"

"Some. But I've learned to refocus my energy on other things."

"Like?"

Getting closer to killing him.

Tearing him apart limb from limb.

Making him beg for mercy, and then refusing to give it to him.

I force a smile, not wanting to ruin the moment. "Like you three."

A larger wave hits our feet. This one reaches my ankles, soaking the bottoms of my pants. Wren shifts from foot to foot.

"You okay?" I ask.

She nods, but I'm not sure I believe her.

"Sweetheart..."

"Kiss me," she whispers, tugging my head down until my lips are mere inches from hers.

She doesn't have to ask twice. My arms wrap around her waist to hold her steady, and I close the distance between us. If a distraction is what she needs, I'll happily give her one.

The kiss lacks urgency. It's an act of affection, not desperation, or at least that's how it feels. Still, I keep a tight hold on Wren, just in case she loses her balance.

With a contented sigh, Wren pulls away first. She keeps her eyes closed, and I use the moment to look at her. As I do, I realize she seems less worn down. It seems like she's been sleeping well, minus her usual nightmares. I hope we'll be able to quell those soon, too.

"We should head back," I say eventually. "Ell and O are probably already working on dinner."

Her hand slides into mine. "Okay."

After retrieving our shoes, we start meandering back to the hotel. It's too hot to go fast, and I think we're both enjoying the time together anyway. I know I am, especially since the pleasurable part of this trip is about to end.

As we near the end of the beach, I glance back at the condos one more time. Ludo will be here soon, if he and Aubrey haven't already arrived. My skin crawls at the thought of them watching us from their condo.

Six more months.

By the end of summer, this will all be behind us. Sammy will have her justice. We'll be able to do whatever we want. None of us will ever have to think about Ludo Holloway again.

I avert my gaze and bring it back to Wren.

Most importantly, I realize as she grins up at me, *Wren will be much safer.*

Chapter Seven

Wren

Back in the penthouse, we leave our shoes at the door. Thankfully we were able to wash all the sand off our feet at one of the outdoor showers.

Oliver is seated at the piano. His fingers move nimbly over the keys, and he plays with such confidence and passion that I find myself standing in the middle of the two couches, staring at him. There's no sheet music in front of him. Not that it would matter, considering his eyes are closed.

Elliot is in the kitchen, a dish towel slung over his bare shoulders while he chops up vegetables on a cutting board. When he sees us, his face lights up. "There you are. I was starting to get worried."

"We ended up walking the beach," Rhett says.

As his eyes flit to me, Elliot doesn't even try to hide his surprise. "Oh?"

"I think I handled it pretty well."

"You did." Rhett places a hand on my back and kisses the top of my head. "I'm proud of you, sweetheart."

Elliot gives me a long look, searching my face, before going back to cutting vegetables. "Food should be ready in a half hour."

Rhett disappears into our bedroom, and a minute later, I hear the shower running.

"Do you need help?" I ask Elliot.

He shakes his head. "I've got it covered. Just relax, love."

Lowering myself onto one of the couches, I angle myself to watch Oliver, only to find he's already watching me. He's still playing the piano, filling the room with a soft, light melody. When our eyes lock, he swiftly ends his song.

"You didn't have to stop."

He stands, not taking his eyes off me for a split second. "There are other things I'd rather do."

Desire curls through my stomach. "Oh?"

"Like I said, princess. You're too pretty not to kiss." He leans over me, placing his hands on the back of the couch on either side of my head. The last thing he says before sealing his lips to mine is, "Can't fucking help myself."

In an instant, the heated need I felt on the plane comes crashing back. I grip Oliver's shirt, dragging him closer until he's straddling me. His hands move to my face, angling my head however he pleases.

Moaning into his mouth, I arch upward. He smells clean, like he's freshly showered and lotioned, and his skin is soft when I grab his arms.

"I've been thinking about this all day." His mouth leaves mine, and he presses a trail of kisses down my body as he sinks onto the ground in between my legs.

"So have I," I pant.

Now his lips are against my lower thighs, at the spot where the skirt of my dress ends. "Tell me you want me, princess."

"I do."

He groans. "Thank fuck." Slowly, ever so slowly, he kisses up my thighs. The fabric of my skirt bunches up in his fists until he flips it over my stomach. "I like it when you wear dresses. Gives me easy access."

"Good thing I packed lots." I slip my panties down my legs without him even asking. As he watches, his eyes flare with lust, so I slow my movements.

He clicks his tongue. "Tease." The second I have them all the way off, he snatches my panties and slides them into his pants pocket.

"Hey!"

Oliver shrugs. "Should've held onto them tighter. They're mine now."

Elliot laughs from the kitchen. "Are you really surprised, love?"

I do a poor job keeping my smile hidden. "No."

Oliver grabs my thighs, shoving them up and open, forcing me onto my back. He's seemingly too focused on me to care about what Elliot just said. "So fucking beautiful," he mutters, shaking his head slightly. "Unbelievable."

With that, he leans down and gives me a single lick. I'm so sensitive, so desperate, that my body jerks in response. He does it again, spreading my arousal to my clit, before he sucks on it gently.

"Oh, *shit*."

He moans deeply before pulling away. "Hold your legs open."

I grab them, keeping them spread as his hands trail down my inner thighs. Oliver bows his head, flicking his tongue over my clit repeatedly. I do my best not to squirm, but it's hard to stay still when it feels so good. When he slides a finger into me, I can't help but whimper.

He slips another finger inside me, pumping them in and out. For a few seconds, he tries out different angles until one has me gasping. Then he sucks on my clit, continuing to work that angle with his fingers.

I'm not one to come quickly, even if it feels really good. My body just needs time. But today, I've been ridiculously turned on since my make out session with Oliver. All the tension and neediness forces my orgasm to slam into me much faster than normal.

I'm not sure how soundproof these walls are, and I doubt our neighbors want to hear me coming, so I move to cover my mouth. But my hands are instantly ripped away.

"Don't you *dare*," Elliot growls just as I cry out. He pins my wrists to the back couch cushions, watching me as I fall apart.

Pleasure courses through my veins, chased by embarrassment. What if someone heard? Oh god, what if someone figures out it was me?

"Ell," I whine, and even that's too loud. "Ahhh, someone could . . . *fuck,* Oliver!"

Oliver hasn't slowed his fingers at all, although he's moved his mouth away from me. He licks his lips and grins. "Delicious. You want a turn, Ell?"

"You really think I'd say no to that?" Tossing his towel onto an empty cushion, Elliot rounds the couch. "Move over."

I get about two seconds of relief before Elliot is kneeling in between my legs. He circles my clit with his tongue, keeping the movement slow and gentle.

Oliver sits on the opposite couch. He crosses his legs, relaxing and stretching his arms out on the back cushions. As he watches us, he smirks at me.

For a few minutes, I'm able to keep my moans quiet. But as I get more and more worked up, they get louder. I clamp my hands over my mouth again, praying desperately no one heard me the first time.

Elliot lifts his head and glares. "I'd move your hands if I were you."

"What are you gonna do, punish her?" Oliver teases.

"No, I'll let Rhett do that."

My eyes widen, and I let my hands fall onto the cushions. I have no desire to get spanked today.

"That's what I thought," Elliot murmurs before dipping his head down and catching my clit between his lips. He sucks, yanking a cry from my lungs that I've been trying to hold back.

"Ell," I sob. "Someone's going to hear."

"They'll live."

I groan as he dives back in.

When I come, I manage not to scream, but my moans are still loud. In retaliation, I grab onto Elliot's hair, pulling harder than I need to. The joke's on me, though, because when he pulls away, he's grinning.

Leaning back, his heated gaze rakes over me. "If we had more time, I'd . . ." He stops, laughs to himself, and shakes his head. "Never mind."

I push myself into a sitting position. "What?"

He's still smiling. "Nothing, love. You'll find out eventually."

I narrow my eyes at him, but then Oliver stands and meanders over to us. He kneels on the couch cushion next to me, takes my chin in between his thumb and forefinger, and presses his lips to mine. The annoyance I'm feeling dissolves instantaneously, and I stretch upward to get closer.

"I want to fuck you," Oliver says in between kisses, "while Ell fucks me. How does that sound?"

Those two orgasms may have knocked the breath out of me, but I still manage an enthusiastic nod. I've thought about it—fantasized—looked it up and watched it. Never in a million years did I think I'd get to experience it.

Until them, anyway.

"Please," I say.

Oliver turns to Elliot. "Did you pack lube?"

He swats Oliver's ass. "Of course I packed lube. Who the fuck do you think I am?"

Elliot stands and immediately tears Oliver's shirt over his head. I go for his belt buckle, undoing it swiftly before pulling his pants and boxers down.

"I've been waiting for this." Oliver steps out of his clothes. "I don't usually get to be in the middle."

Elliot shoves Oliver back onto the couch so he's on his hands and knees, facing me. Framing his face with my hands, I kiss him.

"You'd better be a good boy and do what I tell you, Ol," Elliot says. "Otherwise I'll have Rhett punish *you*."

Oliver whimpers, but it's one of anticipation, not fear. I pull away from him just in time to see Elliot spit in between Oliver's ass cheeks. Then he leans in, swirling his tongue.

Oliver pushes against him and groans. "Do we have time for this?"

With a glance at the clock in the kitchen, Elliot grins. "Just enough. Wren, you keep getting him ready. I'll be right back."

I replace Elliot in a flash. Spreading Oliver's cheeks, I run my tongue over his hole, making him grunt.

"You're going to feel so good, princess," he pants. "Feeling you wrapped around my cock while I fuck you and fuck myself on Ell's dick."

Liquid heat spreads through my stomach at the thought. I moan, continuing to rim him, wondering how different this will feel.

When Elliot comes back, he's fully undressed, and he already has the cap popped off the lube. "Hold out a finger."

I do, and he first squirts some onto Oliver's asshole before adding some to my finger.

"Spread it around. Then slide in nice and slow."

Oliver groans as I follow Elliot's instructions. I start with one finger, then two, smiling when Oliver whines into the couch cushions. By the time I've worked three fingers into him, he's acting like I've been teasing him for hours.

"If we go much longer," Elliot says, "he'll start negotiating."

"Negotiating?"

With a chuckle, Elliot says, "You'll see it at some point. Honestly, if you tell him you're willing to peg him, he might do it on the spot."

Oliver groans. "I'm ready, please. I need you both."

I wash my hand, and Oliver gets up. Thankfully, the couch is pretty wide, otherwise I don't think we'd be able to do this here.

Grabbing a throw pillow, Elliot places it on the couch. "Lie down with this under your hips, love."

I follow his instructions, pulling my knees up to my chest as Oliver climbs over me. He shudders as he slides into me, pushing my legs apart. At the same time, Elliot coats his dick in lube and gets on the couch behind Oliver.

"You ready, princess?" Oliver asks, smiling down at me.

"I think the better question is are *you* ready?" Elliot says, grabbing his ass cheeks and pressing inside.

"Fuuuuck," Oliver groans. His eyes roll back into his head. "More."

"Patience," Elliot says, grabbing onto his shoulder. "Let's ease you into it."

I keep my legs open as much as I can to leave room for them. As Elliot fucks into Oliver a little more, I stare up at them both, although I can't see a lot of Elliot. It takes a minute, but once we're all situated, Elliot starts moving more consistently. The force of his thrusts makes Oliver move inside me.

With a grunt, Oliver rasps, "Let me."

Elliot slows. After adjusting himself for better leverage, Oliver does exactly what he said he would—fucks me while fucking himself on Elliot's dick. Oliver lets out a long string of strained expletives before slamming his lips to mine. He kisses me sloppily, groaning and panting into my mouth, and it might be the hottest thing that anyone's ever done to me.

"Oh my god," he moans when Elliot starts thrusting into him. *"Shit, I forgot how much I love this."*

I grab his head and kiss him again. My tongue slides into his mouth as he lets Elliot take over. It's so different than any other position we've been in, probably because Oliver is writhing in pleasure just as much as I am.

"Wren," he grits out. "Can you touch yourself? I can't, I have to hold myself up."

Oliver's body is pressed too closely to mine for me to be able to reach, but I'm okay with that. Oliver is hitting a spot inside of me that feels like heaven, and if he adjusts to give me room, the angle will change. I won't come from this, but I don't want him to stop. Besides, I kind of like the thought of not coming again.

"I don't need to," I say.

He frowns. "But—"

"Use me. Please."

Oliver grunts, his eyes lighting up. "You want to be our plaything, princess?"

I nod, keeping my gaze on him as Elliot's thrusts make Oliver move inside me. *Fuck,* it feels good.

"You *do* make a pretty toy," Elliot says. "Both of you do."

Just then, Elliot picks up his pace. It forces a gasp out of me, and I grab onto Oliver's arms and hold on for dear life.

"Shiiiit," Oliver groans. He tries to move too, but he can't match Elliot, so he stops.

"That's it," Elliot pants. "Just take it. I'll use you, and you use her."

"I . . . can't . . . last . . ." Oliver is barely able to get the words out. He shudders against me and lets out a helpless moan.

"Kiss him, love. Make him come."

Wrapping a hand around the back of his neck, I tug Oliver down. When our lips meet, his body goes stiff. Elliot is still pounding into him, holding onto my ankles for leverage, and it has all of us breathless.

I never want this to end.

Oliver cries out against my lips. Then his cry dissolves into a series of moans as he comes. I wrap my arms around him, kissing him until he's an unraveled, limp mess in my arms.

Ell pulls out of him. "On the floor on your knees, now. Both of you."

Groaning, Oliver pushes himself off of me. He's still too sated to go quickly, so I end up kneeling first. With one hand, Elliot runs his fingers over my hair, and with the other, he continues stroking his cock.

"You want my cum?"

I nod.

"Or should I give it to Oliver?"

Dropping onto the floor next to me, Oliver says, "Please, Ell."

Elliot grabs a fistful of Oliver's hair and pulls, forcing him to crawl closer. "Shit, I love having both of you like this. So eager to please, aren't you?"

"I'll do anything you want," Oliver begs. "I want you to cover me with your cum."

Elliot smirks. "See what I mean about the negotiating, love?"

Oliver whines impatiently.

"You can have it," Elliot says soothingly. "No worries, Ol."

Arching upward, Oliver watches intently, waiting. My eyes flit between the two of them, loving Oliver's eager expression and Elliot's pleasured one. His gaze doesn't leave Oliver, even as he starts to fall over the edge and he has to fight to keep his eyes open.

"Fuck," Elliot groans. His cum falls onto Oliver's chest, and his hand slows. "You're so fucking sexy with my cum all over you."

Once he's finished, none of us move for a moment. Elliot hasn't stopped staring at Oliver, and I'm still looking between the two of them, caught up in the intense moment they just had.

"Look at all of it," Oliver says, gazing down at his chest. "Fuck."

"Clean him up," Elliot commands, and it takes me a second to realize he's talking to me.

After crawling in front of Oliver, I start licking up Elliot's cum from his chest. Elliot gathers all of my hair up so none of it gets dirty. I savor the salty taste as my tongue travels up Oliver's torso, catching every last drop. When my tongue laves over one of Oliver's nipples, he groans.

"Don't swallow it all, love," Elliot says when I'm close to being done. "Keep it in your mouth."

I obey, and when I'm finished, I look up to him questioningly. Elliot lowers himself to his knees, still holding onto my hair, and kisses me. It's hot and open-mouthed, and a mixture of saliva and cum enters his mouth. A tiny bit dribbles from my chin onto my dress.

Never in my life did I think doing something like this would be hot, but my god, it really is. Especially when Oliver moans as he watches us. And then *especially* when Elliot breaks off our kiss, grabs Oliver's head, and fuses their mouths together in a searing kiss.

That's when I see Rhett watching us from our bedroom door. He's leaning against the doorframe, a half-smile on his face, which for Rhett is a full grin. He doesn't look turned on, necessarily. It's more that he's happy to see us happy—I think, anyway.

Wiping at my chin and mouth, I smile at him. This is probably the most relaxed he'll be for the rest of the week, so I let my gaze rest on him. For a split second, I wish we could kill Ludo today so the guys can put this behind them. But that's not how this works, so I let the thought fade.

The oven timer goes off, pulling all of us back to reality.

"Shit," Elliot groans, reluctantly ending his and Oliver's kiss. "What horrible timing."

"I've got it," Rhett says, walking into the kitchen area. "You guys get cleaned up."

We all stand, and I look down at the cum spot on my dress. *Good thing I overpacked.*

Oliver gives me a tired, happy smile. "You were perfect, princess. I'd like to do that again if you want. Except we'll make sure you get to come next time, too."

With a shrug, I peck him on the cheek. "Or not. I quite like being used by you."

. . .

After we've all eaten and showered, it's time to head over to Ludo and Aubrey's condo. I have pretty simple instructions: stay friendly, stay close, and try to leave the sunglasses in a central part of the house.

The guys stressed that if I can't make it look like a natural, absent-minded thing to do, then to not even bother. It's better to potentially try again at a later time than to raise suspicion by doing something odd.

They say it's not a big deal if I don't get a chance, but we all know they're lying. This is important to them for a multitude of reasons.

On the walk over, I hold onto Elliot's hand, hoping some of his confidence will transfer into me. I've never seen him interact with Ludo, but he's the only one who looks unbothered by tonight. Rhett has been quiet ever since his shower, and Oliver keeps shooting him worried looks.

And me? I made sure I look nice, but I feel like a wreck. Knowing that Ludo was supposedly watching me at Evolve—and that I'm *his type*, whatever that means—has me thoroughly creeped out.

At the condo, Ludo answers the front door and greets us. "Ah," he says when he lays his eyes on me. His smile widens. "I see you got your woman back. Followed my advice, Oliver?"

"Worked like a charm," Oliver replies with a jovial tone as he shakes Ludo's hand. It's shocking to see him look at Ludo with anything but malice, but he hides it well.

Elliot and Rhett follow suit, and then I do too. Except Ludo turns my hand and presses a lingering kiss to my knuckles. It's an odd move and entirely too old-fashioned to make sense, but I give him a friendly smile anyway.

"Lovely to meet you, Miss Taylor."

He doesn't mention that we've met before—and that he left me to die.

"You as well," I manage to say smoothly.

I wonder what he did with Andrew.

"Well, let's not waste any time," Ludo says. "Aubrey is already out on the back patio with drinks."

I move to follow Ludo as he heads deeper into the house, but Rhett grabs my arm. He pulls me back, going first. No, not going first, exactly.

I think it's more that he's placing himself in between me and the man he hates most in the world.

As Oliver takes my arm, he whispers, "You're doing well, princess."

At least one of us thinks so.

On the patio, there are two men in black suits standing off to the side. Ludo's security team, I imagine. There's a large, round daybed on the far end of the patio, decorated with lots of pillows and half-covered by an overhead canopy. Lounging on it is a woman with deep brown skin wearing a light pink romper. Aubrey, I assume.

When she spots us, she jumps to her feet. "Oh, you're here! Perfect!" As she walks over to us, her curly black hair bounces against her bare shoulders. The second I'm in reach, she throws her arms around me and pulls me into a hug. "It's lovely to meet you all."

After some quick introductions, Aubrey grabs my hand and pulls me away from the guys. Ludo looks mildly annoyed but doesn't try to stop her.

"I was *so* hoping you'd come tonight," Aubrey tells me as she pulls me toward the outdoor bar. "Ludo told me a little about you, and I know tonight is supposed to be about me getting familiar with your boyfriends, but whatever. I'm used to having bodyguards I don't know."

"Oh, wow."

She shrugs as she busies herself by making two drinks. "I come from a family of lawyers. My parents take a lot of high-profile cases, and they want me to follow that same path. Between that and being engaged to Ludo, I can't remember the last time I left the house alone."

I swear I detect a hint of bitterness in her voice, but I'm not sure if I'm imagining it or not. "Well, hopefully you'll be able to relax this week."

"I'll be able to eventually," she says with a conspiratorial smile.

I'm not sure what the smile means, but before I can think about it much, Aubrey slides one of the two matching drinks in my direction.

"We can hang out on the daybed together," she says. "I'd love to get to know you more. Do Ludo and the guys work closely together?"

Following her to where she was lounging earlier, I say, "I'm not entirely sure."

I am, of course. But I'm curious what led Aubrey to ask that.

"Oh. Ludo talks about them often enough, so I just assumed." She situates herself on the large cushion, moving a journal and a book with a light pink cover over to make room.

"Oh, is that a book of poems?" I say as I lean over to get a better look.

"Mmhmm. Why, do you read poetry?"

"Not as often as I'd like. I typically stick to fantasy, romance, and murder mysteries."

"If you ever want to get into it more," Aubrey says, "I can recommend some great collections for you."

"Thank you. I'll keep that in mind."

The water isn't too far away, and the sound of the waves hitting the shore has goosebumps spreading across my skin. If it wasn't for last weekend, I'd probably think it was nice. Earlier on the beach, I think I did just fine, but now I'm wondering if that's because I had Rhett with me. The sky is darkening, and it makes the waves look much more menacing.

"That's a lot of water." My voice wavers.

Aubrey catches on. "Oh, are you afraid of it? I used to be when I was younger until I did mommy-and-me swimming lessons."

"Something like that," I mutter into my drink before taking a sip through a cute paper straw. It's sweet and fruity, helping to cover the taste of some of the alcohol.

"So, I know you're with all three of them." Aubrey nods to the guys. "Are they all with each other as well?"

"Yeah. They've been together for a long time. I'm a more recent addition."

She hums, watching as the guys and Ludo converse. Then she turns and looks at me. Up close, I can see just how deep brown her eyes are. They're soft, too, like she spends a lot of time smiling.

"How'd that happen?" she asks. "All four of you ending up together?"

"They met in high school. I work at the coffee shop they swing by once a week. After a couple months of awkward flirting, we ended up at a Valentine's Day ball together. And somehow I found the courage to go home with them."

"No way."

"What?"

Aubrey shakes her head. "That's way too cute of a story to be real. And way too fun of a night."

"It was a whole weekend, actually."

"Damn," she says on a laugh before taking a sip of her drink. Her smile fades almost immediately, because Ludo calls from where he and the guys have gathered around the unlit fire pit.

"Hey you two, come over here. You're supposed to be getting to know your new bodyguards, darling."

Aubrey makes a face when Ludo calls her *darling,* probably because the canopy shields her from his line of sight. Then she sits up, a bright smile on her face. "Just give us a couple minutes. I want to get to know Wren, too."

Ludo doesn't look too happy at her disobedience, but Aubrey easily ignores his soured expression.

"I am so *sick* of him ordering me around," she tells me quietly.

This doesn't sound like it's going to be a happy marriage.

"Why does he expect you to listen?"

She gives me a blank stare for a second, and then she laughs. "You know who you're talking about, right? That man always gets what he wants. But it doesn't matter. I've already chosen to pick my battles for now. And spending a couple minutes over here is one I can win."

"Do you . . ." I trail off, realizing it's probably rude for me to pry into a stranger's love life.

Aubrey must sense my unease, because she nods her head in a way that indicates she wants me to go on.

"Do you want to marry him?" I whisper.

"God no. But it'll be worth it."

"Oh?"

"My parents have a solid reputation and a network of friends and colleagues that Ludo wants access to. Mainly a couple judges, for whatever reason. As for my parents, they took a case that made them some pretty dangerous enemies. They're looking at a couple years before everything is over, and they need protection.

"Ludo has the power to keep my parents' enemies from hurting us, simply through a familial connection. Who would touch us if they knew Ludo would come after them as a result? This is the solution both parties agreed to." She gestures between him and her.

"A marriage of convenience."

"Basically. It keeps my parents safe. And I . . ." She gives me that smile again, like she thinks I'm in on something I'm not. "I'll be just fine."

I'm not sure I believe her, but then again, it doesn't seem like I have the full picture. I tuck that all away in the back of my mind to tell the guys later.

"So if you two aren't in love or anything, why take this vacation together?"

"Appearance and all that. We have to post pictures together on social media." Aubrey rolls her eyes. "For everyone to get what they want out of the arrangement, it has to appear real. That way my parents' inner circle will think Ludo is trustworthy so he can get close to them, blah blah blah. But a pre-wedding vacation is the last thing I wanted to do. It was Ludo's idea because it's convenient for *him*."

"Why?" I try to keep my tone light, hoping I don't come across as too curious. This sounds like it could be helpful, but I don't want Aubrey to get suspicious.

"Hmm? Oh, Ludo has a new employee. A personal one, not one for the club. There's a lot that goes into training someone new. Ludo's process is supposedly more on the grueling side, especially the first few days. Honestly, I feel bad for the new guy. He's practically a kid."

My stomach turns.

"Ludo has a few trusted allies down here who he uses for training," Aubrey continues. "The idea is to put this guy through a series of tests to make him prove his loyalty or some shit. I'm fuzzy on the details, but it sounds like hell. Supposedly, the last time Ludo tried to recruit someone, they died."

Holy shit. Is it going to be this easy to gather information on Ludo?

"That sounds horrible."

"It is. But I'm not surprised. Ludo is heartless."

"It seems like he trusts you, though," I say. "Sounds like you know a lot about his operations."

She laughs. "Oh, that has nothing to do with trust. When we announced our engagement, I moved in with him for security reasons. In an old mansion like his, it's easy to eavesdrop through vents and cold air exchanges, all that shit. The asshole won't tell me anything, so spying on him is the only way I can ever figure anything out. Ludo has no idea how much I know."

This is suspiciously easy.

"So you—"

"Ladies," Ludo calls, his impatience overt this time.

Aubrey rolls her eyes before grumbling, "I can't wait for this whole thing to be over with."

. . .

We end up sitting around the fire pit for an hour or two, lighting it as the sun goes down. The conversation stays casual for the most part, and I notice that Aubrey is considerably different now that we're around Ludo. Her demeanor is still bright and happy, but she's much quieter. She doesn't let on that a single intelligent thought has ever gone through her brain, even though that's how she acted around me.

How odd.

I struggle to pay attention because no matter how loud everyone talks, I can always hear the waves lapping against the shore. By the time it's fully dark, I've crept as close to Elliot as I can. He's been telling stories about winter ski trips and summer backpacking adventures, probably trying to make Aubrey comfortable. He's good at that.

Elliot's voice is the only thing keeping me tethered to real life. Well, that and the way he has an arm securely anchored around my waist. His thumb rubs up and down my side comfortingly. It's a reminder that I'm here, on dry land, a perfectly safe distance from the ocean. Next to him, I have nothing to be afraid of.

Still, all I want to do is bury my face in Elliot's chest and dissolve into anxious tears. I can't—I know that. But it's getting harder to breathe with every passing minute.

Ludo starts talking about a childhood experience he had that's similar to one of Elliot's. It's odd, thinking a monster like him was ever a child.

Since Ludo's attention is diverted, Elliot leans down and kisses my temple. He glances at the ocean. "We need to get you out of here."

"I'll just go inside for a few minutes," I mumble.

I excuse myself and head into the house. On my way to the bathroom, I pass by a small table and set the sunglasses on it, praying they'll go unnoticed since there's a set of keys already on it. It looks like one of those surfaces people would absentmindedly set stuff on, and that's exactly what we're going for.

In the bathroom, I shut myself in and stare at my reflection in the mirror. Every once in a while, I get overwhelmed by all the horrible things in the world, and all my thoughts feel like they're crushing me.

That's how I feel now. Everything is too much. My fears, and how stupid they make me feel. Ludo, and how much I want to watch the life slowly bleed out of him. Jordan, fucking Jordan, and how I wish he was still alive so we could kill him again.

Slowly, I draw in a deep breath. I can be angry later. But right now, if I stay inside the house too long, Ludo or one of his bodyguards might get suspicious.

Think of something nice. Something to calm you down.

My mind instantly goes to the first night I had with the guys. They were so sweet at the ball. As I remember the way Oliver said I looked like a princess, I smile. Then it widens when I think of Rhett. Rhett, who hates crowds and doesn't know how to dance, but did it with me anyway. And of course, there was Elliot, who pulled me away from the ballroom and kissed me and then made sure I felt safe the whole night.

My god, I love all of them so much.

I sigh. Some of the emotional weight has dissipated, and my chest feels lighter. After another long breath, I step out of the bathroom. *I can do this.*

Before heading back to the patio, I stop in the living room. There's a set of large windows that overlooks the beach. I wonder if watching the water from the safety of the house will help ease me into getting back outside. As I watch the waves, I fiddle with the fabric of my skirt, trying to talk myself up.

It's far enough away.

The guys would never let you drown.

There's nothing to be afraid of. Not really.

"You don't seem to like the ocean," Ludo says from behind me.

I jump, focusing on his reflection in the window as he walks closer to me. "Didn't realize you were in here."

He doesn't reply, and we stand next to each other in silence. I go back to staring at the dark water, trying to find the courage to go back outside. Somehow, Ludo is the less-scary option, and I hate it.

"There's nothing wrong with fear, you know," Ludo says. "It's cowardice that's your problem."

If I wasn't already struggling to control my emotions, I'd probably be able to hold my temper. But his accusation is like throwing gasoline on my already-smoldering anger.

"I'm not a coward," I snap, whipping around to face him.

"Whoa, easy there," Ludo says smoothly. He looks me up and down in a way that can only be described as judgmental. "You're acting pretty defensive for someone who has no reason to be."

"You called me a coward. Don't know what else you were expecting."

The door to the patio opens and shuts.

Ludo shrugs. "Seems like it'd be pretty easy to prove to me that you're not one. Or . . ." He smiles, like he knows something I don't. "To prove it to yourself."

I bite back my retort, turning away from him. The last thing I want to do is give him the satisfaction of toying with me. He doesn't actually care about me—he made that very clear when he left me wet and shivering in the snow.

"What are we proving?" Oliver comes up and slings his arm around my shoulder.

How the hell can he manage to be so cheerful around this asshole?

"Just how brave one could be," Ludo says, still smiling. "Or not."

The door opens again, and everyone else files into the condo. Aubrey gives me an apologetic grimace when she notices how close Ludo is standing to me.

"We're gonna head out," Elliot says, and I almost cry with relief. "Gotta get some rest before tomorrow."

"It was lovely talking to you," Aubrey says as she hugs me. "Have a good night."

"You too. Thanks for the drink."

As soon as we're out of the house, I feel like I can breathe fully again. Based on the way Oliver relaxes, I think he's experiencing something similar. He hasn't stopped touching me in some way since he found me with Ludo. Right now, my hand is clasped tightly in his.

"Princess," he asks as we walk back to the hotel, "are you okay?"

"Just overwhelmed, I think. Being that close to the water was . . . um. Hard."

"I'm sorry," he murmurs, squeezing my hand. "We shouldn't've stayed that long."

"I'll be okay. Especially once we're farther away." I fail miserably at keeping the tiredness out of my voice.

He makes a concerned noise, picking up our pace so we can get back to the hotel sooner. I barely notice.

It's cowardice that's your problem.

With a scowl, I glance at the ocean one last time. The sight makes my heart rate spike, and I hate it. I hate it, I hate it, I hate it.

My eyes are still glued to the ocean when I stop, forcing Oliver to pause as well.

"Hey." His touch is gentle as his knuckles run across my cheekbone. "What are you thinking?"

Elliot and Rhett stop behind us, and in my peripheral vision, I see Oliver give them a confused glance.

"I'm going to get over this," I say quietly. Then again, more forcefully. "I'm going to get over this. I'll work through the fear for however long it takes, until I can be around water again without a second thought. I'm not a coward."

I'm not. I refuse to be. And even more than that, I refuse to let a monster like Ludo Holloway be right about me.

Chapter Eight

Rhett

Once we're in the penthouse, none of us stay up for long. Oliver has to be at the condo by six since that's when Ludo and his men are leaving. We're only guarding Aubrey for the first three days of the trip, and only until mid-afternoon. The easiest way to split it up is one of us with her a day, and Oliver volunteered to take the first shift.

We might all end up together, though, considering how well Aubrey and Wren seemed to hit it off. I guess that depends on Wren, though. After her declaration outside, I was hoping she'd be able to sleep peacefully. But unfortunately, *peaceful* is the last word I'd use to describe her as she gets ready for bed.

She's quiet, but she's restless. While she brushes her teeth, she shifts from foot to foot. And once she emerges from the bathroom in her pajamas, she's frowning.

"Sweetheart."

"Hmm?" She focuses on pulling back the blankets on the bed so she doesn't have to look at me.

"What did he say to you?"

At the anger in my voice, she looks up. "He . . ." Her voice wavers, so she clears her throat. "He called me a coward."

"What?"

"He's wrong," she says decidedly as she climbs into bed. "And what he thinks doesn't matter."

"Wren..." I lower myself onto the edge of the mattress and place my hand on her thigh.

"Do you think it's true?" she whispers.

I almost laugh. "Oh, absolutely not. You've had so many brave moments over the past couple weeks, sweetheart. You're far from a coward in my eyes."

That seems to give her some amount of peace. With a sigh, she pulls the blankets over her shoulders. "Are you... are you coming to bed?"

"No. But I'm staying in here with you, don't worry."

She relaxes even more. "Thank you."

I kiss her forehead before shutting off the light. "Goodnight, sweetheart."

"Goodnight."

There's a desk in the corner of the bedroom, so I sit there, angling my laptop away from Wren and lowering the brightness so it doesn't disturb her.

If I'm going to stay up, I might as well work. Lately I've been focusing on doing deep dives into Ludo's inner circles. First, his peers and allies, and second, his trusted employees. Security, his right-hand man, his most favored enforcers, et cetera.

Over the past week, I've found a few things of interest. Possibly the top one is that the Stallards—Aubrey's family—are close friends with a couple of the judges in the Philadelphia area. On its own, it's nothing of importance. But when it's paired with the fact that Ludo had lunch with two different judges last week, a pattern starts to emerge.

Everything I find, I meticulously add to our shared spreadsheet. It's where we keep everything of importance in regards to Ludo's downfall. For a plan as complicated as ours, we have to keep our facts straight.

For about an hour, Wren tosses and turns in bed. Her breathing doesn't even out, so I don't think she even dozes off. When I glance over at her, she's staring at the ceiling, but I don't think she's registering it. In fact, I don't think she's here at all. Not in the ways that matter.

"Wren?"

She blinks. "Yeah?"

"What do you need, sweetheart?" I keep my voice low, not wanting it to carry to Elliot and Oliver's room.

"For my mind to shut off," she whispers. Slowly, she turns her head so she's looking up at me. "It won't stop. It's one chaotic, anxious thought after another, and I can't seem to break away."

"And how do you get your mind to shut off?"

"Reading, usually. But I don't want to turn a light on."

For a moment, I'm not sure what to do. But then an idea forms in the back of my mind. It's one I might regret—I'm not sure—but I'm a man of my word. I'll always do what I can for them.

I pull my shirt over my head and climb onto the bed. "Can I touch you?"

The blankets rustle as she turns to face me. "Yeah."

Pushing the covers back, I slip my arms underneath her and pull her into my lap so she's straddling me. I lean against the headboard, placing her hands on my chest and covering them with my own. "Explore me."

"Explore you?"

With a nod, I murmur, "Use your hands. Touch whatever parts of me you'd like. And ask whatever you want."

She has questions—I know she does. Opening up is like pulling teeth for me, but maybe if I know it's going to help her, it'll be easier to stomach.

"You're sure?"

"I don't say things I don't mean, sweetheart."

Her fingers brush over a small scar on my chest. There's no way she can see it in the dark, which means she's noticed it before. "What's this from?"

"Tripped and fell in the woods when I was a kid. Wouldn't've scarred, but I couldn't stop picking at it."

With a low hum, her hands move up my pecs to my shoulders. Her hands are warm and soft against my skin in a way that soothes some of my pain away.

As her fingers skirt across my cheekbones, I blow out a slow breath and close my eyes. She touches my jawbone, then my chin, and then I feel her thumb brushing over my lips. I try to focus on the way she feels against me instead of on the act of closeness.

You're in control now. She'll listen if you tell her to stop.

Eventually, Wren moves back to my shoulders and down my arms. Once she reaches my wrists, she pulls them upward, and her lips press against the back of my right hand. Again, it's too dark to see my tattoo, but she knows it's there. Her kiss is reverent, almost mournful, and her tone matches when she asks, "Why a butterfly?"

"Sammy loved them." My throat instantly aches, and my voice is hoarse as I continue. "The day she died, we were going to take her to an indoor butterfly garden back home. Me and the guys."

Wren lets out a distressed sound, taking my hands in hers.

"She was so excited. It was all she talked about from the moment we told her we were going. I guess that was our mistake." I try to swallow down the lump in my throat. "She was supposed to wait for me after school. She stayed there for their childcare program, and then when I was done with classes, I'd ride my bike over to the middle school, and we'd walk home together. My dad didn't give a shit, so it was on me to get her home safely."

Wren stiffens, bracing herself as she puts the pieces together. "Oh my god," she whispers.

"There were chronic under-staffing issues at her school. The people in charge of the after-school program were spread too thin, so when Sammy slipped out, no one noticed for a couple minutes. By then, she was gone. She was so excited, and she just wanted to see the butterflies sooner. Who could blame her?

"By the time I got to the school, they'd called my dad three times, but he hadn't picked up. No one thought to call me even though I was always the one who came for her. When they told me they couldn't find her, I fucking panicked. Rushed home, praying I'd find her skipping down the sidewalk, but I never did. I called Ell and O, and they immediately showed up to help me look, but it was pointless. She was gone by then."

"Rhett," Wren whispers, her grip on my hands tightening.

"The police showed up later that night. Sammy had gotten lost and ended up a few blocks off course. Police say maybe she saw something she shouldn't've, or maybe she caught a stray bullet during a hit job. We lived in a fairly violent neighborhood. Cops barely even batted an eye at a little girl dying. Don't think they particularly cared."

"They never figured it out?"

"Oh, they did," I say bitterly. "They just didn't tell us anything. I'm pretty sure they were paid off. We never stopped looking for answers, though. It took us a while, but eventually we got a name—Redback."

"Ludo," she murmurs.

I nod. "We've gathered a lot of information on him throughout the years. Once we realized that Ludo and Redback were the same person, we were able to put together a timeline of his career. When he killed Sammy, he was rising fast in the ranks as an enforcer. Ironically enough, he was working for Edgar Williams at the time."

Silence fills the room as I try to breathe through all the emotions clawing up my throat. Everything is so much more potent tonight. Being this close to Ludo feels like all the happy parts of my life are shriveling up, withering away. The only thing left is an all-consuming hate. Too often, I get lost in it.

I don't want to do that tonight.

"I wish you could've met her." The words are nothing more than a raw rasp. My hands find Wren's hips, and I hold on to her, wondering if I can use her as an anchor so I don't drown in all the anger and hate. "I think you two would've gotten along well. If we'd just kept it from her for a little longer . . ."

"It's not your fault."

"It is. I came to terms with it years ago, Wren. It's okay."

"You were a *child*."

"I was seventeen. Barely a kid. I was the only one who was there to protect her, and I let her down."

"No!" she exclaims. There are tears in her eyes, and the force with which she shakes her head makes them fall onto her cheeks.

"Shhh," I whisper, thumbing the tears away. "We have to keep it down."

"You shouldn't have to feel this way. Shouldn't think that of yourself! There's no way you could've known, Rhett." She's clutching my arms, practically pleading with me.

It's the same stuff I've heard over and over again from Elliot and Oliver, which is ironic. Hell, even Finn has tried to reason with me. Maybe they're right, but how can I fully believe that? I'm her big brother. I was supposed to keep her safe.

"It's funny, though, how different people place blame in the midst of a tragedy," I say quietly.

"What do you mean?"

"My dad blamed me. Of course he did. But Elliot and Oliver, they both found ways to blame themselves instead of me. Elliot for not pressuring his parents more to pay for Sammy and Maria to go to better-funded schools, and Oliver . . . he's the one who told her we were going to take her to the garden. He just wanted to make her happy, that's all. But it backfired tremendously."

"Do they still blame themselves?"

"Sometimes, I think. But it's . . . a different kind of blame. A *what if*-type blame. When it comes down to it, Ludo is the one who pulled the trigger. Regardless of our mistakes, he's the one who killed an innocent child, not us."

Wren leans her forehead against mine as her hands travel back up my arms to rest on my shoulders. "I'm sorry, Rhett. I'm so sorry."

I sigh. In hindsight, this was a horrible idea. The hopeless panic may be gone from Wren's eyes, but an inconsolable sadness fills them now. "I shouldn't've dumped all of this on you tonight," I murmur. "Not when you were already emotional."

"It's okay," she replies softly. "I needed to know at some point."

"Yeah, but—"

She presses a finger to my lips, silencing me. "*Thank you*, Rhett. For opening up to me. I know it's difficult."

There's nothing to say to that, so all I do is nod. Her arms slip around me in a reassuring embrace, and I tighten my hold on her as well.

I can barely remember the time in my life when I liked being hugged. Fucking craved it. Now I have to fight past the memories, past the gut-instinct repulsion. Maybe one day I'll want it again.

I hope.

As Wren presses her face into my neck, she murmurs, "He'll get what he deserves."

I hum in agreement and close my eyes. I'm not sure how long we stay like that, trying to find solace in each other's arms. At some point, I worry that I'll have to wake her when I inevitably have to slide her off my lap.

There's something about our interaction that makes me want to keep her here all night, though. The absence of maliciousness? Her insistence that Sammy's death wasn't my fault? No—no, that's not it.

It's that she didn't touch me until I told her twice that she could. She's such a stark contrast to my father that she creates this sense of safety wherever she goes. I think I'll always admire that about her.

I rub her back as a thread of guilt slivers through me.

Why her? Why can I touch her more but not Elliot and Oliver?

For a split second, I'm worried. Terrified, even. I don't want to love Wren more than the guys. I want to love them all with the same passion, the same care. But just as soon as the thought enters my mind, I realize I could never feel for one more than the other. Elliot and Oliver are essential parts of me. Wren may not be yet, but we'll get there.

Before I can dwell on it more, Wren nestles into me, like she's trying to get closer even though she's as close as she can get. When a small moan escapes her lips, I pause my hand on her back.

"Are you awake?" I whisper.

"Mmhmm. Are you tired?"

"Not enough to sleep."

She angles her head upward and kisses my neck. "Is there anything I can do to help you?"

"No. But thank you."

She sits up and strokes a hand over my hair. "Of course. I . . . I'll always help if I can."

"I know you would," I murmur.

She releases a long breath, tilting her head as she watches me. I'm sure I'm nothing more than a shadow—that's all she is to me, considering how dark it is. But I can just barely make out a gleam in her eyes, a reflection of the little light that's made its way through the curtains.

"You're beautiful, you know that?" Her voice is low, almost timid.

"You can't see me."

She laughs, although it's more like an amused exhale. "I know what you look like, silly. I'd never forget a face like yours. But I . . . I guess I meant *you*." She taps her finger against my chest. "Life hasn't treated you fairly, and you could've let yourself be consumed by bitterness and anger. You could've turned into such a hateful person, but you didn't."

Now it's my turn to laugh, although it's more sad than anything else. "Depends on the day, sweetheart."

"You try," she says gently. "That's all anyone can do."

"I suppose."

"And I admire you for what you're doing. For fighting to get justice for Sammy."

"She deserves justice."

"So do you," she whispers. "And I'm here with you every step of the way until you have it." Her breath skates across my cheek, her lips so close to my own it's almost a kiss.

Once again, I'm struck by how well Wren has adjusted to our life. She's having her troubles—of course she is—but none of them are because our goal for the last ten years has been to dismantle Ludo's life and then kill him, slowly and sweetly.

She's too fucking perfect.

Ever so slightly, I shift, catching her mouth with mine. She lets out a surprised sound before relaxing and grabbing at my hair. My own hands travel farther up her waist, careful to move over her shirt instead of dragging it upward.

I'm not sure who deepens the kiss, or who feels the potent, heady need first. But one moment the kiss is perfectly chaste, and the next Wren is panting into my mouth and I'm groaning into hers.

As I cup her breasts, her grip on my hair tightens. I almost stop, worried I've gone too far when she doesn't want me to, but then she grinds against my hardening cock. My thumbs swipe over her peaked nipples, and she whines.

So goddamned hot.

Almost as if it has a mind of its own, one of my hands continues up her body until my fingers are wrapped around her throat. I keep my grip firm without squeezing, groaning as she rolls her hips again.

Her whine turns into a series of whimpers as I play with one of her nipples and hold her while she continues grinding against my dick. I'd keep her like this until she's crying and begging for more, but that's not what either of us need right now. What we need is—

Fuck. Not this.

Shit, this is a bad idea.

It's the last thing I want to do, but I break off the kiss. "I don't want to use you. Not when you're upset."

Her shoulders sag at the realization. "I don't want to use you, either," she whispers. "But I want to give you a distraction."

As I peer at her through the darkness, she places her hands over mine where they've slid to her waist. I want her—how could I not? My problem is that I don't want her to feel obligated to make me feel better. That's no one's responsibility but my own.

Sensing my hesitation, she smiles, and I swear it actually lights up the room a bit. "I think I could use one too. But only if you want."

Relief billows through me. "Of course I want to, sweetheart."

Instantly, I'm grabbing her throat again, pulling her forward and fusing my mouth to hers. She sighs against my lips, and it's such a sweet sound.

She deserves justice.

So do you. And I'm here with you every step of the way until you have it.

The guys and I have made it clear that we don't own each other. We've done the same with Wren, except a time or two in bed. Secretly, though, I've always disagreed. Elliot and Oliver each own a piece of me, pieces I never thought I'd give to anyone. And now, with Wren, I don't think I even have a choice in the matter.

I belong to the three of them, body and soul. Irrevocably.

"Wren, fuck." I shift us, pushing her onto her back and shoving her legs open more. It's not until I'm covering her body with mine and pinning her wrists to the mattress that I even realize I've done it.

She cranes her neck upward, searching for me, and I oblige her with my mouth on hers. It's harder than I normally kiss her, but how can I stop myself? Everything seems to be falling into place, and she fits so goddamn perfectly.

Wren's legs wrap around my waist, pulling me down until I'm pressing into her so much I'm afraid I'm crushing her. If I am, she doesn't seem to care, too focused on keeping her lips moving against mine. Slowly, I ease up, turning our kiss into a bunch of smaller ones.

"Rhett," she moans. She tries to follow me, but I have her held down enough that she can't. After struggling for a moment, she gives up.

"We're with you too, you know."

"W-what?"

I kiss her again—can't help it. "You said you're with me. We're with you, too. Through everything, Wren. Processing what you had to go through with Jordan, dealing with your family, figuring your life out, all of it."

Forever.

"I know," she whispers. This time when she reaches for me, I let her wrap her arms around my neck, and I lean on my elbows. "It's hard to believe sometimes, but I . . . I know."

"What do you mean, hard to believe?"

She lets out a quiet, nervous laugh. "I'm not used to being so thoroughly cared for."

I smile, dropping my forehead until it's touching hers. I know the feeling. Oliver and Elliot did the same for me. "Now you'll never have to go a day without it."

Before she can respond, I'm kissing her again. I grab at her hair with one hand and snake the other between us. She has to unhook her legs from around me to make room, but the moan she makes when I press the heel of my palm to her clit makes me think she doesn't mind.

"Rhett," she gasps, rubbing herself against my hand.

"Shhh. You have to keep it down. Ell and O need to sleep."

With another moan, she presses a hand over her mouth. The other clutches my arm as she works herself against me. Her panties are already soaked through, and I groan as she coats my palm with her arousal.

"Please take them off," she whispers. "Please, Rhett, please."

Hooking my fingers into her panties, I slide them down her legs before tossing them to the side. Gripping her thighs, I hold them open, wishing a light was on so I could see.

For a second, I stay frozen like that, unsure of what to do first. I somehow need to devour her while simultaneously burying myself inside her.

Wren sits up, pulling at my shorts and boxers until they're halfway down my legs. I have to fall back on my ass to get them off the rest of the way. As I throw them onto the floor, Wren crawls in between my legs. I can just make out her silhouette as she takes my dick in her hand.

It takes a conscious effort to keep my groan quiet when she sucks on the tip of my cock. Her hand moves up and down in time with her head, pulling sensations out of me that make it hard to stay upright.

"Fuck," I mutter, leaning back and resting on my elbows. Her moans only add to how good it feels. "Wren, I need . . ." I don't finish the sentence—don't know how to. The words to describe how I'm feeling are lost on me, or maybe they don't even exist.

She lifts her head up. "Tell me."

"I . . ." With a shake of my head I know she can barely see, I sit up again. "You. I need you."

She gasps when I throw her onto her back. I hover over her, rubbing my thumb back and forth on her inner thigh. When she squirms and whines quietly, I finally move in and brush a finger over her clit. Trying to not make much noise, she clamps both hands over her mouth to stifle the sounds she can't help but make.

"I love having you all to myself," I tell her lowly. "Getting all your moans and your desperation and your needy little cries. Fuck, Wren."

Wren whimpers, and one of her hands comes up to grab my arm. Like this, I know she's mine—I know I own a part of her just like she owns a part of me. I don't plan on letting her forget it.

After a minute, I switch to rubbing her clit with my thumb. One of my fingers slips into her, curling against her front wall.

"Oh my god!" Wren's hand flies from her mouth to grip the comforter.

"You have to stay *quiet,* sweetheart."

"I'm trying, but the way you—*ahhh,* fuck—" she gasps out when I add a second finger inside her. "It feels . . . too good."

"Put your hand back over your mouth."

She does, but her cries only get louder as I add more pressure inside her. They're barely muffled, and it's definitely enough to wake Elliot and Oliver.

"Fuck," I grunt, pulling my fingers out and crawling over her. "Open your mouth."

Once she does, I shove my fingers inside, and she instantly starts sucking them clean. Her tongue flicks against them, and she moans.

Why is that so hot?

Withdrawing my fingers, I grip her jaw and keep her mouth open. Then, lowering my face until it's hovering just above hers, I spit into her mouth. "Swallow it."

She obeys with a whimper before parting her lips and sticking out her tongue. Shit, I didn't even have to ask.

"Such a good girl," I murmur, grabbing her panties and dragging the soaked part across her tongue, forcing her to taste herself more.

"Now we just need to make sure you don't make any noise." I shove her panties into her mouth.

Her surprised cry is muffled by the fabric and my hand, which I keep clamped over her mouth.

"You can take them out once you've proven you can stay quiet. Now replace one of your hands with mine. It stays there, understood?"

She grunts in frustration, but she nods, holding a hand over her mouth. All she has to do is keep it down, and I'm pretty confident this will help her remember.

Backing off, I settle in between her spread legs. Her shirt has ridden up some, exposing her stomach, so I pull it back down. I don't move to take it off, and she doesn't either.

Neither of us mention it, and that realization has my heart beating faster. Weeks ago, when we were first together, I'm pretty sure she would've asked permission to leave it on. Now she knows she doesn't have to ask.

Thank fuck.

Grabbing her legs, I move them so I basically fold her in half. Her knees end up by her shoulders, and her ass is in the air. At this angle, there's just enough light getting past the curtains that I can see how soaked she is. I let myself stare at her for a second before diving in.

Wren squeals, but she cuts it short. Not that it was that loud, anyway, thanks to her panties and her hand.

I lick her from entrance to clit, groaning against her. She tastes heavenly. It's been too long since I've done this.

As I work her clit with my tongue, Wren moans helplessly, squirming against my hold. I keep her there, exactly how I want her, the perfect position to eat her out for however long I feel like.

When I suck on her clit, I expect her to scream, but she manages to bring it down to a wanton sob. Even when I don't relent, she's able to keep quiet.

Raising my head, I whisper, "You're doing so well, sweetheart. I know you can keep it up. You can, right?"

"Mmhmm." The sound comes out differently than normal, but it's still clear enough that I understand what she means.

I bend over her, careful not to crush her, and kiss the tip of her nose. "Good girl."

I swear, she practically melts into the blankets. Until I start circling her clit with my tongue again. The moment I do that, she tenses up, and I can almost feel how hard she's trying to stay quiet.

I'm not sure how long it takes, but she comes faster than I wanted her to. If I could, I'd never stop, but I doubt this position is comfortable for her long term. So after she comes—and manages to only whimper quietly through it—I bring her legs back down.

She's doing better, but it hasn't been enough time to determine whether or not she'll be able to stay quiet, so I don't move to take her panties out of her mouth. Instead, I flip her onto her stomach and direct her to get onto her hands and knees.

Once she's in position, I massage her ass, and she moans in anticipation. She doesn't have a hand over her mouth anymore, but I think her panties stuffed in there serve as enough of a reminder.

Taking my dick in my hand, I rub it against her clit. She shudders. When I slide into her an inch, she immediately tries to take more, pushing back. I let her, smiling at her impatience as I fill her to the brim.

"Look up," I command, pulling out and sliding back in as she does. Then I lean forward and grab her hair. I hold onto it as an anchor as I pump in and out of her, listening to her strained whimpering.

If I could, I'd be sweet and gentle. It's the kind of intimacy our previous conversation would lend itself to. But just like she's struggling to stay quiet, I'm struggling to hold myself back. A need has taken over me—a need to claim her, to mark her, to make sure she knows I'm as in this as she is.

A couple days ago, I was doubting her feelings for us, worried this was just a rebound for her. I was wrong. So, so wrong. I know it now, but this conversation confirmed it more. She's fucking ours.

"I need you up here." I release her hair, snaking my arm around her and hauling her up so her back is touching my front. I thrust into her, and the new angle has me groaning into her neck. "So fucking good."

The second my fingers wrap around her throat, she relaxes into me so fully it feels like she's melting. It may seem like a little thing, but to me, it's a signal of absolute, complete trust. She's allowing me the power to take her life into my hands because she knows I'd never come close to playing with it.

With my free hand, I brush a finger over her hard nipples before traveling farther down. When I find her clit, she bucks against me, moaning a little too loudly.

"Shhh," I whisper soothingly in her ear. "You can do it, sweetheart. I know you can. Come for me again, quietly."

Both her hands grip my arm. I wonder what this feels like from her position—being choked, fucked, and fingered at the same time while not being able to make a noise. Good, I'd say, from the way she's squeezing my dick.

As she gets closer to reaching her peak, her breathing grows more labored. I pick up my pace, and my god, she does so well keeping all those noises contained.

"I should fuck you like this more often," I murmur in her ear. "My beautiful whore."

A strained, tense noise escapes her. I'm so used to her screaming through her orgasms that it takes me a second to realize that phrase pushed her over the edge. Her body convulses against mine until I let up on her clit, still sliding in and out of her. It feels too good to stop.

I slow down, though, letting her recover and catch her breath. She slouches into me as a shudder runs through her.

"You think you can manage to stay quiet for one more?"

She whimpers, but she nods against my chest.

"And will you be good if I take your panties out of your mouth?"

Another nod, this one more enthusiastic.

"Open up." I take them out of her mouth, and she coughs. The fabric is soaked in drool, so I toss them into the hamper in the corner of the room.

"Fuck," she gasps. "I . . . *fuck*."

Nuzzling my face into the crook of her neck, I start to pick up the pace of my thrusts again. It causes Wren to moan, but she keeps it soft enough.

"Rhett," she whispers, and I grab her chin and turn her head so she can look at me.

"Say it again."

"Rhett," she groans, right before I slam my lips to hers. I love the taste of my name on her lips mixed with her arousal.

As I continue to fuck her, Wren's breathing grows heavier and heavier. I touch her clit with my free hand, groaning when she clamps down on my dick.

"You're staying so quiet, sweetheart," I murmur against her lips. "I'm so proud of you."

She whimpers, clutching my arms. I'm not sure if I'll be able to last long enough to make her come again, not like this, so I ease out of her.

"Please don't stop," she whispers. "Rhett, please."

"C'mere." I pull her with me as I sit against the headboard. She turns around and straddles me, and I help guide my cock back into her. "Shit, Wren."

Slowly, she moves up and down. She's panting and moaning softly, lost in the sensations. This is exactly what I wanted—what she wanted. Both of us are so wrapped up in each other that our worries are barely distant thoughts. All I'm focused on is her, and all she's focused on is me.

"Touch yourself," I command, smiling when she does so immediately. "Such a good girl, Wren. Now give me your other hand."

Once she does, I grip her wrist and move her arm so it's behind her and pressed securely to her lower back. My other hand moves to her throat, holding her there as she fucks me.

"That's it," I say lowly. She needs the reminder that she doesn't have to think, doesn't have to do anything other than what I tell her to. I've got her. "You're going to make yourself come just like this, aren't you?"

Her sob is weak as she continues. My hand tightens on her wrist, keeping it pinned behind her back, while her other hand continues to work in between her legs. She's gripping my dick tightly, so tense and needy.

"You . . . Rhett, you feel so good," she gasps.

"You love my dick, don't you? Love fucking yourself with it and taking everything I have to give you like the cum slut you are?"

"Yes," she whimpers as her movements grow faster. "I want your cum, Rhett, please."

With a groan, I say, "You're so goddamn sexy when you beg."

Under any other circumstances, I wouldn't be able to stand it. Her begging would crack my heart in two. But in bed? Fuck, I'll never get enough of it.

"Please give it to me, Rhett," she whispers. "I need it."

I click my tongue. "Aww, was Oliver's cum not enough for you earlier? You need more? So greedy, Wren."

"I am," she says, barely able to keep her voice low. "I'm your greedy slut, and I need you to fill me up."

"Then you'd better be a good girl and come on my cock, hmm?"

Desperately, she nods. I adjust my legs for better leverage, and then I start thrusting up into her. She gasps, and I can tell it's taking everything in her to stay quiet. Her body gets impossibly tense, her back arches, and then she throws her head back.

"Oh, *fuck*," I groan as she comes. The contractions feel like heaven, and they pull me closer to my own orgasm. "That's it, sweetheart."

"Rhett," she whimpers as her fingers slow over her clit. "God, Rhett."

I pull her down until her mouth crashes against mine. When she whines into my mouth, I pump into her one last time before giving her a break. "Can you handle more?" I ask.

"Use me," she whispers. "Fuck me like I'm your toy. Please."

Holding her to me, I move us so she's on her back again, all while staying inside of her. She moans into my shoulder and wraps her arms around my neck, pulling me close.

I prefer being able to see her in a position like this, but even with the lights off, it's pure ecstasy. I start off with slow, deep thrusts that have me holding back a groan. "Do you know how good you feel? Fucking hell, Wren. If I could keep you like this forever, I would."

Her legs come around my waist, keeping my body as close to hers as she can. Her skin is temptingly soft, and I find myself burying my face in her hair. The floral scent of her shampoo fills my nostrils as I inhale deeply.

I don't last long—rarely do in this position. Wren holds onto me as I come with a stifled moan.

"*Fuck.*" I press into Wren one last time. As I shudder through the tail end of my orgasm, my lips find hers. The kiss is uncoordinated and sloppy because I can't manage anything else. My mind is blank, all except for a single thought of *her*.

I can't hold myself up, so I hold onto her and roll onto my back. Only then do I let myself relax. With Wren on top of me, it makes it harder to catch my breath, but I don't care. I love feeling her limp, trembling body against mine, knowing I'm the one who did that to her.

"I'm pretty sure you already know this," she mumbles sleepily against my chest, "but you're really fucking good at that."

"So are you." I raise my head to kiss her forehead. "My pretty toy."

She yawns, already half asleep, before muttering, "I like being yours."

My heart stutters. Really, I don't know why. I've told her she's mine. *Ours*. And I'm already hers as well. But hearing her say it out loud . . . it makes everything feel so much more real. Irreversible.

Easing into a sitting position, I say, "We need to get you cleaned up before you fall asleep."

She grumbles some sort of protest, but at the same time, she drags herself out of bed and heads to the bathroom. After she pees, we take a quick shower, and then she falls back into bed. I'm not tired enough to sleep, but I think I might be able to get there, so I shut off my laptop and climb in with her.

The second I touch Wren, she snuggles up to me. Her arm flops over my stomach, and within minutes, her breathing evens out. For now, it seems like I fucked the anxiety right out of her. If she's dreaming, she's not having nightmares.

I hope she has a peaceful night. I always hope she does. Fuck, what I'd give to keep her happy and safe from the things that haunt her. Carefully, I pull her even closer to me and kiss the top of her head. She moans, nestling her head against my chest.

"I think," I whisper to her sleeping form, "I think I'm falling . . ."

Fuck. I can't even say it out loud when she's not conscious. Oliver has already said it, and I can't imagine Elliot will be far behind. How will she feel if it takes me a lot longer? Will she understand? Or will she view it as me not caring for her?

What if I'm never able to say it?

Then you'll show her. You'll show her just like you do with Ell and O. You'll do everything you possibly can.

The thought doesn't calm my worries completely, but it helps enough that I can relax. I kiss Wren's temple and close my eyes.

It takes an hour, or maybe longer, but eventually I drift off to sleep with my arms locked around the only woman on this planet I'd willingly lay down my life for.

Chapter Nine

Elliot

In the morning, I get up with Oliver. It's still dark outside, and I normally don't get up this early, but I don't want him to have to eat breakfast alone.

I check my phone and notice that I have a text.

Sparrow Belgrave: Don't underestimate Aubrey.

What the hell? I shouldn't be surprised that somehow Sparrow knows we're Aubrey's bodyguards for the next few days. Not only is she a master at making people disappear, the woman knows *everything*. That's why we couldn't turn down the Wyoming job when she offered. Inevitably, Sparrow has dirt on Ludo that we'll need. It's good to be in her circle so that when the time comes, we can buy it from her.

Still, it's a potential safety problem that the information made its way to her.

Elliot: How did you find out Ludo hired us?

She doesn't respond immediately, so I slip my phone back into my pocket.

As Oliver pours himself a bowl of cereal, he asks, "Did you sleep okay?"

"Like the dead. You?"

He shrugs. "Woke up a lot."

It's classic for him, especially in a situation like this. No doubt, he's worried about Ludo being suspicious of us. We've made sure to keep our relations with him civil and professional, but that all changed when Oliver accused Ludo of knowing where Wren was when she got kidnapped.

"We'll be okay. We just have to tread carefully."

"I will. I . . . I'm sorry, Ell. I just—I fucking lost it when we watched those videos Jordan sent us. I wasn't thinking straight." He bows his head.

"We were all desperate to get her back."

"But what if I ruined everything? What if this whole job is a ruse, a test of loyalty we're bound to fail? What if Ludo never trusts us?"

"It doesn't matter." I grab his shoulders, turning him so he's facing me. "One way or another, we'll be the end of him, O. I don't care what we have to do or what we have to sacrifice. As long as the four of us stay together, we'll find a way. I promise you that."

His brows are furrowed and his eyes are still full of doubts. But when he meets my gaze, I spot just enough of his usual determination—just enough that I know he'll be okay.

"Okay," he murmurs.

It doesn't take too long for Oliver to eat his cereal, and by then, it's time for him to head to the condo. Just as he's putting his shoes on, the door to Rhett and Wren's bedroom opens and shuts quietly. Rhett slips out, padding across the room toward us.

"Where's Wren?" Oliver asks, peering behind Rhett.

"She's still asleep. I just came out to say bye before heading back in."

"Oh," Oliver says softly. "You didn't have to do that. I—"

Rhett catches him in his arms. Cradling the back of his head with one hand, he leans down and kisses him. Oliver clings to him, to the notion of safety and peace that comes with being inside Rhett's embrace, before sighing.

"I love you both," Oliver says as he pulls away.

Rhett kisses him again before murmuring, "I know. We'll see you later."

When Oliver turns to me, I kiss him. "Love you too, Ol. Text us if you need help."

"I will."

I hate watching him go. It's one of the things I dislike most about our life—having to split up to get a job done. At least he won't be far.

Once Oliver is out the door, I head into the kitchen area. As I go about making some coffee, I ask, "Did you get any sleep last night?"

"Some. I woke up after a couple hours and started going through the audio from the bug Wren planted." Rhett steps up to me, standing oddly close.

"Oh? Find anything of note?" I go through the cabinets until I find the mugs, pulling out two. I'd get three, but I doubt Wren will be up for a while.

"Ell, stop." Rhett catches my wrist and spins me around to face him. He pins me against the counter, his hips pressing against mine.

"What...?"

"I'd like a proper good morning, that's what." He says it like it's the most obvious thing in the world before tilting my chin up and kissing me.

Warmth floods my veins. There's something about getting kissed by Rhett that leaves me feeling special. Right now, I bask in it, grabbing his hips and keeping him tightly against me. When he starts to pull back, I follow him, drawing the kiss out for another couple seconds.

I keep my eyes closed after we pull away, smiling. "That was nice."

"Why are you acting surprised?"

Why is he surprised that I'm surprised?

Rhett isn't the most physically affectionate person, and he knows it. The amount of touch he's able to handle ebbs and flows, but he usually keeps to himself. I'm not used to good morning kisses and hugs from him. But, I suppose, this tracks for how Rhett's been acting recently.

"You've just been more physically affectionate lately. I'm not used to it. I'm perfectly happy about it, of course."

Relief overtakes his features. "I have been?"

"Yeah. You haven't noticed?"

"Not . . ." He rubs the back of his neck, staring at the floor. "Not entirely."

For a minute, we stand together silently, awkwardly. *That's* a surprise for both of us. Awkwardness doesn't often show up in our relationship these days.

Reaching behind me, Rhett pours our coffee. His free hand lingers on my waist as he does. And fuck, I love it.

"I should get back to Wren," he says. "She hasn't had any nightmares yet, which either means she won't or one is still coming. I'd love to say it'll probably be the former, but . . ."

I nod in understanding. During the time she's been with us, I can count the nights she hasn't had a nightmare on one hand.

"I'll update the spreadsheet with a link to the doc I'm transcribing everything into."

"Thanks."

With one last kiss, Rhett heads back into the bedroom. I grab my laptop and set up at the kitchen table. By the time I have it on, Rhett's already added the link. Sipping my coffee, I open the doc and immediately start scanning the text Rhett has typed out.

The conversations in the condo last night are nothing of note, and then there's silence until around five in the morning. Rhett includes that there are a whole bunch of indecipherable noises, which is normal. At some point, though, Ludo speaks. He's the only one talking, which makes me think he's on the phone.

Ludo: Morning. Did you get the child? [laughs] Unlike me? Oh, this has nothing to do with sympathy. [pause] You'll see. He'll make an excellent backup plan if we need one. But we most likely won't. Aubrey has taken a liking to Wren, so I'm sure they'll be best friends by the end of the week. If the two of them bond, it'll give me even more influence. [pause] Good, good. I'll talk to you soon.

I narrow my eyes at the screen. That confirms my hunch. Ludo either wants or needs us close to him for some reason. Whatever is going on with this kid is concerning, especially since it seems like it's somehow connected to us.

There's nothing else of interest in the transcript, but I go over it again anyway. Then I start wracking my brain, trying to think of any kids Ludo could possibly use as a backup plan. The only one I can think of is Maria, and she's far from a child. She's only a few years younger than Oliver.

No matter how hard I try, I can't think of any child Ludo could be talking about. Somehow, that makes it all much more unnerving.

At some point, I hear Wren and Rhett get up. I never heard her screaming or crying, which is a good indicator that she didn't end up having a nightmare. Fuck, I hope so. She could use a good night's sleep.

When their bedroom door opens, I drag my eyes away from my laptop and take her in. She has a throw blanket wrapped around her shoulders, and she looks like she needs to go back to bed. "Morning, love."

With a sleepy groan, she sits in the chair next to me. "Morning."

"You didn't have to get up if you weren't ready to."

She starts to reply, but a yawn overtakes her before she can. Then, "I tried to get back to sleep but couldn't."

"Too much on your mind?" I ask as Rhett comes out of the bedroom and grabs himself more coffee.

Guilt shrouds Wren's features as she fiddles with the edge of her blanket. "Yeah. I think . . . I think I have some stuff to tell you guys."

I'm bracing myself before I even realize I am. Never in my life has that phrase led to anything good. It means fights, yelling, slamming doors, and an underlying hostility that never truly fades. So when I turn to face her, I'm already preparing for the worst—although I'm not sure what that would be in this situation.

"Rhett?" Wren says. "Can you sit with us?"

Based on his hardened expression, he heard what she said to me. He sits across from us and folds his hands, resting them on the table. "What do you have to say?"

"Aubrey is . . . very trusting." Wren squirms. "She told me some stuff about Ludo. Stuff I don't think most people would tell a practical stranger. I think she could be really helpful."

"You don't sound too happy about that," I say, hiding my relief. If all she has to talk about is her conversation with Aubrey, that's so much better than whatever I was gearing up for.

"I wasn't expecting to like her," Wren says. "I thought I'd hate her as much as I hate Ludo. And now I don't know what to do or what to feel. I know we can't let her in on our plans. It just feels wrong to use her for information, that's all."

Pulling her chair closer, I put an arm around her. "I know, love."

Over the years, we've had to make a lot of sacrifices. One of the hardest things to let go of was the adherence to a strict set of rights and wrongs. We're murderers for hire, for fuck's sake. Of course we do questionable things. A *lot* of questionable things. Still, I'm familiar with the struggle. It took me a lot of time to get past it.

"But my priority is you guys and your plan," Wren says. Her eyes lock with Rhett's. "To get justice for Sammy. If getting close to Aubrey helps get us closer to our end goal, then it's worth it. Besides, Aubrey seems to hate Ludo. I think she'd agree with our cause."

"Why don't you tell us what she said," Rhett suggests.

After taking a steadying breath, Wren outlines her conversation with Aubrey last night. The things that stick out to me the most are why Ludo is here and how much information Aubrey volunteered without Wren even asking. It almost sounds like a trap.

"How the hell does a kid fit into all of this?" Rhett mutters.

"And what's Ludo need a backup plan for?" I add. "I don't like this."

Rhett's jaw is set, and his arms are crossed. No doubt, he's thinking about the last child we know who crossed paths with Ludo.

"What are you guys talking about?" Wren asks.

"Here." I pull up the doc again and angle my laptop so Wren can read it. "This is the audio from the sunglasses."

She perks up. "It worked?"

"Yeah." I kiss her forehead. "You did a good job, love."

That seems to lift her mood significantly. Unfortunately, it only takes a few minutes, and then she's frowning again.

"Ludo wants me and Aubrey to become friends? That's . . . weird."

"I agree," Rhett says darkly. "I'm not going to tell you who you can and can't hang out with, but there's absolutely no way you're spending time with her without one of us present. You're not going *anywhere* by yourself."

Wren doesn't protest. At the moment, I think she prefers it this way. If I got kidnapped from my own apartment, I'd probably want someone around to keep me safe at all times, too.

My phone buzzes, and then Wren's and Rhett's do as well. Grabbing my phone, I see a notification from Oliver in the group chat with the four of us.

Oliver: Aubrey wants to hang out with Wren???
Wren: Sounds good to me!
Elliot: Nothing near water.

Wren hums when she sees my text. "That's probably a good idea."

Oliver: Aubrey suggested shopping. She needs stuff for the honeymoon.
Rhett: Two of us should go.

The fact that he's not volunteering means he doesn't want to. Fair enough—Rhett has always hated shopping and dealing with other people. Stresses him out.

Elliot: I'll come with you guys.

"Thank you," Rhett mutters.

"I don't mind." I let my arm fall from Wren's shoulders and kiss her cheek. "Maybe it'll even be fun."

And maybe—*hopefully*—we'll be able to learn something more about Ludo's plans for us.

Chapter Ten

Oliver

My morning with Aubrey is pretty uneventful. I'm not sure how I feel about her and Wren getting closer, but it could be a great way to weasel our way into Ludo's personal life more. The closer, the better, honestly.

Aubrey and Wren are both hungry, so we stop for food first. By the time we arrive at a little plaza full of cute, upscale stores, it's already afternoon. We're only supposed to keep an eye on Aubrey until around three—that's when Ludo gets back from whatever he's doing—but obviously if we stay out later, she's still our responsibility.

When we enter the first store, I'm immediately drawn in. So many vibrant articles of clothing hang on the racks. It's an explosion of color.

"Oh, wow," Wren says, stopping in front of a romper. "This is pretty."

I already know what she's going to do, and so does Elliot. We watched her do it over and over again when we took her shopping weeks ago. Instead of further inspecting the romper or looking for one that's her size, she immediately goes for the paper tag hanging from the side.

Elliot catches her wrist. "Ah ah. Don't bother checking the prices." He slides his card in between her fingers and kisses her cheek. "Get whatever you want."

Wren laughs nervously, staring at the credit card like he's playing some practical joke on her. "You sure you want me to hold this? What if I lose it?"

He shrugs. "I trust you."

As Wren and Aubrey look through the store, chatting and laughing with each other, Elliot and I watch from a distance.

"The two of them seem to be getting along well," I say quietly.

Elliot nods. "Ludo wants them to."

"What?" I hiss. "And we're just letting it happen?"

"I think it'll be good for us, too," Elliot murmurs. "Rhett has a transcript of the conversations in the condo last night, so you'll be able to read the whole thing soon. But the basic gist of it is that he wants Wren to get attached to Aubrey so Ludo has another attachment to *us*. Which is exactly what we want. Aubrey doesn't seem to know about his plans, though. She genuinely likes Wren."

"Makes sense."

"Oh?"

"I happen to think Wren is a very likable person."

With a quiet laugh, Elliot puts his arm around my shoulders. "No shit."

"Wren is in on this whole getting close to Aubrey thing, right?" I watch her face, noting how intently she's listening to Aubrey. Her smile is sincere as she nods, adding in a comment here and there. "I don't want to use her like that."

Gently, Elliot squeezes me. "She is. Practically volunteered to do it, but it's definitely making her uneasy."

"Understandable," I mutter.

When Aubrey and Wren head to the dressing rooms, Elliot and I stay back. I may have fallen in love with this place the second I stepped inside, but I wasn't distracted enough to miss the man who walked past and spent just a second too long peering through the windows.

On its own, that's not a big deal. Lots of people peer into windows, and this place is definitely eye-catching. What's bugging me is that the man has made a second appearance. He crossed in front of the store again, and now he's hanging out at one of the outdoor tables of the cafe next door.

"Did you text Rhett?" I ask in a hushed tone.

"He's ready with the car just in case. We can leave this area and see if he follows."

I nod, letting my gaze fall on Wren as she steps out of the dressing room wearing the romper. Since Aubrey is still getting dressed, Wren turns to us.

"I love it, princess," I tell her.

Aubrey comes out in a pair of linen pants and a pastel pink shirt that she tucked in. Her and Wren take each other in, giving their opinions and such. It reminds me of shopping with my mom and Maria. No matter what, my mom was always supportive of us finding our own styles. Even her negative feedback was laced with kindness and encouragement.

Fuck, I miss them. I should make time to see them as soon as we get back. If we can plan it around her work schedule, maybe Wren can meet them, too. Or, if I have things my way, she'll never go back to her job unless she absolutely wants to. We can take care of her—as long as she won't find that stifling.

While the girls finish up trying on clothes, Elliot and I keep a close eye on the man outside. He finished his drink a long time ago, but he's still sitting there even though he's not doing anything.

"He's not bothering to be very subtle," I whisper to Elliot before realizing he's smiling. "What? What are you—"

I follow his gaze. Wren is at the counter swiping Ell's credit card. Based on the way she's shifting from foot to foot, the total was more than she anticipated.

"You like it when she spends your money?"

"Our money," he corrects, still smiling. "And yeah. I like it when any of you do."

Once all the clothes are packed up, Wren tries to hand the credit card back to him. "The total was—"

Elliot cups her cheeks and kisses her. "I don't care about the total, love. Spend however much you want. And keep the card."

With a surprised squeak, Wren puts the card back in her wallet. "You—you're sure? It—what if—that's—"

"I'm positive," he says gently.

Aubrey watches the interaction with amusement before turning to Wren. "Okay, so I know we're supposed to be shopping for clothes, but there's a really cute bookstore over—"

"We have to leave the plaza, actually," I say.

Aubrey frowns. "But I think Wren will really like the shop. It looks really nice, and they have this poetry collection I wanted to show her."

"Oooh," Wren gasps, "I've been wanting to start reading poetry again."

"We can come back," Elliot says. "But first we have to leave."

Aubrey's face falls, and her eyes dart to the windows. "Are we being followed?"

"Potentially," I say. "But it's nothing to worry about. We're perfectly capable of keeping you both safe."

That seems to help Aubrey relax some. We get a cab, and as we're piling in, the man gets up from his seat and heads to an SUV. While Aubrey directs the driver to another boutique she wants to check out, Elliot texts Rhett.

Wren takes my hand. "What are we gonna do?"

"You don't have to do a thing," I say before whispering in her ear, "except maybe try to keep Aubrey calm."

Not letting go of my hand, Wren turns in her seat to look at Aubrey. "Hey. You okay?"

"I'm too close," Aubrey mumbles. "It can't end here."

"What? Nothing is ending here. The guys will keep us safe."

As we drive, Wren does her best to reassure Aubrey. By the time we're pulling into the parking lot of another strip mall, she seems less worried.

"The plan is to act like nothing is wrong," I say. "We're gonna go inside, you two are gonna keep shopping, and we'll let you know what to do from there. The only thing you have to do is stay away from the windows at the front of the store."

Aubrey gulps. "Got it."

We pay the fare and then head inside. The man following us stayed a few cars behind us the whole time, but it was still obvious he was tailing us. Honestly, I'm a little disappointed he's making this so easy. The challenging ones are always more fun.

In the shop—another boutique about the same size as the first—Aubrey and Wren avoid the very front of the store. The man makes no move to get out of his vehicle, instead taking a parking spot that gives him a view of the front door.

Aubrey and Wren pick out a few articles each. Thankfully we're the only people in the store, which makes things less dangerous for anyone else around.

I meander toward the back of the boutique, smiling at the woman who's meticulously folding a box of shirts at the counter. There's a cute little spot with two dressing rooms, and then—bingo—another door. Quietly, I open it and step into the back storage room.

It's small and cramped in here, so I find the exit easily. That door leads to behind the buildings. The perfect place for delivery trucks, employee parking, or a getaway car.

Back inside, I give Elliot a nod before texting him and Rhett one last time. The next part of our plan is sure to unnerve the girls, but it's the safest option for them.

"Why don't you guys put these in the dressing rooms?" I nod in that direction. "Then it's time to get you two away from that guy."

As Wren hangs her stuff in the first dressing room, I notice one of the pieces she picked out is a deep, dark green. No doubt, she did that *very* intentionally.

"Okay," Elliot says, brushing his fingers down Wren's arms comfortingly. "Most likely, that man is going to come inside once I leave."

"You're leaving?" Her voice sounds so small, so scared, and her brows are knit together.

"I'm only going far enough that the guy outside feels comfortable coming in. Once he moves, I'm coming right back. Just do what Oliver and Rhett tell you, and everything will be fine."

"Rhett? But Rhett's not here, I don't under-"

"I'll explain in a minute, princess." I pull Elliot away and ask quietly, "This isn't real, right?"

"I don't think so," he says in a hushed tone. "But we need to treat it that way regardless. And keep your eyes peeled for an actual threat."

"Got it."

He kisses me lightly before heading for the front of the store.

Grabbing Wren and Aubrey, I pull them into the storage room. "Rhett is waiting outside to get you two out of here. Then Elliot and I will deal with the guy out front."

Wren tries to protest, or ask questions, but we don't have time. I shove the back door open. Rhett is already waiting with the car running. He opens the door to the backseat silently.

"In you go," I say, ushering Aubrey into the car. "I'll see you guys later."

"Oliver." Wren pauses even though Aubrey tries to pull her into the car.

"I'll be okay." Gently, I kiss her, and then Rhett pushes her into the backseat and slams the door.

"If I don't hear from you in five minutes, I'm coming back," he says as he rounds the car. "Be careful."

"Always am," I say lightly before slipping back inside. "Love you."

"I love—"

The door slams before Rhett can finish. *Shit.* I'm not used to him saying it back, so I didn't think to give him time. But right now, I don't have extra time to waste. I'll make it up to him later.

Rushing back into the store, I close the curtains to both of the dressing rooms before plopping onto the couch across from them. Just then, the bell on the front door jingles, signaling someone coming in. Involuntarily, my leg starts bouncing. Can't help it. I hate being alone like this. If I fuck up, there's no one to save me. Not until Ell comes back, anyway.

As I hear the woman up front greet the man, my conversation with Finn yesterday morning replays in my head. *Don't leave room for mistakes in your head, or you'll find yourself making them.*

We can't afford to fuck up today. Not when the girls' safety is on the line, and not when we have so much riding on this job. I have to do this.

Finn's right. I can handle this—I *know* I can handle this.

I stare at my phone, pretending to scroll, until I see the man appear in my peripheral vision. My blood pressure spikes, but I don't show it.

"Don't move." His voice is hushed yet commanding.

I look up, plastering on a surprised expression. "Whoa, hey, there's no need for a weapon like that."

Stepping farther into the dressing area, he growls, "I'll be the judge of that."

Raising my hands slightly in surrender, I give him a quick once over. Short, thinning hair, solid build, and pink, sunburned skin. He looks like a regular tourist except for the gun in his hand. He's holding it expertly, like someone who's handled one thousands of times before. Still, he walked right into our trap, so he's not the brightest.

"Which one is she in?" he demands.

I give him a confused look. "Who?"

With an annoyed growl, he rips open the first curtain. When he realizes the dressing room is empty, he quickly moves onto the next one. "You motherfu-"

I'm already on my feet and advancing toward him. He sees me in one of the mirrors, but it's too late. With a series of practiced, fluid movements, I disarm him and drop him to the floor.

Stepping back, I aim his gun directly at his head, not bothering with my own. "Stay on your knees."

Behind me, Elliot laughs. "Damn. I guess there was no need for me to rush back."

At the sound of his voice, my anxiety dissipates. I did it—*of course I did it*—and now Elliot is here in case something goes wrong.

Behind us, we hear a feminine gasp. Elliot turns, but I don't want to take my eyes off this guy, so I don't move.

"Ma'am, so sorry to scare you like this," Elliot says. "We're not going to hurt you, I promise. There's no need to call the police."

"Are—are you here to steal stuff?" she asks in a trembling voice.

"No," Elliot says. His tone is calm yet commanding. "We're just trying to keep our client safe." There's a pause, and I think he gestures between me and him. "We're bodyguards."

"Oh," the woman breathes out. She still sounds scared, but not as much.

"I'm gonna pay for everything in those two dressing rooms," Elliot says. "And then we're gonna take this guy and get out of your hair. Again, sorry to scare you. Can you start ringing everything up for me?"

She gulps. "Sure."

After she gathers up the clothes, Elliot grabs a couple scarves and starts tying the man up. "We'll have her add these to the bill as well."

"Listen," the man says. "I didn't want to hurt anyone. I just want Aubrey."

"Sucks to be you, I guess," I say with a shrug. "Because you're not getting her."

"Hear me out," he says. "Whatever your boss is paying you, I'll double it. We can make it look like you fought your hardest."

"Not a chance," I spit out.

"Fucking piece of shit," Elliot mutters, bending down and searching through the man's pockets. He pulls out a set of car keys. "I'll grab his car and bring it around back."

"Sounds good."

"Wait," the man blurts. "What are you going to do to me?"

"What do you think we're gonna do?" I taunt. "Let you go?"

His eyes are wide and pleading, and he even clasps his hands together. "Don't kill me. I work for Ludo. He sent me to test you guys. Trust me, you passed! Just please don't kill me."

Elliot rolls his eyes. "You really think we're gonna believe that?"

We most definitely *do* believe him. Hell, we practically predicted this would happen. But we can't let on that we know that.

"Please!" the man begs. "Just call him and ask."

When Elliot chuckles, I brace myself. The only time he laughs like that is when he's dealing with someone who's severely gotten on his nerves. I've heard it countless times at Hayes family gatherings.

"Oh," Elliot says through a tight grin, "I'll do you one better than that."

...

Getting the guy tied up, gagged, and into the trunk of his SUV isn't hard. Neither is leading him around Ludo's condo and up onto the patio. No, what's hard is seeing Wren sitting on the bench by the empty fire pit holding Aubrey, with Rhett pacing behind them. All I want to do is go to them, but I can't. Not yet.

When Ludo sees us, alarm flashes over his features, quickly followed by intrigue. He's sitting in an Adirondack chair, a drink in one hand

and a tablet in the other. Once we're close enough, we shove the man toward Ludo, and he falls at his feet.

Slowly, Ludo sets his tablet down on the arm of his chair. Before even acknowledging the man before him, he takes a long sip of his drink. "Elliot. Oliver." He takes his sunglasses off and hangs them on his shirt. Finally, he looks down. "Samuel."

Samuel grunts.

Motherfucker. He really was testing us.

Ludo huffs out an amused breath before addressing us. "I was expecting you to take a lot longer to notice him. You three really are as good as everyone says."

Elliot's face hardens. "We're *better* than everyone says."

Ludo smiles, and it's that dark, sinister smile that I hate. "Good." Pulling out a knife, he cuts through Samuel's gag and restraints. "How'd they do?"

"Just fine, sir."

"I want a full written report by dinner."

"Yes, sir."

Samuel drags himself to his feet. He turns to us and holds out his hand. "I'll be needing my car keys back."

Elliot tosses them to him, and we watch him go. I wonder how many other men Ludo has down here that we don't know about.

"Let me *go,* Wren."

As Samuel rounds the house, my attention is drawn back to the girls. I watch as Aubrey stands, even as Wren desperately tries to hold her back.

When I first looked over, I thought maybe Aubrey was crying. Now I realize I couldn't be more wrong. She's glaring at Ludo, so angry she's shaking.

"*You,*" Aubrey seethes. Her fists are clenched tightly as she marches right up to Ludo. "You orchestrated this whole thing, and you purposefully kept it from me!"

Ludo leans back in his chair, following her movements with a disinterested, lazy stare. "And?"

"And?! I was terrified! Why didn't you tell me?"

"Didn't want to give it away, obviously."

"Seriously? Would it kill you to think about someone other than yourself every once in a while?"

"Unless it's beneficial to me, darling, I see no reason to."

"You repulse me. *Repulse* me, Holloway." Aubrey turns on her heel and storms inside, slamming the door behind her.

"Aubrey," Wren calls, following after her.

With an eye roll, Ludo settles back into his chair. He directs his attention toward us, seemingly having forgotten about Aubrey and Wren already. "You three did well today. I'll get my report from Samuel, but I'd love to hear the sequence of events from you as well."

As Elliot walks Ludo through our afternoon, Rhett wanders over to us slowly. He's taking controlled, even breaths, and his mask of tolerance is slipping. We need to get him out of here before he loses it.

"Well done," Ludo says once Elliot is done explaining. "And clever planning."

"Thank you," I reply as I grab Rhett's hand. "I'm glad you're happy with the results of the test. I for one am fairly tired, and I'm in the mood for a nap. Same time tomorrow?"

Ludo nods. "Same time tomorrow."

"I'll stay with Wren," Elliot says. "Make sure she gets back okay."

"Got it. See you." I flash them one last smile before dragging Rhett off the patio and around the condo.

Once we're on the path back to the resort, Rhett slows us down. "You don't seem tired at all."

"I'm not. Just needed to get you out of there. You looked ready to burst."

"That's about how I felt," he says darkly. "All I could think about was strangling him. I told Aubrey and Wren it was a test after you called and confirmed. Ludo didn't care at all—not that he scared the girls, not that he divided our attention, nothing. He's a fucking dick."

"Quiet," I say as I glance around. It looks like we're alone, but who actually knows. "Wait to say stuff like that until we're in the penthouse."

He grunts. "Whatever."

I pick up our pace again. If Rhett is getting sloppy, that means he's too pissed to care. The last thing we need is for him to give away our true feelings toward Ludo just because he's in a bad mood.

With a sigh, I glance back toward the condo. Hopefully Elliot and Wren are having better luck controlling themselves.

Chapter Eleven

Elliot

I'd much prefer to leave with Oliver and Rhett, but there's no way in hell I'm letting Wren stay here by herself. So I pour myself a drink from the bar and then lower myself into the chair next to Ludo. It's too goddamn hot out here, but the view is nice.

"You four are quite loyal to each other," Ludo says.

"We are."

"Maybe to a fault sometimes."

"I suppose that's how it could look to an outsider."

Ludo hums thoughtfully. "Care to explain?"

"No, not particularly. But in that same vein, I do have something else I'd like to explain to you."

Ludo tilts his head toward me, one eyebrow raised in curiosity. "Go on."

Before I continue, I take a sip of my drink, hoping the alcohol will get rid of some of my annoyance. It doesn't. "I was expecting tests of loyalty from you. It's the only thing that makes sense. But what I wasn't expecting was for you to go about it in a way that could've gotten your fiancée hurt. Or worse."

"Oh?"

"Samuel. You now know what we did, how much we prioritized Aubrey's safety, that we can't be bought, etc. But while you were testing us, you were also distracting us from possible *real threats*. Nothing happened, and even if something had, we probably would've been able to handle it. But life doesn't have many guarantees.

"I understand how important it is to know who you can trust. Test us all you want, Holloway. I don't care. But the next time you do it, it'd better be in a way that doesn't endanger Aubrey—or Wren."

Ludo is silent as he stares at me. Whatever he's feeling, he's hiding it well. For a minute, I'm afraid I've gone too far. But then, slowly, he asks, "What are you really saying, Hayes?"

"I'm saying that there's little I wouldn't do to keep the woman I love safe. So the next time you send one of your men after us like that, we won't be bringing him back alive."

Ludo's mouth curves upward. "Noted."

The tension—at least for me—is unbearable. I stand. "I'm going to check on Wren and Aubrey."

With a sigh, Ludo follows me. "I suppose I should come with you."

Inside, the girls are sitting on the couch. Aubrey looks just as pissed, and when Wren glances up and sees Ludo, it takes her a second too long to school the hatred on her face.

My pulse picks up as I wait for Ludo to notice, but his attention is elsewhere.

"Shopping," Ludo says, surveying the bags that Samuel must've brought in from his backseat. They're all in the entryway, placed rather haphazardly. "An interesting past time when you're in paradise. Pools, hot tubs, the ocean . . ."

Wren stiffens as Ludo's gaze finally rests on her. "There's plenty to do."

"Yes, plenty. It'd be a shame if you left it all unexplored because of a little—"

"Oh, shut *up,* Ludo," Aubrey snaps. "No one cares about your opinion." Standing, she smiles softly at Wren. "Thank you for coming after me. I appreciate it."

"Will you be okay?" Wren asks, grabbing Aubrey's hand.

"Oh, I'll be fine, no worries. I'd like to take you to the shop we didn't get to go to this week, if you want? It's this Black-owned bookstore that I'd love to support, and they have an amazing fantasy section."

"I'd like that."

Once we've said our goodbyes, we hurry to the penthouse. We have audio to sort through, and I want to spend some time relaxing before going to bed early. Wren silently chews her bottom lip the whole way back.

In the elevator, I cup her chin. "What's wrong?"

"I'm worried for Aubrey. She doesn't want to marry him, Ell."

"Who would?" I mutter. "He's a piece of shit."

Still, the whole situation isn't sitting right. Aubrey told Wren she's only marrying Ludo so her parents will be under his protection. It seems like Aubrey is getting the short end of the stick here.

"The worst thing is that I don't know if I can trust her," Wren says with a sigh. "I like her a lot. But I'm so worried this is another test from Ludo, that she's secretly on his side but pretending not to be. But . . ."

"But what?" I prod when she doesn't continue.

"I think she has something up her sleeve. Not with Ludo, but *against* him. There have been a couple things she's said that make me think she already has a way out of this planned. Maybe that's just wishful thinking on my part, though."

"Or you could be onto something. I know some people are phenomenal liars, but in my opinion, I don't think Aubrey is faking how much she likes you."

Wren's expression brightens. "You think so?"

"I do," I say as I pull out my phone. This conversation has reminded me that there's someone who could help us figure out whose side Aubrey is on.

Sparrow hasn't answered my text—which is fair, honestly. If I was the keeper of everyone's deepest, darkest secrets, I wouldn't reveal my sources either. So I try a different question.

Elliot: Did you mean don't underestimate Aubrey as an enemy or as an ally?

Her response is almost immediate.

Sparrow Belgrave: Don't you think I'd tell you if she was an enemy?

That's a good point, I suppose.

I angle my phone so Wren can see. "I'd say she's trustworthy."

"Oh, thank goodness. But . . . uh, who's Sparrow?"

Right. I forgot we didn't tell her a lot of details about Wyoming. It was for her safety, but we forgot to fill her in afterward.

"Someone we can trust when it comes to Ludo," I say. "It's in her best interests to take him down as well. She's the one who hired us for the Wyoming job."

"And she knows Aubrey?"

"Or she knows something *about* Aubrey. It's kind of her job to know things."

"But either way, we can keep hanging out? As actual friends?"

"Looks that way."

"And it'll be a way to get closer to Ludo?"

"That too. As long as you're okay with it, love."

"I want to help bring him down."

Fuck, I love her.

In the penthouse, Rhett is sitting at the kitchen table. He has one earbud in, and he's typing furiously on his laptop. When he sees us, he pauses.

"Anything good?" I ask.

"Nothing of use, but there's still plenty to go through."

"Keep us updated."

I leave Wren in the living room to take a shower. I know it's stupid, but I feel like I need to wash Ludo off me.

As I step into the bedroom, Oliver comes out of the bathroom. When he sees me, he makes a relieved noise. "I'm glad you didn't stick around for long."

"Couldn't've. I was already about to lose it."

Humming in agreement, Oliver plops onto my lap like it's the most natural thing to do—probably because it is. "I think Rhett was about to punch him. He was pissed when he picked up the girls."

"At least Ludo is more confident in our abilities now. And I'm glad we all made it through safely."

Even though we knew Samuel most likely wasn't a true threat, I didn't like leaving Oliver alone like that. I never like it when we have to split up.

"Agreed," Oliver sighs. He kisses my cheek before standing. "I'm gonna check on Wren. Take your time in the shower. You're tense as hell." He pokes my shoulder.

"It won't help," I mumble after he's gone. I've got too much to worry about, too much to plan. At this rate, I probably won't even sleep tonight.

For the hundredth time, I find myself wishing this was all over. I want to know what life is like without all this external pressure and stress.

"Six months," I whisper as I turn on the shower. But even as I say it, I can't help but feel that even that time frame is going to be agonizingly long.

...

When I get out of the shower, Rhett is sitting on the bed waiting for me. I pause in the doorway, momentarily confused, but then I remember our conversation from the other day.

I'd fuck the stress out of you if we had time.

Rhett stands, prowling toward me. "You don't look relaxed."

"You here to change that?"

He captures my chin between two fingers, gazing down at me, and kisses me gently. "If that's what you need."

Thank fuck.

I nod.

"Do you need to struggle?"

"Please."

I like being in charge. Being the strong one, the leader, the one everyone can rely on. Even when it does nothing but drain me, I can't shut it off. I can't be that person all the time, no matter how much I want to be.

At some point, Rhett figured out he could take it from me. I may put up one hell of a fight, but he always wins. It's what we both usually want, and it's easier for me to let go when he forces me to submit to him. It's rare that things go the other way. Rhett doesn't tend to enjoy giving up control.

Rhett kisses me again, still keeping it gentle and loving. "Your wish is my command, pretty boy."

Already, I feel myself relaxing. *I love this man so much.*

Without warning, Rhett yanks my towel off and shoves me onto the bed. I'm caught off guard, so my attempt to roll away fails. Rhett pounces on top of me, grabbing my wrists and pinning them to the mattress. I try to buck him off, but he barely budges.

Clicking his tongue, he leans down and murmurs in my ear, "Disappointing. I was hoping for an actual challenge."

With a grunt, I manage to free one of my hands. I grab the back of Rhett's neck and yank him down. Pure heat courses through my veins as I kiss him fiercely. He nips at my bottom lip as I work myself into a better position to dismount him.

He grabs my wrist and pins it back down. "You think I don't know what you're doing?"

"You said you wanted a challenge." With all the force I can manage, I knock him off me. I'm not able to gain the upper hand enough to get on top of him, but when he tries to grab me, I'm able to dodge.

I fling myself toward the edge of the bed, and Rhett follows. When he lands on top of me, it pushes us too far, and we fall to the floor. Somehow, we manage not to hurt ourselves, but it makes a lot of noise. Worth it—I end up on top.

I pin Rhett to the floor and lean down. My lips are a mere inch from his as I whisper, "Don't tell me I'm being *too* much of a challenge for you."

"You little—"

There's a knock on the door, and then it opens. "Hey, are you guys okay—ah. Yeah, they're fine, princess. *More* than fine." With a laugh, Oliver steps back out and closes the door.

"You're going to pay for that comment," Rhett growls. He rips his hands free from my grasp, grabs my head, and pulls me down.

The moment his mouth meets mine, everything shifts. I can feel myself starting to relax. My body softens against his as he bites my bottom lip hard enough to draw blood. I grunt at the pain, simultaneously wishing for more and wanting to pull back.

Rhett flips us so I'm on my back and he's straddling my hips. "Is that all it took? One rough kiss, and you're ready to comply?"

Just like that, I'm struggling again. He always taunts me like this. If I give in too easily, I can't get out of my head enough. What I need is for Rhett to completely overpower me—to take away my ability to make any independent decisions. Only then can I truly let go.

"Let me up," I grunt as I push at his shoulders.

"If you wanna get up, you're going to have to fight for it."

Again, I push at him, but it doesn't do much. Rhett is bigger and stronger than I am, and he's also gotten very skilled at putting—and keeping—me in my place.

"Aww," Rhett says with mock sympathy. "You're trying so hard, but it's futile, isn't it? I'll give you an A for effort, at least."

"Fuck you," I grit out.

Never in getting to know Wren did I think she'd teach me something about fighting—playfully or not. But here I am, about ready to take a page from her book.

"Why are you smiling like that?" Rhett demands.

"Can't help it." Quickly, I go for his armpits, tickling him and praying I'm not about to get myself killed.

Rhett reacts immediately, shouting and scrambling off me. As soon as we're both on his feet, he smiles sadistically. "Oh, you're gonna pay for that."

There's nowhere for me to run. I try to jump and roll across the bed, but Rhett follows me. Just as I'm about to put distance between us, he pulls me back with a strong grip on the back of my neck.

Rhett throws me onto the mattress before covering my body with his. Our heaving chests are pressed up against each other as he leaves another hot, fierce kiss on my mouth.

"Do I need to restrain you?" he growls. "Force you into cuffs and make you take whatever I decide to give you?"

I groan. Desperately, I move my head toward his for another kiss, but he pulls back.

"Maybe," he says with a sadistic grin, "I should mark you up so everyone knows just who you belong to."

"Fucking hell, Rhett," I gasp. "Just do *something*."

On the last syllable, Rhett grips my jaw and forces it open wider. He spits into my mouth, and his eyes darken with satisfaction as I swallow. "Such a good boy," he murmurs. "You want my dick?"

"God, yes."

He kisses me, and his tongue delves into my mouth and tangles with my own. And just because I can—just because he thinks I'm finally done fighting—I buck him off of me. He lands on his side, so I quickly force him onto his back and straddle him.

"But first," I say, grinning, "maybe I'll make *you* work for it."

"Oh, really?" Since I'm not holding down his hands, he's easily able to grab my cock and stroke it. He only does it enough to pull a groan out of me before he stops.

"Rhett," I pant.

"You want more of that?"

I let out a frustrated grunt and move to replace his hand with my own, but he catches my wrist before I'm able to get to my dick. "You know I do."

"Then get on the floor on your knees, pretty boy." He shoves me to the side before I can even move.

As I get into position, Rhett gets up and grabs something from his bag. Leather cuffs linked together.

"Since you're being a pain in my ass today," he says as he secures them to my wrists behind my back. "Maybe these will remind you who's in charge here."

"In charge? You? Are you sure?"

"Goddammit, Ell. You've got no idea what you're getting yourself into."

Oh yes I do.

Rhett yanks his clothes off, and my mouth waters at the sight of him. Not just his cock, but his body. Beautiful, rounded, sharpened, and for the moment, all mine to enjoy. There's a safety that comes with losing ourselves in each other's bodies, and it's been far too long since Rhett and I did so alone.

"Open your mouth," he commands.

I smirk.

"You're really gonna make this harder on yourself? Fuck, of course you are." He brushes the tip of his dick against my lips, teasing me, and I almost open my mouth for him just so I can get a taste.

But I don't. I just need a little more.

When I turn my head away, Rhett chuckles darkly. "If you don't start listening, I'm going to spank that ass of yours until you can't sit right for the rest of the week."

"I'd like to see you try."

"Oh, I'll do more than *try*."

I can't struggle as much with my wrists restrained, so he hauls me up with ease and throws me face down onto the bed. I roll onto my back quickly.

Sadistic delight flashes in Rhett's eyes. "You're asking for trouble."

"Give me hell."

He shoves me back onto my stomach. Before I can brace myself, he smacks my ass so hard I jump. My skin stings, and the pain is met with another hit—and then another.

"Fuck," I grunt.

"You'll take it," Rhett growls as he spanks my other ass cheek. "Won't you, pretty boy?"

"Yes," I groan, flinching at the next smack.

And just like that, I'm his. Pliant, mindless, and lost in the painful bliss Rhett is so good at dishing out. He spanks me until there are tears falling from my eyes and my ass is on fire.

"You finally ready to be a good boy, Ell?"

"Yes," I say into the blankets. "I'm yours. Do whatever you want to me."

He massages my ass, easing the sting. "Oh, I will."

I expect him to bring me back to the floor, but he doesn't. Effortlessly, he pulls me so my head is still pressed into the mattress and my ass is in the air. I brace for another smack, but instead he spreads my cheeks and circles my asshole with his tongue. I grunt.

Rhett doesn't spend a lot of time rimming me, probably because he's too impatient, but I don't mind because I am too. Once he's prepped me and washed his hands, he smacks my ass one last time.

"Owwww," I groan.

"Your ass is too fucking sexy. Couldn't stop myself," he says as he disconnects the cuffs. He flips me onto my back before redoing them so my hands are in front of me. "I'd keep you like that so I could bounce off it while I fuck you, but I want to look at you."

After pulling me right to the edge of the bed, Rhett coats his dick with lube. I open my legs for him, and he lines himself up. As he pushes inside, he groans and closes his eyes.

"Thought you were gonna watch me," I taunt.

"I'll get to it." His hand wraps around my cock, moving up and down.

When we finally lock gazes, Rhett smirks. He's working his way farther into me so slowly it's torturous. I've been waiting for this moment ever since he gave me that massage Sunday night, so I'm having trouble staying patient. I don't beg, though. Don't want to. I trust Rhett to give me exactly what he knows I need.

Once Rhett is seated all the way in me, he finally leans over. One hand is still stroking my cock, and he places the other by my head to hold himself up. "Look at you, so ready to let me have my way with you. Completely at my mercy."

"Like I said, Rhett. Give me hell."

"Oh, I plan on it." He pulls out and slides back in, and a groan tumbles from his lips. "So tight."

We stay just like that, him thrusting into me and stroking my cock while I take it. He doesn't let me look away, not for a single second, and I've never loved being trapped in his gaze so much.

I don't know how much time passes. Don't particularly care, either. All that exists is us, free from expectations and drunk off each other.

"You feel how well I fit inside you?" Rhett pants as I feel myself reaching that tipping point. "It's like you're made for me, pretty boy."

"Rhett," I groan. "I'm gonna come."

"Fuck yes. Give it to me. Come everywhere."

With a shudder, I finish, and hot cum coats my stomach and Rhett's hand. *Fuck,* it feels so good.

"Don't you dare," he says when my eyes start to slide shut. "You look at me through the whole thing."

Even though it feels like I'm drowning in all the sensations, I manage to hold eye contact until Rhett stops stroking my dick. My head feels light, and my thoughts are fuzzy. "Rhett," I pant as I lift my head.

He isn't far behind me. His hand moves from the mattress to my throat as he says, "Stay like that. Just like that, Ell. Oh, fuck."

He pounds into me for another minute before pulling out. Within seconds, he's coming all over my stomach with a deep groan. I gaze up at him, watching as all his walls come crashing down, just for a few brief seconds.

"I love you," I whisper.

He smiles, and it reaches his eyes. When he kisses me, my stomach flips, like I'm a teenager falling in love again. "Love you too, Ell."

Chapter Twelve

Rhett

Murder probably isn't the best thing to think about to get myself to relax. Somehow, though, it's the thing that helps the most often. Fantasizing about standing over Ludo's limp, tortured, unmoving body is one of the only things that can calm the constant fury stirring in my chest.

There are other things that help, of course. Being with Elliot, Oliver, and Wren is the best thing. But right now, the penthouse is dead quiet. Everyone's asleep, which means if I don't distract myself, I'll end up going off the deep end.

As I lie in bed, killing Ludo is where my mind defaults to. I've done this so many nights it's practically habit. But tonight, not even thoughts of avenging Sammy are enough to bring me peace.

Gently, I move my hand under the covers until I find Wren's arm. She's out cold, so I don't want to move her too much, but I doubt just touching her a little will wake her up.

Since thoughts of killing Ludo aren't enough to get me to sleep, I try to think of the future. Normally that scares me—I've put little thought into what life will be like once we have our revenge. But tonight, I try to think of the happy things.

Everyone will be less stressed. Maybe I'll be able to work through my aversions more. I'd like to be able to accept every hug or little touch that comes my way. I'd like to say *I love you* more often. Fuck, that'd be nice.

I'm not sure how long I lie in bed for, but sleep doesn't come. I keep perfectly still, trying to trick my body into drifting off, but it doesn't work. Just as I'm about to give up, grab my laptop, and move into the living room, Wren's breathing changes.

At first, she inhales sharply, which is usually a telltale sign that she's having a nightmare. But then she groans and sits up. For a second, she doesn't move. Then she grabs her phone from the nightstand and checks the time.

When she gets up quietly, I assume she's going to the bathroom, but she starts going through her bag. She slips out of her T-shirt, and I avert my eyes until she's done changing. Maybe she's cold so she's putting something warmer on.

"You're not a coward," she mutters to herself. "It's time to stop acting like one."

Footsteps sound, and I realize she's not coming back to bed. I almost call out to ask her where she's going, but I stop myself. During my teen years, I did my fair share of sneaking out. If I was caught, I never would've admitted to what I was doing. Best to follow her.

When Wren opens the bedroom door, I swear under my breath. She must think I'm asleep. But still, why is she leaving like this? Where is she going? It doesn't make sense.

Once she shuts the door, I get out of bed. There's no way in hell I'm letting her get far by herself. I throw on some clothes, gritting my teeth when I hear the hallway door close. She should know better than to go out alone.

I stay in the penthouse until I hear the elevator open and close. Only then do I slip outside and hit the downward button. I keep an eye on the floor indicator for Wren's elevator, watching the number descend until it hits the ground floor.

What the hell is she thinking?

One of the elevator doors opens, and I hurry inside, hitting the button to take me to the lobby. The thing takes forever to get down, and when I step out onto the ground floor, Wren is already gone.

Fuck. *Fuck!* Where could she have gone?

Just then, I hear a door close. Peering down a hallway in that direction, I catch her through the door's window. She's outside now—in the pool area.

Dread fills me as I rush down the hallway. Wren is just in my view, setting a towel on one of the chaise lounge chairs. She pulls her dress off, revealing a bikini underneath.

Despite this being a god-awful idea, I can't help but drink in the way the moonlight illuminates her body. She couldn't be more beautiful if she tried.

When Wren starts heading toward the pool, I move outside, closing the door slowly so she doesn't hear it. The stairs into the water are on the far side, and I watch her pause at the top. Her hand is gripping the railing tightly.

She said upstairs that she's not a coward. Is this because of what Ludo said to her? Did he say something else today that set her off?

I stay in the shadows where she can't see me. However much I want to stop her, I won't. Only Wren can be the judge of what's pushing herself too far. This is her decision—even if I think it's a stupid one.

"You can do it," I hear her say. She's staring into the illuminated pool, still standing at the top of the steps. "You're *not* a coward, dammit."

Hesitantly, she steps into the water. She squeezes her eyes shut and takes a deep breath before moving down another step. Both of her hands are on the railing, grasping at the pole like she'll drown instantly if she lets go.

I keep my eyes trained sharply on Wren. I've seen what happens to Oliver when his anxiety overtakes him. If Wren starts panicking in the pool, it's likely she'll lose control and drown. I need to be able to pull her out of the water as quickly as possible.

Odds are, she'll feel a lot safer if she knows she's not alone. But she obviously wants to do this by herself. I don't want to make myself known unless I absolutely have to.

For a second, it looks like Wren is going to back out of the pool. But then she takes a steadying breath and moves down the stairs until she's touching the bottom. It's just the shallow end, so Wren's head is far above the water, but she's still clutching onto the end of the railing.

She stands frozen before taking a step into the pool. Her hands fall from the railing. Another step. Then another.

She stops, looking around. "See, it's not so bad. Not scary at all. Not... not... fuck." Her voice breaks, and she rubs at her face with her shaking hands. The next couple breaths she takes are choppy and uneven, but then she's able to get it together. "Just don't think about that. Think about... think about... them." Her voice softens on the last word.

It takes a minute, but she manages to avoid whatever breakdown was about to happen. She walks stiffly to the edge of the pool, where she grabs onto the side and slowly lowers herself down. But when she gets to the point where her shoulders are immersed, she stops.

Wren is facing away from me, so I can't see her expression, but the tension in her body is enough of an indicator.

"This was a bad idea," she squeaks out. Then she's moving toward the stairs, retreating from her fears, and I can't even blame her.

We should've offered to do this with her. We should've been more supportive.

As I watch her ascend the steps, I can't help but think that I'm still ridiculously proud of her. How many times did Jordan shove her head under water and hold her there? And how many of those times did Wren think she'd never take another breath?

Fuck. We should've tortured him for longer.

Wren is over by her stuff now, her towel in her hands. But she's just standing there, dripping wet, staring down at it.

"Goddammit," she hisses out. "Wren Marie Taylor, you know how to swim. For fuck's sake."

With a newfound fervor, Wren throws her towel back onto the lounge chair and marches over to the deep end of the pool. She doesn't even pause—just jumps in.

Panic sears through my veins, and I'm already kicking off my shoes when she surfaces with a gasp. She pushes her hair out of her face and lets out a victorious laugh. Then she dives under the water again, swimming toward the bottom before coming up for air.

With a breath of relief, I slide my shoes back on. *She's fine. She's doing it. Fuck, she's okay.*

Just as Wren is gaining her bearings, a shadowed figure steps up to the far edge of the pool. It's dark, but I'd recognize that red leather jacket anywhere.

"Not a coward, I see," Ludo says, slipping his hands into his pants pockets. As he looks down at Wren, the pool lights illuminate his face. The way he's looking at her has all my panic flooding back, but I stay hidden.

"Ludo," Wren says, meeting his gaze.

To her credit, her voice is only a tiny bit surprised. She stays in the middle of the deep end, treading water. The other options are moving closer to him, which I highly doubt she wants to do, or moving farther away. And with a man like Ludo, backing away from him is a terrible idea. The man can practically smell fear.

"You know," Ludo says, crouching down and clasping his hands in front of him, "you're a smart little thing. You kept your mouth shut about my visit, didn't you?"

What?

Wren stays silent.

Ludo laughs. "I was expecting your men to say something. Demand answers. Anything." He shrugs. "But to my surprise, they never asked. And when I hired them for this job, my suspicions were confirmed. You never told them I could've saved you."

"Based on my limited knowledge of your character, the thought of helping me probably never even crossed your mind," Wren says dryly.

"Smart woman," Ludo replies. The grin that creeps onto his face is more predatory than amused. It's all teeth and dead eyes. "I can see why they're all attracted to you."

Wren ignores his latter comment. "You don't want them to trust you? It was a perfect opportunity. Save me from Jordan, earn their gratitude."

At that, Ludo laughs. It's a sound that's haunted me since the first time I heard it. "Oh, Wren," he drawls, "why would I grovel for their trust when they're already so willing to do whatever I ask? Besides—I'm far from trustworthy, and you'd do well to learn that sooner than later."

She doesn't respond, just nods silently.

If they say anything else, I miss it. The chaotic clamor of my thoughts drowns out the world around me.

He was there. He was there, and he could've gotten her out sooner.

But the bastard didn't. He was going to let her die.

And she didn't even tell us.

My mind is going a mile a minute trying to think of a reasonable explanation. Something, anything. But I come up short.

She lied.

She fucking lied to us.

I'm already working through the different ways I can cause Ludo pain. What I can do tonight, or tomorrow. After this, I can't wait any longer. He's caused too much damage, put my family in danger one too many times.

I'm going to kill him.

Ludo walks away, whistling to himself, and Wren shudders in the water. Only once he's out of the pool area does she move to the edge of the pool and hoist herself out of the water. She pads over to her stuff, glancing in his direction warily.

Stiffly, Wren dries off and puts her dress back on. After she gathers her stuff in her arms, she starts heading back inside.

She doesn't make it, though. I step out of my hiding place, crossing my arms and blocking her path. Wren gasps, stumbling backward.

"Rhett?" As she takes me in, she doesn't relax. And why would she when I know my face is clouded over with a thousand different emotions. "Rhett, I..."

My voice is gruff, and there's no mistaking the anger in it as I say, "You've got some explaining to do, sweetheart."

Chapter Thirteen

Wren

If I had to choose between standing under Ludo's chilling gaze or Rhett's angry, disbelieving glare, I'd choose Ludo a thousand times over. Nothing he could ever say to me would hurt nearly as much as the look Rhett is giving me right now.

"What," he grits out, "the *actual hell*."

"I—"

He holds up his hand to silence me, his glare sharpening. "First, you come down here in the middle of the night by yourself. And then you get in the pool when you know very well that you could've panicked and drowned."

With a sigh, I squeeze my eyes shut, willing the betrayed look on Rhett's face to fall away. But when I glance at him again, it's still there.

"And then," Rhett continues, laughing bitterly, "it turns out that you've been keeping a *vital* piece of information from us. Why would you do that, Wren? Fucking why?"

"I didn't want . . ." Shifting from one foot to the other, I let my gaze drop to his hands. They're clenched into fists at his sides. *Fuck.* How do I explain this to Rhett without him thinking I don't trust him?

"I'm doing my best not to jump to conclusions here, Wren. But I'm struggling to come up with a reasonable explanation as to why you'd keep it to yourself that *he* was there." Rhett shakes his head, blowing out a harsh breath. "God, I'm going to kill him. I can't believe he thought he could get away with this."

Fuck. He shouldn't be saying stuff like that out in the open.

"That's why," I say softly. I take his hand, relieved when he doesn't pull away, and guide him back into the hotel. The air conditioning is cold against my still-damp skin, and I want nothing more than to huddle into Rhett's warmth, but I have a feeling he'd push me away if I tried.

The thought breaks my heart.

"I don't understand," Rhett says, frowning at me.

Keeping my voice down just in case someone can hear us, I say, "I didn't tell you guys that Ludo was there—that he easily could've saved me but didn't—because of *you*."

The second we're closed into the elevator, Rhett drops my hand. "That doesn't make sense. I should've been one of the first people you told. But instead, you hid the fact that he was there. That doesn't look good for you, Wren."

I let out an exasperated noise as I turn to face him. "Rhett! Just look at yourself. When you find out that someone you care about has been hurt, your first instinct is to find the person who harmed them and hurt them back. You did it with Adam. And if he'd been a little bit more knowledgeable about the gun that was in his hand, he could've killed you."

"He didn't though."

"It could've been Oliver," I remind him gently. "It almost was."

His nostrils flare.

"And don't insult my intelligence by pretending I don't know you want to do something to Thomas, too."

Rhett opens his mouth to protest before snapping his jaw shut.

"I understand you're angry at Ludo—for lots of reasons. But going off without a plan over this one thing likely would've gotten you hurt, if not killed. It would've ruined your overarching plan as well. I was going to tell you. Just not yet."

The elevator comes to a stop, and the doors open. Neither of us move. His expression goes from pissed to understanding to irate in a matter of seconds.

"You thought that's what I'd do," he says flatly. "That I'd ruin everything we've spent a decade working on, for you."

"I wasn't one hundred percent sure," I whisper, watching him shake his head. "I didn't want—"

"You severely underestimate how much avenging Sammy's murder means to me," he says, and his voice is so icy and scathing at the same time that it has the hair on the back of my neck standing up.

The elevator doors start closing. Rhett jerks his arm out, stopping them, and they slide open again.

"Go to bed, Wren."

"But—"

"*Now.*"

The finality in his voice sends a wave of dread through my system. I step off the elevator, swallowing down the need to ask him where he's going. I hold his gaze as the doors shut, even though he's looking at me with so much disappointment it makes my throat feel like it's closing in on itself.

Was I wrong to worry about what Rhett's reaction would be? To assume I meant more to Rhett than I do? The thought causes a tangible, painful weight to press down on my chest.

Inside the penthouse, I shut the door quietly, frowning. Some of the lights are on.

"Wren?" Elliot calls. "Rhett?" He comes into view, shirtless and in sweatpants.

With the windows framing the dark ocean behind him, Elliot looks larger than life, like something out of a movie. If things were different, I'd probably enjoy staring at him right now. As it is, though, I'm fighting to do anything but burst into tears.

"There you are. I thought I heard someone leave." As he moves closer to me, he narrows his eyes. "Were you swimming?"

"Yeah. Rhett followed me down."

Elliot glances behind me. "Where is he?"

"I don't know."

This would be a good time to explain everything to Elliot, but I can't bring myself to do it. Having him look at me the same way Rhett was mere seconds ago would be too much. I can't handle disappointing both of them in one night.

I try to move past Elliot, but he grabs my arm and tugs me back.

"What happened?"

"I . . ." *Fuck, Ludo was right. I'm nothing more than a coward.* "I can't, I'm sorry." I slip out of his hold, heading into mine and Rhett's room. As I start to close the door behind me, Elliot puts a hand out and stops it.

"Why am I getting the feeling that something really bad happened?"

I try to push the door shut, but it doesn't budge. "I really don't want to talk about it, and you need to get some sleep. Aren't you taking the morning shift with Aubrey?"

"Wren, you look like you're about to start crying. Do you really expect me to leave you alone?"

Goddammit.

"If you want someone to comfort, Rhett probably needs it more than I do. Go find him. I need to wash the chlorine out of my hair."

"Love, just tell me what happened."

"I can't." I push at the door again, but Elliot shoves it wide open and steps into the bedroom.

"Why not?"

I try to explain, but I choke on the words. Slowly, I back away from him and try again. My voice shakes. "Because I'm afraid you'll hate me afterward."

Elliot shakes his head. "I could never hate you." Realization crosses his features, and then he's stepping toward me, slipping an arm around my waist and pulling me against him. "What did Rhett say? What did he do?"

For a moment, I squeeze my eyes shut and stay silent. But at this rate, Elliot isn't going to leave me alone, so I might as well get this over with. I look up at him, at the way his brows are furrowed in worry and his eyes are burning with concern. There's nothing I can do but try to soak it in, to try to remember everything about this moment. If he reacts like Rhett does, it might be the last time he looks at me with any kind of care.

Before speaking, I take a deep breath, trying to steady my voice. "Rhett didn't do anything. I . . . I did. When Jordan kidnapped me, Ludo stopped by his house one day, I think for some kind of business meeting. When Ludo saw I was there, he broke off the deal and left."

The moment I mention Ludo, Elliot tenses, his arm around me tightening. When I finish, he looks up at the ceiling, taking a deep breath. Then he looks down at me, confusion and anger replacing the concern in his eyes.

"He left you."

I nod.

Elliot releases me, rubbing at his face. "I know I shouldn't expect anything from that miserable piece of shit. But he... Jesus fuck. He just *left* you there. Goddammit, I knew he was lying."

"I—"

"Wait. Wait, did you just tell this to Rhett?"

"Yes. He—"

"Fuck." Pulling his phone out of his pocket, he taps the screen a few times before holding it to his ear.

Why isn't he angry? He should be furious with me.

"Rhett isn't answering. Shit. There's no way he's thinking straight. If he tries to get back at Ludo..."

"What? No, he won't."

"We need to find him before he does something he'll regret." Elliot is already rushing out of the bedroom and into his.

"Elliot! He's not going to do anything." I follow, lingering in the doorway while he pulls on a shirt. Oliver is still sound asleep in the bed.

Turning to me, Elliot says, "This is what he does, love. Every single time. You saw it with you and Adam."

"I know. I—"

"Just trust me, Rhett is—"

"He won't," I shout, causing Oliver to wake. "Just *listen* to me for five seconds. Rhett found out that Ludo was there. And when I explained that I didn't tell you guys because I was afraid Rhett would deviate from the plan out of anger, he got mad at *me* for even thinking that. So he's not going to do anything."

Elliot pauses, frowning. "That doesn't make any sense."

Oliver groans. "What's going on?"

Still giving me a blank stare, Elliot says, "Rhett got mad at you because you assumed he'd continue acting the same way he's acted for years?"

"I . . . I guess, yeah."

Absentmindedly, Elliot runs his thumb across his bottom lip. Then he's right in front of me again, stroking my hair. "We'll figure this out."

I cringe away. "Why aren't you mad at me? I lied to all of you."

The question seems to take him aback. "I . . ."

"Guys," Oliver says. He's sitting up and rubbing his eyes. "What the hell is going on?"

With a sigh, Elliot says to me, "I'll explain it to him. Why don't you shower."

"Are you sure? It might take longer than normal, I should probably do a hair mask because of the chlorine—"

"It's okay, love. Take your time."

"Okay. Thank you."

After he kisses me on the forehead, I give Oliver an uneasy glance before I all but flee the room. In mine and Rhett's bathroom, I turn on the shower, trying to stop myself from shaking.

They're never going to forgive me. I shouldn't've kept it from them. I shouldn't've tried to keep Rhett safe.

In the shower, I thoroughly wash the chlorine from my body and go through my normal haircare routine, plus the hair mask. Like I told Elliot, it takes longer than normal. I think most of the reason why is because I'm avoiding the conversation I know will come once I'm done.

Even so, I'm still finished before I'd like to be. Slowly, I open the bedroom door and step out. Elliot and Oliver are both sitting in the living area with solemn looks on their faces.

Elliot looks up. "Rhett texted me. He's okay, love. He just needs some space."

I cling to the small thread of relief, but it's not enough to quell my uneasiness. I twist my fingers into my oversized T-shirt. "I really am sorry."

Oliver doesn't look at me. It's understandable. This was a vital piece of information for them to have, and I kept it from them. Still, it causes my heart to ache.

"Come here," Elliot says, patting the couch cushion next to him. When I sit, leaving some space in between us, he threads an arm around me and pulls me closer.

On the couch across from us, Oliver continues staring at the ground. He's leaning forward with his elbows resting on his knees, keeping his head bowed.

"I get why you did it," Elliot says. "For the most part, anyway. You were afraid of how Rhett would react?"

I nod silently.

"Okay, that makes sense, given his track record. But if you'd told all of us together, Ol and I would've been able to stop him until he calmed down."

How did I not realize that on my own?

"I'm sorry," I say quietly. "I didn't think it through."

"It's okay." Elliot's voice stays soothing and calm, and I just don't get it. How the hell is he not angry? "We've thrown a lot at you the past couple weeks, love. You judged the situation the best you could."

I stare at him blankly. Is he serious? Considering Rhett's reaction, I was expecting Elliot and Oliver to be just as angry. "You understand?"

"Honestly? It's something I probably would've done when we were younger. *But,* just so we're clear, it can't happen again."

"It won't," I say quickly. "I promise."

With a tired sigh, Elliot nods. "I need to get some sleep. But tomorrow, after my shift with Aubrey and after Rhett cools down, let's talk this out. You can tell us everything that happened when Ludo showed up."

"Okay," I whisper, scrunching my eyes shut when he kisses my forehead. "Goodnight."

"Goodnight, love."

After kissing Oliver's forehead, Elliot heads into their bedroom and shuts the door softly. Silence takes over the penthouse, and I have to force myself to breathe while I watch Oliver. He's still in the same position, head bowed, with one of his legs bouncing. No acknowledgment of my presence, no words—nothing.

He hates me. My god, he hates me. What if he never gets past this?

"Oliver?"

His leg freezes, and he heaves in a heavy breath. "Princess..."

"Please don't hate me," I whisper.

Oliver's head snaps up. "What? Hate you? Princess, why would I—" His eyes widen when he sees my face. "Oh god. Wren, no. I don't hate you."

Disbelief ripples through my thoughts. "But you...you..." My throat clogs up, and I have to blink back tears.

"Fuck," he mutters. He rubs his face. "C'mere, princess."

Hesitantly, I stand and step up to him. I hover a few inches away, unsure of what he wants. "I didn't want to keep it from you."

Oliver takes hold of my wrists and draws me onto his lap. His arms encircle me, holding me in place, like he knows I'm two seconds from running away and sobbing into my pillow. "I know."

"Are you angry?" I whisper.

"Not exactly. Your intentions were pure, and I can follow the logic. But..."

When he pauses, my stomach turns. *This is it. He's never going to trust me again.*

Oliver looks up at me, and I expect to see hurt or betrayal written all over his face. But the only thing I find is . . . worry. "I think there are some things you need to know."

Chapter Fourteen

Oliver

Wren is so nervous she's practically vibrating. As I try to figure out how I want to phrase this, I trace my fingers up and down her spine. "Have you ever noticed how important it is to Elliot that you trust us?"

"I have," she says.

"We don't keep things from each other. Not... not important things. I get that's a fairly normal thing in most relationships, but we take extra care to not keep secrets."

"I promise I won't do it again, Oliver," she whispers. "Never again."

"Hey, I know," I say gently. "I just need you to understand where we're coming from. Or, more specifically, where Elliot is coming from. His parents didn't trust each other, and it led to a really toxic environment. Instead of working things out, they were constantly going behind each other's backs, accusing each other of shit, yelling at each other, the works. Elliot swore he'd never be like that.

"When it came to us, Elliot worked hard to earn our trust. We were kids, so of course we all fucked up. But we eventually got to the point we're at now. We trust each other with our lives, and with every little thing that comes our way. That took a lot of work."

Wren sags against me. "I really messed this up, didn't I?"

"Not as badly as you think." I try to sound as reassuring as I can. "You're allowed to make mistakes. We all do. And the thing is, what you did is understandable. You were trying to protect Rhett."

"He didn't see it that way."

"He'll . . . he'll come around."

I'm not completely sure what's going on with Rhett. Wren's logic is solid for the most part. If anyone other than Ludo had left Wren at that house, they'd be dead by now, thanks to Rhett. I don't get why he can't see that—he already knows it.

What I said doesn't seem to help Wren's nerves at all. "Are you sure Elliot isn't mad at me? If trust is really important to him, and I lied, then—then how is he *not* mad?" Her voice sounds panicked, like she's afraid he's hiding it—or that it'll come later, when she's least expecting it.

I let out a tired laugh. "He has a lot of practice dealing with his partners fucking shit up." I point to myself. "Exhibit A."

"I've just never seen someone move on from getting hurt so fast."

"Yeah. He had to do that growing up. Since his parents were constantly fighting or nitpicking at every little thing he did, he learned to brush things off quickly. Otherwise he never got a break from all the negative shit they threw at him."

Her expression saddens. "That's awful."

"He found ways to escape. And now he doesn't talk to his family often, so it's not as much of a problem. But he's always the first to cool off after a fight."

"What about you?" she asks softly.

"I take a bit longer to process things." My gaze falls. It's the last thing she wants to hear right now, but I don't want to lie to her. That's what got us into this mess in the first place. "Can I ask you a question, princess?"

"Anything."

"If you were worried about Rhett's reaction, why didn't you come to me? Or Ell? We know him a lot better, so we could've predicted his reaction better. Or, as Ell said, we could've stopped him from doing something stupid."

She blinks rapidly, like my suggestion is a completely new thought to her. "I . . . I don't know."

"Was it because you thought we wouldn't be able to help?"

It's a stupid question to ask. Of course that's not what she thought. But my own insecurities have a tendency to shine through at the worst possible times.

"Not at all," she says. "I guess that since it matters to all of you, it didn't occur to me to only tell one of you. There wasn't much conscious thought put into it. My mind's been pretty full lately."

I nod. Ell is right—we've thrown a lot at her. With the amount of stress she's been under, I can't even fault her for not thinking straight. Maybe I should be more hurt, but the feeling that's dominating my thoughts right now is how pissed I am at Ludo.

How could he just leave her? How could he be so heartless?

"I want to talk to Rhett," Wren says quietly. "I want to explain."

"That's not a good idea tonight, princess."

"I don't want him to hate me."

"He doesn't."

She doesn't respond. Her brows are furrowed, and her eyes are blank. She's getting lost in worried thoughts, which is a feeling I'm all too familiar with. Once that ball gets rolling, the thoughts only get worse and worse, until there's little you can do to stop them.

"Hey." I nudge her. "I promise he doesn't hate you. Now, we both need to get to bed. I'm gonna sleep with you tonight, okay?"

"You don't have to. If you need more time—"

I cut her off with a kiss. Yes, she lied, but she's obviously broken up about it. If I was in her position, sleeping alone would only make things worse. "I don't need more time to show you that I love you, and that I'll always love you." Standing, I pull her with me. "No matter what, Wren."

Tears spring to her eyes, but she blinks them back. "I love you, too."

I text Rhett to update him on our sleeping arrangements. Odds are, he won't come to bed tonight, but there's always a chance.

"I promise I'm not hiding anything else," Wren says as I get under the covers with her.

"I believe you, princess." I pull her body into mine. "Now go to sleep."

...

In the morning, I get up after Elliot is already gone. Wren is still sleeping, so I leave her be, wanting her to get some more rest. I slept like shit, which is typical when one of the guys is away for the night. I only hope Wren slept better than I did.

As I make myself coffee, I notice movement on the balcony outside. Rhett is pacing, his head bowed. He looks like shit. I'm pretty sure he didn't come back last night, so odds are, he didn't sleep at all.

Abandoning the coffeemaker, I head outside. When I open the sliding door, Rhett pauses and looks up. Yep—I know that look in his eyes. He's had no sleep and too much time alone with the things that haunt him.

I don't even get a word out before he says, "Please don't lecture me."

I bite my tongue before I make a joke about that being Ell's job. This isn't the time for that. "Are you going to fix things with Wren?"

He turns away.

"Rhett, come on. You can't say what you said last night and just leave her like that. It's cruel."

"I need Sammy to be my priority," he says darkly.

"That doesn't change the fact that Wren's logic was solid. She was afraid of what you'd do. None of us like that she lied. *She* doesn't like that she lied. But she's still new to this. To us. And she did her best."

"It doesn't matter," he grits out.

"It does."

He shakes his head.

"Don't be an asshole, Rhett. You can't expect her to be perfect. *She did her best.* You can't tell me that doesn't mean any-"

"It doesn't matter because she's right, goddammit," he yells, whipping around to face me. "I'd ruin everything for her. For any of you."

His admission takes me by surprise. Avenging Sammy's murder has been his one and only life goal since we were teens. I know Rhett would never sacrifice one of us for our plan, but sacrificing the plan for one of us? When we've all worked so hard to get here? I don't want him to have to do that.

"Sammy deserves better than that." Rhett's voice is laced with a cocktail of shame, defeat, and disappointment. He turns around again, gripping the railing and lowering his head. "She deserves better than what we've given her. It's been *ten years*. She shouldn't have to wait that long."

When I step up next to him, he tilts his face away from me. I don't force him to look at me. It'd only push him further away. "Sammy will get her justice. And if you think she's up there somewhere, looking down on us and wondering why we haven't taken Ludo out yet, I guarantee she's not."

"What if she is?"

"Rhett, if she's watching you, there's no doubt in my mind that she doesn't give a shit about Ludo. I'll never forget the way she looked at you. You were everything to her. And if she could see you right now, she wouldn't be disappointed in you. She'd be worried that her big brother was making himself miserable. She'd want you to focus on trying to be happy."

"I can't, O. I can't move on while he's still alive."

Fucking hell. I can't even fight him on that. I've thought the same thing too many times myself.

"I'm worried about you," I say softly.

"By this point, I'd say we're all worried about each other."

"That doesn't make it any better."

He shrugs. Typical—his default setting is deflecting. Over the years, he's come so far in managing his anger and sharing his burdens. But my god, at times like these, I wish he was further along.

"You can't avoid Wren forever."

"I'm not planning on it. I just need a little more time."

"How much?" I don't want her to be miserable all day.

"I . . . I don't know. Elliot texted me and said Wren has more to explain, that he was thinking we could do an early dinner once he's done with Aubrey. That's, what, six hours from now? Seven?"

"She thinks you hate her, Rhett."

He swears, so quietly I almost don't hear him. Then he's heading for the door, grumbling something about being an idiot.

"Rhett, wait, she's sleeping." I follow him back into the penthouse, but I don't make it far.

Wren is standing in the doorway to the bedroom, frozen. Her eyes widen as Rhett advances toward her.

"I lied." The words don't come from Wren's mouth—they come from Rhett's. "I'm so sorry, sweetheart. The things I said... I was lying to myself. Lying to you. And I don't hate you, Wren. I'm not capable of it."

She frowns when he stops a few feet in front of her. "Lying to yourself?"

"You were right." It sounds like it pains Rhett to admit that—it probably does. "My first thoughts were of how I could make Ludo regret leaving you there. I wanted to storm into that damn condo and kill him right then."

Wren grips the doorframe to steady herself. Her voice is hesitant as she asks, "So why did you... you said..." Averting her gaze, she presses her lips together like she's trying to stop herself from crying.

"I didn't want to believe that I'd skip over our plans," he says. "It feels like a betrayal to Sammy, not giving her the justice she deserves. But you're right. I would. If it came down to it, I'd do it without a second thought."

"I don't want you to do that," she whispers.

"Neither do I. Ludo deserves every ounce of pain we're going to give him. But I shouldn't've said it the way I did. Those words never should've left my mouth. I *would* ruin everything we've worked for. For you, for Ell, for O. And I'm sorry I couldn't admit it to you."

Wren looks like she wants to throw herself into Rhett's arms, but she stays planted in the doorway. A tear slips down her cheek. All I want to do is wipe it away and hug her until she's smiling again, but I can't. This moment is for her and Rhett.

Slowly, like Wren will bolt if he moves too quickly, Rhett steps up to her. "I'm so sorry, sweetheart." He brushes away her tear.

Her face scrunches up, and more tears fall onto her cheeks. "I'm sorry, too. I didn't want to lie to you."

"I know. It's okay." Again, he wipes at her tears. "I understand."

As Wren hiccups and does her best not to cry, Rhett shifts uncomfortably.

Do something, I want to tell him. *Hold her, touch her, anything.* I know it'll be hard for him. Touch during or after arguments usually sends him to a dark place, but god, the look on Wren's face is heartbreaking. She really, truly thought he hated her.

"Wren . . ." He lays a hand on her shoulder. "Fuck, c'mere."

Her forehead hits Rhett's chest as he circles his arms around her. When she grabs onto his shirt and leans into him, relief billows through me. They both need the mutual reassurance from each other.

"It's okay," Rhett says quietly. He's rubbing her back gently with his face buried in her hair. "I'm so sorry, sweetheart."

When they finally pull away, she looks up at him with shining eyes. "I already told O and Ell, but I want to make sure you know, too. I'll never lie to you again, Rhett, I promise."

"I know," he murmurs. His lips feather against her forehead. "Thank you."

She's still holding onto his T-shirt to keep him close. Gently, he takes her hands and removes them from his body, squeezing as he does.

"Do you have to sleep?" she asks.

"I should try," he says as he glances at me. "We're having dinner when Ell is done, yeah?"

"Yep," I reply. "I'm planning on keeping up with the bug in the condo today, and we can go over everything of importance then. As well as whatever Wren has to say."

"Okay." After a moment's hesitation, he runs a hand over Wren's hair. "You gonna be okay?"

She nods.

He leans down and drops a kiss to Wren's lips. "I'll see you both later. Goodnight."

"Night," I say as he slips past Wren, holding her hand until the last possible moment.

Once the bedroom door is shut, Wren rubs at her eyes and sniffles. I'm worried she's about to start crying again, but when she turns to me, she gives me her best attempt at a smile.

I want to ask if she's really okay or if she needs a hug, but I know that look in her eyes. She's still right there on the edge. Anything could push her back into tears again. And if she starts crying, Rhett will inevitably hear, and then he won't be able to get any sleep.

So all I ask is, "You want coffee?"

"That sounds nice."

As I pour it, I say, "I have to get some work done, so I can't go with you if you want to head out. You could try to do something with Aubrey if you'd like, and that way Elliot will be with you, but otherwise you're kinda stuck here."

"I'm not sure I'm in the mood to be social. I'll just read."

Handing her a mug, I press my lips to her forehead. "Okay. Just let me know if you need anything."

"I will." With another smile, she retreats to the couch and grabs one of the books she brought with her.

I watch her for a second. She looks worn down, but like she's trying to hide it. It makes my chest ache with worry. Last night, she just... went swimming all by herself. Fuck, she could've died. She can't do it again—we can't let her. It's too dangerous.

Before Wren notices that I'm watching her, I turn away and grab my laptop. I don't know how to fix this, not exactly. But I know where to start. First, we need to figure out why she snuck down by herself. And then somehow—quickly—we need to find a way to remind her that we're here for her. Because my anxiety can't take another scare like last night. Not ever, ever again.

Chapter Fifteen

Elliot

I meet everyone at the resort restaurant for our early dinner. The place isn't too busy considering we're in between the standard rush hours, which is good. It means there's no one around to overhear our conversation.

"Sorry I'm late." As I slide into our secluded corner booth, I wince at the painful reminder of Rhett spanking me. *Fuck,* it hurts. After I kiss Oliver on the cheek and rest one of my hands on his thigh, I say, "Ludo and his guys didn't get back at the time they said they would. Looked like they left immediately after I did, too."

Rhett raises an eyebrow. "Oh?"

As I look over the menu, I say, "Aubrey was chatty. Said today is the last day of training for their guy, which makes me wonder where Ludo is going to be tomorrow. As for tonight, Ludo is taking Aubrey out to meet some people."

"Interesting." Oliver places his hand over mine. "I've been keeping up with the feed from the bug, and I haven't caught anything about tomorrow."

"Has there been anything at all that might be helpful?"

Oliver shakes his head. "No. But Ludo only hired us for three days. Starting the day after tomorrow, he's gonna be at the condo more, right? We should be able to catch something then."

"Hopefully." My tone doesn't sound convincing. It's very possible that we won't get any more information out of this trip.

"I think we need to talk about the guy they've been training," Wren says. Her posture is pin straight as her eyes dart between the three of us. "I'm pretty sure I know who he is."

"Go on," Rhett says. He's sitting in between Wren and Oliver. One of his arms is around Wren, keeping her close to him.

"Do you guys remember the nineteen-year-old I told you about? The one who Jordan almost killed because he gave me a blanket?"

We all nod.

Wren swallows nervously before continuing. "The reason Jordan didn't kill him is because Ludo showed up right as he was about to pull the trigger. Apparently, Ludo and Jordan were going to discuss some sort of business deal. But when Ludo saw me, he said the deal was off. Then he saw Andrew—that's the kid—and took him when he left."

I lean forward. "Did Ludo say why?"

Wren shakes her head. "He asked if Jordan knew who Andrew was, but Jordan didn't know, and Ludo didn't bother explaining. Do you . . . do you know?"

"I wish. You didn't get a last name?"

"No. I'm sorry."

I'm about to tell her she has no need to apologize, but Rhett speaks first. "Hold on. Why do you think Andrew is the man Ludo's training?"

"Aubrey said something about him being young," Wren explains. "It doesn't feel like that could be a coincidence. But I . . . I guess it's just a feeling."

"Hunches are always worth exploring, love."

Wren nods silently. I was hoping that getting this off her chest would help her to relax, but she only looks more uptight. When our server comes by to take our orders, I'm pretty sure even they notice.

Once he's gone, Oliver says, "Why don't you talk about last night, princess."

After dragging in a long breath, Wren turns to Rhett. He doesn't look angry. In fact, he looks desperate to fix things.

"There isn't anything left to talk about," he says firmly.

"There's not?" she asks.

"We all understand why you kept it from us, right? You were afraid of how I'd react?" Rhett makes a point of looking at all three of us, waiting until we give him confirmation to continue. "And you've already promised not to keep something like this from us again, correct?"

Slowly, she nods.

"Then we're done," Rhett says with finality. "No need to go digging through it all again. I, for one, would prefer not to dwell on it."

"No," Oliver says. "No, we still need to talk."

The fear in Wren's eyes makes my chest ache. I never want her to be afraid of us. *Ever.*

"What are you doing?" I hiss at Oliver.

He ignores me, reaching across the table and holding out his hand. Only after Wren hesitantly places her hand in his does he continue. "I'm not angry, princess. I just need an explanation."

"Okay," she whispers unsteadily.

"Why did you go swimming by yourself? You could've drowned, Wren."

Oh. In the middle of everything else, I completely forgot about that.

"I wanted to prove to myself that I could do it on my own. Without a security blanket or a crutch, I guess. You guys make me feel brave. But I need to be brave on my own."

"I understand that." Oliver keeps his voice calm as he rubs the back of her hand with his thumb. No doubt he's trying to soothe her. "But why last night? And why such a drastic change? You went from a kitchen sink to a pool. You don't think that's too big of a jump?"

"I..." She falters and tries to pull her hand away, but Oliver keeps his grip firm.

"It's because Ludo called you a coward," Rhett says lowly. "Isn't it?"

"He did *what?*" By the time I realize I'm practically shouting the words, it's too late. The few people in the restaurant glance toward us, but at Rhett's glare, they turn away quickly.

"He noticed that I was being avoidant of water, so he told me that fear isn't my problem, cowardice is. I didn't want him to be right about me."

"Wren," Oliver says, "his opinion of you doesn't matter. Let him be right, let him be wrong. The only thing that's important is that we support you. You're allowed to take your time with this, and you're allowed to let us help you. *Please.* I don't want you to hurt yourself."

After an agonizingly long moment of hesitation, Wren nods. "Okay. I'm sorry."

I don't like how much Wren is apologizing, but before I can say something, our food comes. Wren barely touches her plate while we eat, which I'm beginning to realize is a common occurrence for her when she's nervous. At some point, she excuses herself and heads for the restroom. We all watch her go.

"Was I too harsh?" Oliver asks once she's out of earshot. "That wasn't what I was trying to do."

"You were fine." I reach over and squeeze his arm. "I think she's still feeling guilty, but that will fade."

"She looked scared," Rhett says.

"I hated that," Oliver mumbles into his plate.

"She'll be okay," I say. "This is the first time we've had anything close to a fight with Wren. And it wasn't with one of us—it was with all three of us at once. I hate fighting with either of you, but I hate fighting with *both* of you even more."

"Shit." Oliver rubs his face. "I didn't even think of that. She probably feels awful."

"It's not your fault," Rhett says. "It's mine. I shouldn't have said what I said."

Before they both start to spiral, I cut in. "What matters is that we're past it. From this point on, we need to make sure Wren feels secure in this relationship. In *us*. I don't want her doubting anything, and I definitely don't want her to be constantly afraid that we're holding a grudge against her or something like that."

They both agree, which puts them somewhat at ease. Out of habit, I let my gaze wander around the restaurant, making sure we aren't being watched. Just as I'm about to turn my attention back to Oliver and Rhett, I spot Wren making her way across the room. The problem is, she's not heading for our table.

Wren goes up to the only person sitting at the bar, a young man facing away from us. Upon seeing her, he tenses. I can't hear their conversation, but the concern on Wren's face is clear as day. She reaches out and touches the guy, and he winces before pulling away.

The second Wren makes eye contact with me, I'm out of the booth and on my way over to her. It's then that I hear the man protesting.

"No, stop, you can't—"

"Wren? Love, what's going on?"

The man turns around on his barstool, and the second we lock eyes, I freeze. All of the air is sucked out of my lungs, and I have to blink twice to make sure I'm not seeing things.

"Ell," Wren says, grabbing my arm and tugging me closer. "This is Andrew."

"Stop," Andrew hisses at Wren. "I can't be seen here. Fuck, this was such a bad idea." He starts to stand, but my body miraculously starts working again, and I shove him back down onto the stool.

No way. There's no fucking way.

"Hey! Get your hands off me, man."

I release him, but I don't move away. No, I just stare, taking in the details of his face and trying to put the pieces together. He's a carbon copy of teenage Rhett. There's only one answer for how that's possible. I just don't want to admit it.

"What's your last name?" I ask, my voice hoarse.

Andrew narrows his eyes. "What's it to you?"

I don't have time for his bullshit, so I say, "Is Richard Brooks your father?"

His jaw drops, and dread pools in my stomach. *No. No, no, no.*

"How did you know that?" Andrew demands. He slips from his stool and gets up in my face. "Who the fuck are you?"

"That bastard," I breathe out.

"Elliot!" Wren exclaims. "Don't be rude."

That snaps me out of my shock. Grabbing Wren's hand, I say, "I think you should come with us, Andrew. I have something to show you."

He hesitates, but Wren gives him a pleading look, so he follows.

Seeing Wren talking to teenage Rhett is a mindfuck I wasn't prepared for. Apparently Oliver and Rhett feel the same way, because when they see us approaching, they have similar reactions to my own. Oliver drops his fork, and his jaw goes slack. As for Rhett, he turns into a fucking statue.

"Will you please explain what's going on?" Wren hisses, following closely behind me.

"Not here," I grit out.

Once we're at the table, Oliver stands. "I'll get the bill. Meet you guys upstairs?"

"Let's go. Rhett?"

He still hasn't moved, his eyes glued to Andrew. He's probably thinking the same thing I am.

"I'll bring him up with me," Oliver says. "You guys go ahead."

In the elevator, Andrew turns to Wren. "Look, I'm glad you got out alive, but who the hell are these guys? And why does one of them look like me? Are they who Ludo was talking about before I left with him? When he said Jordan was a dead man walking? It's because of them?"

"Yeah." Wren's eyes stay trained on me as she works with the information she has. "Ell . . ."

The elevator dings, and the doors open. I usher them through the hallway and into the penthouse as quickly as I can.

"How did you know my father's name?" Andrew asks, but I ignore him, pulling up Finn's number in my phone.

"Does Rhett have aunts? Or uncles?" Wren asks weakly, like she already knows the answer is no.

Finn picks up quickly. "What do you need?"

"I need some security footage deleted, mostly from the last hour." I explain the situation, detailing where Andrew was sitting at the bar. "Follow us all the way up to the penthouse. Hell, make it look like we were never at the restaurant in the first place."

"You got it." The line goes dead.

Shoving my phone in my pocket, I turn back to Andrew. He's sweating, his eyes darting all over the penthouse like he's looking for a place to escape or hide. The lighting in the restaurant was dim, but looking at him now, I can't help but grimace. The kid is covered in cuts and bruises.

"Are you working for Ludo?" he asks.

"Yes."

"Are you—" Andrew gulps. "Are you going to tell him about this? Please, I was just bored. All I was gonna do was have one drink, and then I was gonna go back. I promise."

"Go back?" Wren prods.

"To my—to my hotel room. I'm not supposed to leave without supervision. Oh fuck, I'm begging you. Please don't tell him. I need his help, I can't mess this up."

Before answering, I give myself a split second to think things over. It seems that Andrew thinks we have more knowledge and association with Ludo than we actually do. I'm not sure I want to tear down that façade yet. "We'll talk about that later," I say slowly. "For now, we have some other questions for you."

Andrew nods anxiously.

The door to the penthouse opens, and Rhett and Oliver file in. Rhett's expression is still shuttered, and Oliver gives me a worried glance.

"Can someone explain what's going on?" Wren asks.

"I'd like that, too," Oliver says as he eyes Andrew suspiciously. "Princess, how do you know him? Or did you just recognize him because . . ." He waves a hand between Andrew and Rhett.

"This is Andrew," I say, gesturing to him. "Richard Brooks' second son. That we know of, I suppose. Andrew, meet your older brother." I point to Rhett.

Considering the shitshow that the past couple days have been, my expectation is for Rhett to yell. To get angry, to storm off, to take it out on anyone. He's gotten much better at managing his anger, but not in a situation like this.

I suppose that's why we're all taken aback when Rhett does the exact opposite. Pity, or maybe sympathy, ripples across his face before he says softly, "I'm so sorry."

For a second, Andrew just stares at his older brother. Then he scoffs. *"Sorry?* That's it? You're fucking *sorry?"*

Rhett's brows pull together. "What—"

"You left me with that bastard, and all you have to say for yourself is *sorry?"* Andrew yells.

"What, no, I—"

"How could you do that?" Andrew advances toward him. "How could you do fucking *nothing?"*

At the last second, Wren slips in between the two of them. "Stop!" She shoves Andrew back before he's close enough to Rhett to do any damage. "Stop, it's not what you think."

Rhett tries to push her out of the way without being too forceful. "Sweetheart, don't—"

Wren bats Rhett's hand away, keeping her focus on Andrew. "Rhett is twenty-eight."

Andrew rolls his eyes. "So?"

"There's only a nine-year difference between you two. Don't you think you'd remember your childhoods overlapping?"

The anger slowly fades from Andrew's eyes. "Oh."

Rhett pulls Wren back and tucks her into his side. That way he has a hold on her if she tries to get in between them again. "I didn't know you existed until a couple minutes ago."

"Right," Andrew mumbles. "Sorry."

"I would've gotten you out of there if I'd known," Rhett says. "I would've found a way."

"Trust me, I know what you mean," Andrew says darkly. His expression matches one Rhett wears often, and it's uncanny and unsettling.

This is going to take a long time to get used to.

"What the hell are you doing working for Ludo?" Rhett asks. "You have no idea—"

"Rhett," I cut in, holding up a hand. He immediately understands what I'm trying to say—keep all our cards hidden—because he doesn't continue.

"I have to," Andrew says. "He's the only way I can get my—our—little brother away from Dad."

Rhett looks like he's about to keel over. "Little brother?"

"Oh, Jesus fuck," Oliver says under his breath.

"Yeah. And Ludo is my only hope for getting Benny away from Dad, so—"

"Oh, he most certainly is *not* the only option," Rhett snaps.

"Well, he's the best one," Andrew says with an ironic amount of confidence. "Ludo already took him in. It's part of our agreement."

My heart sinks. None of this sounds good. It makes one thing make sense, though—the child Ludo was talking about the other day.

With every second, Rhett looks worse and worse. Wren leads him to one of the couches and has him sit down. For once, he doesn't protest. Probably because he's too numb to try.

I attempt to figure out our best move. We can't let Andrew know we don't trust Ludo—that could lead to disaster. But what are we supposed to do from here?

Andrew's gaze flicks to the door. "Look, I should really get back. I shouldn't be out of my hotel room. If someone comes and checks on me—"

"No one's going to," Oliver says. "Ludo and his bodyguards aren't even on the resort property right now. It's just us."

I start pacing, moving myself in between Andrew and the front door. We're not done yet, and I'm in no mood to chase him through the hotel if he tries to run. "Tell us more about this agreement you have with Ludo."

Andrew narrows his eyes. "Why should I tell you anything? Actually, what the fuck do any of you even want with me? Yeah, I'm Rhett's brother, so what? That doesn't mean my life is any of your business."

Dropping his head into his hands, Rhett lets out a distressed sound. "You have no idea what you've gotten yourself into."

"That's enough, Rhett," I say. Family or not, we can't trust Andrew with any part of ourselves—especially our past.

"I know exactly what I've gotten myself into." With enough fire to set the whole resort ablaze, Andrew casts Rhett a glare. "Now let me leave. I shouldn't be up here anyway."

"Can't do that," I say. "Not until you give us some answers."

"I don't owe you anything," Andrew bites out. His eyes are lit up with fury, and he looks and sounds so similar to the younger version of Rhett that my heart snaps in two.

What's this kid been through?

"Ell," Wren says, standing and coming toward me. "Maybe we should give everyone some time to process. This is a lot for all of us."

"No. This happens now." This may be our last chance to get Andrew alone. We can't waste it.

Oliver takes Wren's spot on the couch. Hesitantly, he places a hand on Rhett's arm, slipping it around his shoulder when Rhett leans into his touch. They start murmuring to each other, quietly enough that no one else can hear.

Andrew protests, spouting something about how we can't keep him here. I barely pay him any attention. Rhett is shaking his head, and it looks like he's struggling to get in enough air.

Did I make the wrong call? Should we let him go?

"Hey!" Andrew shouts. "I'm talking to you. Either let me go, or I'll force my way out."

Wren slides herself in between me and Andrew, holding her hands up. "No, Andrew, don't—"

When I look back at him, it's already too late. The knife is flying through the air, catching the late afternoon light as it spins straight for us. On instinct, I grab Wren and pull her out of the way. But the knife is moving too fast, and my reaction is a second too slow.

Since she still has her hands up to protect herself, the knife doesn't make it past her arms. She gasps at the pain before the blade clatters to the floor, nicking my forearm as it does.

Andrew tries to bolt past us toward the door, but Oliver jumps to his feet and grabs him by the back of his neck. Rhett follows quickly and throws Andrew to the ground. Before Andrew can scramble away, Rhett is on top of him with both hands around his neck.

"You picked the wrong family to fuck with, kid," Rhett growls.

Ignoring the sting from my own cut, I grab Wren's arm. "Love. Love, I'm so sorry. Fuck, you're bleeding."

"It's not that bad." Her voice is tight, and she clings to me while she watches Rhett and Andrew.

"Let me see." As I inspect the cut, I hold her wrist gingerly. Blood flows across her skin, and some drips to the floor.

This shouldn't've happened. I never should've taken my eyes off Andrew.

Thankfully, Wren's cut isn't too deep. I'm about to usher her to the bathroom to clean it when I hear Oliver say behind me, "You have to let up, Rhett."

I whip around to see Rhett still strangling Andrew. His face is hardened with fury, and I can't even blame him.

"Please," Andrew wheezes. "Please don't."

"Rhett," Oliver snaps, shaking his shoulder. *"Stop."*

For a second, I think we'll have to physically haul Rhett off his brother, but he removes his hands. Andrew gasps and coughs before trying to squirm out from underneath Rhett. It's a pointless move.

"What the hell were you thinking?" Rhett barks. He grabs Andrew's wrists and pins them to the floor. "That we'd let you go after that?"

"Just let me up." Andrew's voice is raspy and forced. "I'm sorry."

"Sorry?" Rhett shouts, making Wren jump. "Don't fucking lie to me. You were aiming to kill."

Someone needs to calm him down before this escalates even further. Neither of us are at a risk of bleeding out, so I push Wren into Oliver's arms and crouch down next to Rhett.

"Give me one good reason why I shouldn't kill him," Rhett says darkly. He keeps his glare on Andrew, so potent that even I can feel it.

"You already know why."

Rhett works his jaw as I watch the internal battle play out across his face. Finally, he releases Andrew and gets up. "Don't touch him. Don't fucking touch any of them, or I'll slit your throat and watch you writhe on the floor as you bleed out and struggle for your life. You got it, kid?"

Scrambling to his feet, Andrew snaps, "I'm *not* a fucking kid."

"You're sure acting like one," Rhett growls.

"Hey, that's enough," I say, pushing Rhett farther from Andrew and staying in between them. "We did some stupid shit when we were nineteen, too. Of course he's acting a little green. He *is* green."

It takes a second, but Rhett takes a deep breath. "Right. Do you need to check on Wren? We're fine here."

"Like hell we are," Andrew grouses.

Glancing around, I realize Oliver and Wren have disappeared. "Yeah, I want to make sure she's okay. Andrew, I know this isn't what you want, but you've gotta deal with it. If you try to fight your way out of here again, I won't stop Rhett from doing whatever he wants to you."

Not true. But obviously Andrew isn't going to cooperate voluntarily.

With a huff, Andrew throws himself onto the couch and crosses his arm. He's pouting like a five-year-old, but I don't have time to dwell on it. I'm already halfway out of the room, praying Rhett can find the willpower to control himself.

In the bathroom, Wren is sitting on the counter, and Oliver is gently dabbing at her cut with a cotton ball. Disinfectant and bandages litter the area next to the sink.

"I've got it."

The way I say it holds no room for discussion, so Oliver moves out of my way. He touches my arm, right above my own cut. "Are you okay?"

"Fine. I'll deal with it in a minute. Can you make sure Rhett doesn't hurt Andrew too much?"

As Oliver leaves, his hand trails across my back, but I barely feel it. My only focus is on Wren.

She attempts a wobbly smile. "I'm okay, Ell. The cut isn't that deep."

I step in between her legs and grab onto her waist to hide the way my hands are shaking. Seeing that knife flying toward her—realizing I didn't have enough time to get her out of the way—fuck. I can count on one hand the amount of times I've felt that mind-numbing, no-thoughts-just-act kind of panic.

My eyes lock onto hers. "Never again, Wren."

"What?"

"Don't you *ever* put yourself in harm's way to protect me. If one of us is going to get hurt, it's going to be me. Every goddamn time. You got it?"

"Ell—"

"No, I mean it. I never want to see a weapon aimed at you when it should be pointed at me. Never step in front of me like that again."

She tilts her head down and stays silent.

"Wren. Promise me."

"I can't," she whispers.

"You can," I grit out, "and you fucking will."

She shakes her head.

"Why not?" I demand, fighting the urge to shake her until she sees some sense.

"Because I can't bear the thought of seeing you hurt!" She pokes her finger into my chest. "You don't like seeing a weapon pointed at me? I don't like seeing a weapon pointed at you! How am I supposed to stand by and just watch you get hurt? Or die? Fuck, Ell, I love you too much to do that. I know it's scary—I was terrified. But I was more scared of losing you than I was of getting hurt."

My heart fucking stops. I don't even think she realizes she said it. I stare at her, waiting for it to register, but it doesn't.

"Why are you looking at me like that?" she asks.

"Like what?"

"Like . . . like you're afraid but also happy."

I hesitate, willing my heart to stop pounding wildly, but my pulse only races more. Leaning down, I keep my eyes locked on hers and whisper, "Because I love you, too."

Her lips part from a mixture of shock and realization. When she releases a breathy, "Oh," and slowly blinks, I think that means her mind has caught up with what she said.

Moving my hands from her waist, I hold her face gently and kiss her. Her arms wrap around my neck, and there's something about the way she does it that has goosebumps spreading across my skin.

This isn't how I imagined telling her. I've had some sort of plan forming in the back of my mind—because I plan everything—but I didn't think it'd happen this fast. With her and Oliver, it makes sense that they said it so quickly. Both of them wear their hearts on their sleeves. But I didn't realize I was ready to say it to her until I heard the words leave her mouth.

Reluctantly, I pull away. I never want to stop, but I need to finish cleaning her cut. When she looks at me, there's a glimmer of happiness in her eyes that fills my heart with hope. She's still not fully back, but it's a step closer.

"Elliot . . ." She sounds out of breath. Maybe a touch disoriented, too. That doesn't stop her from tugging me down for another kiss. I let her, too caught up in the moment to stop.

I can't believe I said it this fast. But I can't imagine holding it back any longer.

This time, Wren pulls away to gulp in air. A slow smile creeps across her face. "I can't believe I said it without realizing."

"It's on brand for you." With a chuckle, I give her one last kiss. "Now let's get this cut bandaged up."

As I finish cleaning her cut, she winces. If I could, I'd take the pain and bear it myself. That knife never should've touched her.

"I thought he'd stop," she murmurs as I stick the bandage to her skin. "I thought if he knew he'd hurt me, he wouldn't throw it."

"I know, love. I know."

She shifts restlessly, her eyes filled to the brim with worry. "Ludo has to know they're related. That must've been what he meant when he asked Jordan if he knew who Andrew was."

"Seems like it."

"Why would he know that?"

"I'm not sure."

I have one possible answer, I'm just afraid to admit it. But regardless, many other aspects of Ludo's plan are coming together, and the picture is far from pretty.

Ludo getting friendly with Philly's judges. Him testing our loyalty yesterday. And him keeping Rhett's younger brother as a backup plan.

Wren stares up at me anxiously. "This isn't good, is it?"

In this family, we don't lie to each other. Even though the truth is going to stress Wren out, I refuse to keep her in the dark. So I stroke her hair, hoping she'll find some semblance of comfort in the gesture, while I say, "No. No, not at all."

Chapter Sixteen

Rhett

Once everyone is back in the living room, we don't waste any time. We don't know how long Ludo will be gone for, and by the time he arrives, Andrew needs to be back in his room like nothing happened.

"Let's talk about this agreement you have with Ludo," Elliot says. "What all does it entail?"

"I want legal custody of Benny," Andrew says. "He's only twelve."

I drop my head into my hands. *Fucking hell.*

"But you don't have grounds for CPS to step in."

Elliot doesn't phrase it as a question. He knows. When I was close to turning eighteen, all I could think about was finding a way to get Sammy away from my dad so I could raise her myself. The problem was, we could never get enough evidence of anything to get the authorities to step in. By the time we were close, it was too late.

"The courts don't care about emotional abuse," Andrew says.

"We know." Oliver sounds haunted as he says it. We all are.

"We're getting off topic," Elliot says. "What does this have to do with Ludo?"

"He's gonna help me. He said he could make Benny disappear without a trace until we can legally detach him from my parents. Ludo is going to keep him hidden and hire a tutor so Benny can keep up with his schoolwork."

Raising my head, I glare at Andrew. "So you had him kidnapped? Seriously? Do you know how traumatized he's going to be?"

"I'll be back home soon," Andrew says. "I'm staying with Ludo, and he said my room is right next to Benny's. It was the only thing I could do to get him out of there."

The room feels like it's tilting, or like I'm spinning out of control. Oliver's hand rubbing up and down my spine does little to ground me. If anything, it's making everything worse.

"What does Ludo get out of this deal?" Elliot asks.

At least one of us is able to keep this conversation on track.

"I work for him until I have custody," Andrew says. "I don't get paid much, but Benny stays safe, and we have a place to live."

Oliver shoots me a skeptical look. "That's it?"

"What do you mean, *that's it?* This shit's hard." Andrew holds out his bare arms, showcasing his wounds. "And painful."

"Doesn't sound like Ludo gets much out of this deal. He's not one to have a heart of gold," Elliot says. "And he's not known for being generous, either."

"Maybe not to you." Andrew crosses his arms and arches his brow, like he actually knows more than us in this situation. Like he knows anything at all.

He killed your sister. I almost say it out loud, but I catch myself at the last moment. Currently, Andrew's loyalties don't lie with us. It doesn't matter that he's my brother. We can't trust him.

"Okay, fine." Elliot shrugs. "He's doing this out of the goodness of his heart, then. What are you going to be doing for him?"

"Whatever he asks. Why do you want specifics? What's it to you?"

"Because you're my brother," I say firmly, meeting his glare with a steady, hopefully convincing gaze. "And you're entering into a highly dangerous—and also illegal—field of work. We may not have known that the other existed, but that doesn't change that I care about you."

Andrew rolls his eyes. "You just tried to kill me fifteen minutes ago."

"It was a momentary lapse of judgment. I'd like to keep you alive, and you getting into this line of work is worrying."

"We're practically strangers. Blood doesn't matter. You can't have a bleeding heart in this world, Rhett. Everyone has a sob story, but that doesn't mean you can help everyone. Suck it up, move on, and let me live my life."

My muscles go rigid in an effort not to cringe. For someone who's trying to get away from our dad, Andrew sure sounds a lot like him. "Andrew..."

"I think what Rhett is trying to say is that you might be in over your head," Oliver says. "Do you even know the full scope of Ludo's businesses?"

"Don't underestimate me." Andrew's tone is full of spite, like he's had to prove his worth his entire life and he's sick of it. Considering my own upbringing, that's a likely possibility.

"No one's underestimating you," Wren says. "But working for Ludo is dangerous."

Andrew shrugs. "Working for Jordan was dangerous. I managed just fine."

Shit, that's right. I forgot that's how Andrew even got tangled up with Ludo in the first place. "How did you get involved with the Williams family?"

"I started out working at one of their restaurants. Ended up hearing some conversations I shouldn't've, and when they found out, they were gonna kill me. I volunteered to work for them instead." Andrew spreads his hands. "Everything with Jordan went to shit, Ludo took me in, and now here I am."

He's not thinking this through. Of course he doesn't realize it—he's nineteen with no knowledge of how the world works. The problem is, it's going to get him and Benny killed.

"Do you have a picture of him?"

Andrew's face twists in confusion. "Of Ludo?"

"Of Benny," I say, my voice gruffer than I'd like.

"Oh, yeah." Andrew pulls out his phone and goes through some pictures before handing it to me. "Here."

The second I look down at the photo, my throat closes up. Benny looks so much like Sammy, right down to the sparkling eyes and goofy smile. It's like being transported back in time. *Fuck, I miss you so much, Sam.*

There's a woman in the picture with Benny. His and Andrew's mother, maybe? My mom was still alive when Andrew was born, but he's definitely not hers. Andrew is too close in age to how old Sammy would be if she were still alive. And again—I'd remember him.

I lose track of the conversation happening in the room as a time line clicks into place in my head. My father—that bastard of a man—was having an affair while my mother was struggling for her life. And now, yet again, his youngest child is in danger because of his neglect.

History is repeating itself.

Someone says something, but I barely hear, like they're trying to speak through a thick wall. I can only process one thing, over and over again. *He's going to die. He's going to die. He's going to die.*

Andrew is going to get Benny killed. It's like Sammy all over again, except this time, it's worse. Because this time, I'm equipped to do something about it, but I feel just as helpless.

"... it's too much, Ell. We need to give him time to process."

Andrew's phone is pulled from my hand. I barely register Wren's sweet, floral scent as she guides me to the kitchen table. At some point, a glass of water is placed in front of me, and I manage to swallow down a sip.

Wren stays close. She doesn't touch me, but I can feel her presence.

"We'll continue this another time," I hear Elliot say. "If you breathe a word of this to Ludo, he'll know you left your room. We've wiped the security tapes, but you need to keep your mouth shut."

"I know," Andrew grits out. "I'm not stupid." He mutters something under his breath, and then I hear the door close.

Oliver rushes to my side. He pulls me out of my seat, grasping my shoulders.

"O," Elliot protests, "he's not going to want—"

"I don't care." Oliver wraps his arms around me, and maybe I'm too numb or maybe I'm too worried, but my skin doesn't crawl, and I don't have to fight the urge to push him away.

"Ludo is going to kill him," I mumble into Oliver's neck. "He's going to kill them both."

"We're not gonna let that happen," Oliver says firmly. His arms tighten around me, and I'm pretty sure they're the only thing keeping me from falling apart. "We'll get them out of there and keep them safe."

Doubts flood my mind. *I can't lose them too.* It doesn't matter that I didn't know about their existence until an hour ago. I can't let them suffer the same fate as Sammy.

"What could Ludo want with them?" Fear bleeds into my voice, raw and breathless. "What's he going to do to them?"

No one speaks.

I spin to face Elliot. "I know you have hunches. Don't you dare hide them from me."

"We can talk about that later," he says.

"No. Tell me what you're thinking."

After another moment of painful silence, Elliot sighs. "We've seen that Ludo has been cozying up to judges. Aubrey confirmed it as well. Combine those with the fact that he's promising Andrew legal custody of Benny, I'd say Ludo is trying to get control of the courts. Bribery, deals, possibly even blackmail."

"He can get his men off with reduced sentences or a slap on the wrist," I say as my hands curl into fists. "As for his enemies . . . he could potentially get them locked up for longer."

"You think he'll go after juries?" Oliver asks.

"He's done worse," I say darkly.

"Based on the information we got from the bug," Elliot says, "it sounds like Ludo is planning on using a child as leverage against us. That has to be Benny."

A chill sweeps over my skin. Leverage. *Leverage?* "But that would mean . . ."

"He wants something from us," Elliot says.

Wren tilts her head to the side. "We already knew that."

"Not like this. If Ludo thinks he needs Benny as a backup plan, then whatever he wants from us is something he doesn't think we'll be willing to do. He's planning on forcing us, and . . ." Elliot trails off with a grimace, too uncomfortable to finish.

I do it for him, even though the weight crushing my chest makes it hard to breathe. "And he has no problem putting a twelve-year-old's life on the line to do so."

...

I throw myself into work. Both Oliver and Elliot volunteer to transcribe the audio from the bug, but I brush them off. This is something I have to do.

My anxiety over my brothers' safety is only quelled by distraction. It's like I'm seventeen again, desperately searching the streets and calling out Sammy's name. Except now, I'm looking for some way—*any way*—to save Benny and Andrew. Forget that I threatened Andrew's life. He's on thin ice—anyone who tries to hurt one of us is—but he was scared. Trapped. He doesn't understand we're the ones on his side, not Ludo.

And as for Ludo...

Hurting him means hurting my brothers—*shit, I have brothers*. It means everything is different. Our entire plan is as stable as a house of cards, and Ludo just came through with a fucking leaf blower. He's corrupted everything like the vile, wretched snake he is. Now we're left to pick up the pieces in the wreckage he's left behind.

As I listen and type, I'm peripherally aware of Elliot making Wren eat her leftovers from the restaurant. I don't think she's able to finish them. Somewhere in the back of my mind, my concern for her grows. When she's about to leave the table, I tear my attention away from my laptop.

"Sweetheart." My gaze catches the bandage on her arm. *Fuck*, how did I already forget Andrew did that to her? "Wren, come here."

Hesitantly, she moves closer to me, but she stays out of reach. She's hugging herself, almost like she's afraid. Afraid of *me*.

Immediately, all thoughts of my brothers vanish. Is she still worried about everything that happened last night? *Why do I have to be such an ass?* I turn away from my laptop to face her completely. "Do you think I'm still angry with you?"

Her eyes widen at my forwardness. "I'm sorry, I—"

"No. I said it was okay. I said I understood. *I meant that.*" I'm vaguely aware that my tone is probably too harsh, but I need this to hit home for her.

She wrings her hands while she stumbles over her words. It takes a minute for her to get a full sentence out, even though it's short. "Are you sure?"

"Wren. Of course I am. I will *never* make you beg for my forgiveness. Never, sweetheart." I'm standing and moving toward her all without proper thought. My hands cup her cheeks, and I lean down to rest my forehead against hers. "I'm the one who was in the wrong, not you. What I said . . . it wasn't true. You mean more to me than avenging Sammy. I'd drop everything for you if I had to. For any of you."

"Please—"

"*No.*" Again, my tone is too strong, and I feel her wince. "Fuck, I'm sorry. I just need you to know. I need you to understand. I'm not angry with you, sweetheart, I swear. Even last night, I was angry with *myself*. I never should've taken it out on you."

"*I know.*" She clutches my arms and looks up at me with so much sadness in her eyes that it makes my chest ache. "I just . . . I know feelings can linger sometimes, and it can take a while to process things. Or . . ." She looks away. "I don't know."

I wait for her to continue, but she doesn't. "Wren," I say, managing to keep my voice gentle this time.

She meets my gaze.

"It's in the past." My thumb strokes over her cheek. "We never have to bring it up again."

That seems to make her fully relax. "Really?" she whispers.

"Really." Slowly, giving her time to pull away, I move to close the distance between us. When my lips brush against hers, her arms come around my waist, and she kisses me back.

Thank fuck.

"I told you once that I always mean what I say." My voice is quiet as I murmur the words against her lips. "I'm sorry I went back on that. It won't happen again."

Her arms tighten around me. "I know. And . . . Rhett?"

"Hmm?"

"You don't have to beg for my forgiveness, either." She pulls away so she can look at me. "I'm not going to hold this against you. I hate it when people do that. And I don't want to be like that."

"Thank you."

Despite the sadness in her eyes moments ago, her face lights up with a smile, and she pokes me in the side. "What's that thing you said to me a couple days ago? Don't thank you for the bare minimum? That should go both ways."

"Mmm." I dip my head down to kiss her again. "I suppose so."

We hold each other for another minute before I eventually remember what I was doing before I got distracted. I need to get back to transcribing the audio from the bug.

"You're okay?" My fingers feather over her bandage. "I know today has been hard."

"I'll be fine," she says as she nuzzles her face into my chest. "Already doing a lot better."

I kiss the top of her head. "Okay. I have to get back to work."

With a sigh, she pulls away. "Can we help you?"

"No." Today has been hell. I'm not going to make it worse for the others by asking them to work when they need to unwind. "Go find the others and relax."

She looks like she wants to protest, but all she does is kiss me again. Her hands linger on my body for a moment before she steps away. "You deserve to relax too, you know."

I nod, not giving her a verbal response. I don't know how to tell her that what I deserve isn't important right now. What matters is keeping my brothers safe.

Once she's gone, I sit at the table and dive back into the audio. Considering the condo was empty for most of today, a lot of the feed is just silence. When Aubrey and Ludo get back in the evening, there's bickering over wedding details before she storms off.

And then... *nothing*.

No phone calls. No conversations with his bodyguards. Just the sounds of papers rustling and a keyboard clacking.

Come on. Give me something.

I'm mostly caught up to the present, given how much dead space there was over the course of the day. As I wait, hoping Ludo will say something of use, my thoughts catch up to me.

They're going to die, just like she did.

What is Ludo going to make us do?

How can I keep everyone safe?

Elliot's voice barely breaks through my consciousness. "You need to give yourself a break."

I don't respond.

"Rhett. You can't help them if you're so sleep deprived you can't think straight."

"I'm thinking fine."

"No, you're not."

"Well, I'm not going to stop, so—"

Elliot shuts my laptop. "Yeah, you are."

For the first time in what feels like hours, I look up. It's dark outside, and the penthouse is oddly quiet. "Where are Oliver and Wren?"

"Outside. Which is where *you're* about to be. Put your swim trunks on. We're helping Wren."

That's when I realize that Elliot is shirtless and wearing his own swim trunks. I jump to my feet. "No. She's not going anywhere near that goddamned pool."

"We're gonna be in the hot tub."

"No. *No,* she needs to—"

Fuck.

"Needs to what, Rhett?" The way Elliot says it makes me think he knew this is exactly how this conversation would go before it even happened. His tone holds a challenge, but it's also a loophole out of my stress.

"She needs to take a break," I mumble.

"And?"

Blowing out a sigh, I say, "And so do I. I'll be out in a minute."

After changing, I join the others by the hot tub. The night has cooled off, but it's still comfortable out.

Oliver is already in the hot tub, and his face lights up when he sees me. His smile quickly fades, though.

"This is a bad idea." I pull Wren away from the stairs that lead down into the water. "You're pushing yourself too hard."

"I'm not," she insists, and just as I'm about to argue, she presses a finger to my lips. "Last night was a mistake. I shouldn't've gone down to the pool by myself. But this is different. I have all three of you here with me. And you saw me in the pool. I think I did pretty good."

I look to Elliot for help, but he gives none. "You literally agreed with me two minutes ago that she needs a break."

"We all do," Elliot says, gesturing to the hot tub. "This sounds like a great one."

"But—"

"If it's too much, we'll get out of the water and do something else," Wren says.

"And we'll be right here with her if she needs us," Oliver adds.

Wren tugs me closer. "Please? I want you all to relax before bed."

Relaxing sounds like such a far-off concept that I almost laugh. There's no possible way I'll be able to shut my brain off. But Wren is already pulling me toward the hot tub.

Elliot gets in first, hovering on the steps and holding out his hand for her. When Wren gets to the edge, she hesitates for a second before grabbing onto Elliot and dipping her toes in.

I keep a firm grip on her other arm as we slowly take the first step, and then the next.

"This isn't too bad," she says. To her credit, her voice is only a little high pitched.

"Almost there, princess," Oliver says. He's watching her proudly from the middle of the hot tub. "You're doing great."

Wren stays steady as we make it all the way in. Oliver wraps his arms around her waist and kisses her lightly. I still haven't let go of her, and neither has Elliot, so she's nestled between the three of us.

"How are you feeling?" I can't take my eyes off her. Not only because she looks stunning in her light purple bikini, but also because I'm terrified for her. Just because I'm willing to push myself to my limits doesn't mean I want her to do the same.

Turning, she beams up at me. "I feel good. Safe."

"Good enough to sit?" Oliver asks.

"Um . . ." She eyes the bench warily. Sitting will bring the water level up to her chest. Her hair is up so it won't get wet, but it's still closer to water than she normally lets her face get.

"You can sit on my lap," I suggest.

"And Oliver and I will stay close," Elliot says.

"Then yes."

We all stay close as we move to the edge. Once I'm seated on the bench, I pull Wren onto my lap, and Oliver and Elliot settle on either side of us. My arms encircle her, keeping her tightly and safely against me. With a happy sigh, Wren leans her head against my shoulder.

I drop a kiss to the top of her head, her hair tickling my nose. "Still okay?"

"Still okay. More than okay. This is nice."

However much I don't want to admit it, she's right. The combination of the night air, the hot water, and being with these three is actually helping me to relax. I forget sometimes—too often—how much their presence can calm me.

For the next half hour, our conversation stays light. I keep waiting for my body to rebel against having Wren so close to me for so long, but it never happens. Instead, her skin against mine and my arms wrapped around her only serves to help me feel more grounded. More supported.

Oliver is in the middle of telling a childhood story Wren hasn't heard yet when Elliot and I lock gazes. We've heard it multiple times from his mom, which is how we know he's telling a slightly altered version.

"... and then, after *fifteen minutes* of looking for Maria, I finally gave up. After that, she won every time I was it, and I still don't know where the hiding spot is."

"You're leaving out a detail," Elliot says. "A very important detail."

Oliver can't hide his smile. "No, I'm not."

"If I recall," I say, "there was a bet attached to that game."

Wren gasps excitedly. "Ooohhh! High stakes?"

Elliot chuckles. "Very."

"I don't know what you're talking about," Oliver says on a laugh.

Batting her eyelashes at him, Wren clasps her hands together. "Please tell me?"

He leans in and kisses her. "Fuck, how can I say no to those pretty eyes? But you have to promise not to laugh."

"Promise," she whispers, grinning.

"If I won the game of hide and seek, Maria had to do my chores for two days. If I lost..." Oliver lets out an embarrassed groan. "If I lost, I had to take a shot of the hottest hot sauce Maria could find."

Wren is biting her lip so hard I'm afraid she's going to make herself bleed. Her eyes are full of light as she does her best to contain her amusement.

"You said you wouldn't laugh." Oliver pokes her shoulder.

"I'm not laughing," she squeaks out, but there are tears in her eyes from holding back. "Why did you bet something so *painful?*"

"I was confident I'd win! And after that, I was confident I'd never stop shitting my guts out."

Wren cringes. "Oh god."

"Never touched hot sauce since," Oliver says.

"And Maria has never let him live it down," I add in. Keeping a firm hold on Wren with one arm, I reach over and grab Oliver's jaw. I pull him in for a quick kiss, noting that he doesn't resist at all.

After that, we don't stay in the hot tub for much longer. Once I'm dried off and fully clothed, I head to the kitchen to find a snack. I was so focused on work that I didn't think to eat at all.

Oliver and Wren are still on the balcony. I find Elliot by the fridge, pulling a couple things out.

"You hungry too?" I ask.

"Not really. This is for you."

"Oh. You didn't have to—"

"Drink your water. You didn't touch it all evening."

I grab my glass from the table and take a few sips. As Elliot works, I watch him, trying to gauge his mood. He doesn't look upset, but something is definitely wrong.

After a few minutes, Elliot sets a plate on the table, and we both sit. Only once I've started eating does he quietly say, "We need you."

"I know."

Tiredly, he shakes his head. "I don't want to lose you because of this."

"You're not going to."

"No, Rhett, listen to me. When we were younger, we threw ourselves into getting revenge for Sammy. It consumed us. The guilt, the pain, the frustration, the anger—it ate away at all of us. Don't you remember?"

"I'd never forget." All of those things still linger inside of me, festering, simmering.

Elliot reaches out and places a hand on my arm. "We're going to find a way to get Benny out of there. Andrew too. Or, I don't know, take out Ludo faster. Whatever you want. But in the meantime, don't let this consume you. Not again, Rhett."

I shove around the food on my plate. "I have to protect them."

"We will," Elliot assures me. "All of us, not just you. You're of no use to your brothers if you're exhausted all the time."

Everything in me wants to fight against what he's saying, but I don't. "Just promise me."

Scooching closer, Elliot takes my face in both of his hands and leans in close. "Rhett, I promise you, we're not going to let your brothers die. All four of us are in this together. We've got them."

My throat aches, but I swallow down the pain. I try to speak, but no words come out.

"Trust us with this?" Elliot asks, still holding my face.

I rest my forehead against his. "Always, Ell. Always."

Chapter Seventeen

Oliver

I'm not ready for the night to be over yet, so I stay outside. Wren must feel the same way, because she doesn't go in, either.

After drying off, she leans against the wall that acts as a railing to keep people from falling over the edge. It's dark out, but the resort lights illuminate the ocean some, so she takes in the view.

Coming up behind her, I place my hands on Wren's hips and rest my chin on her shoulder. The past twenty-four hours have been a train wreck. Hanging out in the hot tub acted as a reset of sorts for us, but I still want to check in with her.

"How're you doing, princess?" I whisper as I pepper her neck with tender, loving kisses.

She relaxes into me. "Better than I was earlier."

After finding out Rhett has two younger brothers, Wren's omission of the truth seems so small and far off. I still wish she hadn't kept anything from us, and I know she wishes she hadn't as well, but thankfully we all moved on quickly.

"Did I scare you earlier? In the restaurant?"

"Maybe a little."

Taking a step back, I turn her around so she's facing me. "What were you afraid I would say?"

She squirms, trying to make space between the two of us, so I give her some. She doesn't make eye contact as she says, "I was worried you wouldn't forgive me. Or that you'd hold it over my head. Or . . . or that you were done with me."

A tangible, physical pain pangs in my chest, and it takes me a second to catch my breath. "Wren. No, princess, never. I will *never* be done with you."

"I know, I'm just not . . . used to forgiveness, I guess. Fuck, I'm sorry, that's stupid. There's no reason for me to expect you guys to be assholes."

"Hey, it's okay, I get it."

Finally, she looks up at me with cautious hope. "You do?"

"Rhett and Elliot have been an integral part of my life for fourteen years, princess. Just because I have a good parent doesn't mean I can't recognize the effects of a shitty one's actions in someone else. I have a lot of experience with Ell and Rhett."

"Right," she says quietly.

"Why don't you explain it to me," I say gently. Slowly, I ease back into her space, wanting to be close to her. She seems to want it too, because when I wrap my arms around her, she does the same to me.

After a steadying breath, Wren asks, "When you were a kid and you did something wrong, did your mom always forgive you? Like, *really* forgive you?"

"Yeah. Of course she did."

"Like, she never lorded things over you? Never told you that she wanted to leave you at a bus station because of something you did, or called you a spoiled brat, or made you feel bad for mistakes you made in the past? Even if she said she forgave you?"

"No," I say. "But your mom did?"

Wren nods. "All the time. She'd even say we were okay, and then go complain to her friends about me. She'd do it with me right next to her, and then I'd get embarrassed and try to defend myself. It made her friends uncomfortable too, even though she'd always play it off as poking fun." Wren rolls her eyes, and I realize they're glistening with tears. "Once we were alone, she'd scold me for talking back to her and tell me I was being too sensitive."

"I'm so sorry, princess. No kid deserves a parent who treats them like that."

She sniffles. "It only got worse when she married Thomas. They'd both gang up on me, and it took me way too long to grow a backbone, so I'd just take it until I could run to my room and cry."

My heart breaks for her. I can only imagine how lonely she felt.

"I—I know you guys wouldn't do that type of thing to me," Wren continues. "You wouldn't talk badly about me to other people or tell me you wanted to leave me. You wouldn't say you forgive me and not mean it. Hell, Rhett just told me a couple hours ago *very specifically* that he'd never do anything like that. But sometimes, all I can think of is my mom and Thomas."

"I get it, princess. Sometimes it's hard to remember you're safe when you haven't been for your whole life."

"I want to feel as safe as I know I am," she whispers.

"It'll come. And in the meantime, you've got us no matter what. I'm not letting you go, you hear me? I can't."

"Fuck," she mutters as she wipes at her eyes. "You're going to make me cry."

"You can, princess. It's okay."

She shakes her head. "I don't want to. I just want to be happy." Her fingers trace over the butterfly tattoo on my chest. "I'm not ready for tonight to be over, but I don't want to spend the rest of it being sad."

"I'm not ready for it to be over, either."

"Then kiss me," she whispers, and her lips brush against mine. "Kiss me and make me forget."

With only a moment's hesitation to stroke my thumb over her cheek, I fit my mouth to hers. I know a kiss can't help heal a broken heart, but as my lips move against Wren's, I try anyway. She deserves so much better than what she's gotten out of life.

I move us back so Wren is pressed against the half wall behind her. My body is touching her in every spot possible as I kiss away the lingering memories of her childhood. If I could, I'd go back in time and find her. Comfort her. Take her far away from everything that ever hurt her.

Wren eases back. "Oliver, I need you to know something."

I search her eyes for any hint of what she has to say, but all I find is an earnest care. "Tell me."

"I'm not letting you go, either. The past few weeks have been hell, but they're the best hell I've ever been through. I'd do it all again in a heartbeat, because it meant falling for three men who not only stole my heart, but protect it with their lives. I didn't realize how deeply love could run until you. It's so much it hurts sometimes, but I wouldn't have it any other way."

A smile takes over my face, one that's so wide my cheeks ache. "You—fuck. Goddammit, I love you so much."

Our mouths crash together in a kiss that's almost frantic. There are so many emotions, so many feelings, and the only way to stop them from getting too overwhelming is to pour into each other.

"Wren," I groan. "Hold onto me."

Her arms come around my neck, and I hoist her up so she's sitting on the ledge. Immediately, I steady her with my arms around her waist. It's a long way down to the ground if she were to fall, so I want to make sure she's secure.

She gasps and holds me tighter. "Oliver!"

"I've got you, princess," I murmur against her lips. "I won't let you fall."

The door leading inside slams open, and quick footsteps sound behind me. No doubt, they saw us through the window and freaked out.

"What are you doing?" Elliot's voice is panicked as he rushes toward us. Rhett is close behind him.

"She's safe," I say, kissing Wren when she smiles down at me. "I wouldn't do this unless I knew I could hold her."

Elliot comes up beside me and puts an arm around Wren. Rhett does the same on my other side, securing her even more.

"Love, this is—"

She silences Elliot with a kiss. "You've got me."

"I do," he says. "We all do. But you're not scared?"

She shakes her head. "I trust you, Ell. With my whole heart—with everything in me. Let me show you."

It's almost like Elliot and Wren stay frozen in time for a few seconds. They stare at each other, Elliot in amazed disbelief and Wren with such tenderness and undying trust it's unreal. Something happens between the two of them—something just for them—and for a moment I feel like I'm intruding on something private.

When he's able to move again, Elliot releases a short breath. With his free hand, he takes hold of Wren's chin and kisses her deeply. She matches with equal intensity as one of her hands leaves me to grab

Rhett's shirt. She pulls him closer, breaks away from Elliot, and fuses her mouth to Rhett's.

"Fuck," Elliot mutters. He watches them for a moment before joining in and kissing both of them at once.

A surprised sound comes from Wren, but she adjusts to kissing both of them with ease. I'd join in, but I'm perfectly content with watching, and I want to make sure someone is fully focused on keeping Wren from tipping backward.

When they pull away, Wren is gasping for air. "Oh my goodness."

"My turn," I rasp, rising onto the balls of my feet and stealing a kiss. I keep it short and sweet, because I have something else I'd rather be doing. "You guys have her?"

"She's not going anywhere," Rhett says.

Slowly, I remove my arms from around Wren's waist. Once I'm no longer supporting her, I caress her thighs. "I want to make you come like this. Please?"

Her eyes widen, and she gasps so quietly I almost don't notice it. "Are you two okay with that?" she asks, glancing between Rhett and Ell.

"Oh," Elliot chuckles, "most *definitely*."

Rhett nods.

I grab one of the chairs that's out here and position it right in front of her. She slides her thighs open more as I lower myself into the chair. By the time my eyes lock with hers, her breaths are already coming quickly.

"What do you want me to do, princess?"

"Untie my bikini top."

The lilac strings are double knotted, so it takes me a second to get them undone. I have to stand to reach them, so I kiss her as I undo the knot in the back. Once I have it all the way off, I toss it onto the back of my chair.

As I stare at Wren's mostly naked body, I groan. Her nipples are tight and hard, just begging me to run my tongue over them. "Princess, can I—"

"Not yet," she says. "Now undo the bottoms."

Fuck, I'm already hard, just from her telling me what to do.

Once I've untied the knots at Wren's hips, Elliot and Rhett help lift her so I can pull the bikini bottoms out from underneath her. Wren doesn't even look scared as they do.

"Sit down and bring the chair closer."

I do. I want to touch her, to bury my head between her thighs, to make her scream for me. No matter how tempting those thoughts are, though, I stay still with my hands in my lap. While I look up at her, waiting, she smiles down at me.

"He takes instructions well," she says.

Rhett snorts. "Sometimes."

"I'll be good." The words come out of my mouth quickly, desperately. I can see how wet Wren is, and all I want to do is taste—

"Ah ah." Rhett grabs my hair and pulls me back, and I realize I was leaning in. "Did she tell you that you could do that?"

"Princess," I pant. "Please?"

Elliot swears under his breath, and a cursory glance in his direction tells me he's as hard as I am.

"Go ahead," Wren says.

I don't wait another second. With my tongue, I spread her arousal to her clit. She's so wet already, just from kissing, and I love how much she craves us. I don't say so—I'm too busy focusing on her. Gently, I suck on her clit while holding her thighs open.

When Wren groans my name, it only eggs me on. I immediately move into the things I know she likes. She gasps, and a cocktail of pride and pleasure courses through me.

"Does it feel good, sweetheart?"

"So good," she moans.

"Don't forget to tell him. He needs to know he's pleasing you."

"Oliver," Wren pants as she looks down at me, "you're such a good boy."

In response, I flick the tip of my tongue over her clit rapidly. She melts into Elliot and Rhett's arms, and they keep a firm hold on her so she doesn't have to worry. As Wren's moans grow louder, Elliot leans down and kisses her to capture them with his mouth. Only when Wren's legs start to tremble do I pull away.

"Did she tell you that you could stop?" Rhett arches a brow at me challengingly—almost threateningly.

"Princess," I murmur as I kiss her inner thigh. "May I use my fingers?"

She nods breathlessly. Using the hand that's not currently keeping Wren from plummeting to her death, Rhett grabs Wren's thigh. Once he's helping her hold it up, I let go so I can slide a finger inside her. My mouth goes back to her clit, sucking, and after a minute I add a second finger.

"Oh, shit," Wren gasps. "Oliver, just like that."

As I continue on in the same way, I feel Wren clench around my fingers. She's back to trembling, and her chest heaves with every gulp of air.

"Are you close, love?"

"I am," she whimpers out.

Elliot nuzzles his face in her neck. "We've got you. You can let go."

"Fuck," she whispers. "Oh my god, *ohmygod.*"

As Wren comes, she throws her head back and cries out. Without Elliot and Rhett anchoring her, she'd fall straight to the ground, but she doesn't hold back. She's placed her life in their caring hands, trusting—knowing—that they'd never even let her come close to falling.

I continue sucking on Wren's clit until she begs me to stop. When I pull back, the guys haul her up, and I lock eyes with her and lick my lips. "I want more."

"Inside," Rhett says. "You can keep going while I fuck her ass."

Carefully, Elliot and Rhett move Wren from the ledge. I push back my chair and take Wren into my arms. She grabs onto me for balance, and I kiss her until Rhett pulls us apart.

"*Now,*" he says impatiently. "I've waited long enough."

With a smirk, I kiss Wren again, dipping her backward until she's laughing against my mouth. When I straighten, Rhett sweeps Wren up into his arms and marches toward the door. She lets out a delighted squeal before grabbing onto him.

Inside, Rhett drops Wren onto the couch on her hands and knees. He gets behind her, shoves her ass cheeks apart, and dives in. Dropping to her elbows, Wren groans into the cushions.

I get the lube, and after I hand it to Rhett, I'm grabbed from behind. Elliot spins me around and slams his lips to mine. I almost lose my balance, but he holds onto my hips as his tongue enters my mouth. At the taste of Wren's arousal, he groans.

"You want him and me at the same time? Hmm?" Rhett asks as he preps Wren with his fingers.

"Yesssss," she whines.

"And what about Ell? Make him watch? Make him jealous?"

She smiles at that and hides her face in the cushions.

"You want to make him wait to come the same way he makes you wait?"

She nods into the couch, and we hear a muffled, "Mmhmm."

Elliot clicks his tongue. "Careful what you wish for, love. I can pay that back tenfold another time."

At that, she makes a shocked sound and looks up. "Ten . . . tenfold?"

"He's not joking, princess," I tell her. "He'll tease you for hours without letting you come."

She swallows audibly, and just when I'm sure she's about to back out, she says over her shoulder, "Make him wait."

"Fucking hell," Elliot whispers.

I grin at him. The next time he gets the chance, I'm sure he'll pull Wren away and have his way with her. My guess is he's already deciding all the different things he'll do to her.

Once Rhett is done prepping Wren, he eases inside of her, giving her just the tip of his lubed-up cock. He makes her take another inch before pulling out and sliding in farther.

"Both," Wren begs. "I want both of you."

Rhett ignores her pleas and continues what he's doing. Only once he's in to the hilt does he pull out. "Get up."

Rhett washes his hands before sitting back on the couch. I help Wren balance as she slowly lowers herself onto his cock. She has her back to him, so I get to watch her as she takes all of him. Her eyelids flutter closed, and her lips part as she tries to take a full breath.

"Fuck," she pants.

"Relax, sweetheart," Rhett murmurs. "We've got you." He adjusts Wren so she's leaning against him with her head on his shoulder.

I kneel between their spread legs and watch Rhett's cock slide in and out of Wren. My patience runs out quickly, and I slip two fingers into

Wren's vagina. It pulls a moan from both of them, and when I suck on Wren's clit, she sobs.

Wren tries to sit up so she can see me better, but Rhett grabs her and slams her against his body.

"No," he says. "I want you right here when you come. I want to feel you writhing and moaning, trapped against me."

"Oh, fuck," she groans. Her back arches, and her head hits Rhett's shoulder.

Between him fucking her ass, and me fingering her and eating her out, Wren comes within minutes. She grips my hair so tightly it stings, but I love it. When I pull away, she loosens her hold, and her arms fall to her sides.

"Fuck her, Ol," Elliot says from behind me.

I turn. He's seated himself on the opposite couch and placed his ankle over his other knee. His arms stretch across the back of the couch. The position gives off an air of indifference. I almost fall for it, but the heated need burning in his eyes gives him away.

Elliot nods toward Rhett and Wren. "Don't keep them waiting."

As I position my dick at Wren's entrance, Rhett slows down to make it easier. He's holding her arms and keeping her in place, and as I slide into her, I take her in. Sweaty, panting, and already glowing from her two orgasms.

"You're so pretty like this." As I thrust into her completely, I fuse my mouth to hers. Rhett starts pumping into her again while I stay slow. My mind goes blank for a second, and I break off our kiss to choke in a gasp. *Fuck,* I love this.

"Tell me how she feels." Elliot's voice is a low, lustful rasp.

"So unbelievably tight," I groan. "She's gripping my cock so hard."

"You like having his dick inside of you, sweetheart?" Rhett murmurs in Wren's ear. "You want to feel him pounding into you?"

All she can manage is a moan and a nod.

"Mmm." Rhett kisses her neck, right below her jawline. "I want to feel that, too."

"Please," she gasps.

"She asks so nicely," Elliot says. "Good girls get rewarded, don't they?"

"They do," Rhett replies. His eyes lock on mine as he slowly moves inside of Wren. "So do good boys."

My heart thunders in my chest. The things they're saying to me are making it beat too quickly. For the briefest of moments, I'm worried they're going to give me a heart attack, but then Rhett thrusts into Wren again. It forces a grunt from deep inside of me. As if my body has a mind of its own, I slide out of Wren and then back in.

Rhett holds my gaze as Wren moans in between us. "Harder."

I obey, leaning over them to grip the back of the couch for balance. "Like this?"

"Harder," he demands, "and kiss her while you do it."

Again, I obey. Rhett releases one of Wren's arms to play with her clit, and she cries out against my lips. It's so hot, so goddamned hot, that I find myself pulling back so I can stare at them both.

"I'm gonna come," Wren gasps. "Too . . . too much, oh *fuck*."

"Don't stop," Rhett tells me. "Fuck her through it."

We push her higher and higher until she's screaming and trying to squirm away from Rhett's touch.

"I can't," she cries. "I can't take it, please."

Finally, Rhett pulls his hand away, and I slow down before I come too fast.

"One of you needs to finish," Elliot says impatiently. "I'm not waiting much longer."

"Or," I reply over my shoulder, "we could all fuck her at once."

Wren groans. "Please."

Elliot stands. "Get into the bedroom."

I pull out of Wren and lift her off of Rhett. Her legs are shaky, so she holds onto me as we make our way into the bedroom. Elliot has me get on my back on the center of the bed, and Wren crawls on top of me. Once she's slid all the way down my cock, she cups my face and kisses me.

"Uh uh, no," Elliot says as he climbs onto the bed. He hovers over us, grabs Wren's hair, pulls her head up, and slams his lips to hers. He's far from gentle, taking control of the kiss from the start. Wren keeps herself pliant and willing to succumb to his wishes. When he pulls away, he grips her chin. "This mouth is mine for the night."

"Use it," she whispers. "Use me however you'd like."

He smirks. "Careful what you wish for, love."

In response, she presses her lips to his again. He's gentler this time, probably because Rhett is already behind her and easing into her ass again. As he does, Wren groans wantonly.

Elliot straightens, guiding Wren's mouth to his dick. "Make her scream around my cock."

As he slides into her mouth, Wren whimpers. He's careful not to go in too far so she can still breathe. Slowly, she takes over, sucking and licking his cock. Meanwhile, Rhett is pumping in and out of her ass, and it's all I can do to not come on the spot.

"Why haven't we done this before?" I groan.

"Shit," Elliot pants. "We really should've. I've missed the way your lips feel wrapped around my dick, love."

Her response is entirely incoherent. Hesitantly, she takes him deeper before gagging and pulling back.

"Hey, don't." Elliot strokes her hair. "Save that for another time. Tonight, just enjoy yourself."

"Okay," she whispers. Then she sucks on the tip of his cock, pulling a breathless groan from his lips.

"Can you take it harder, sweetheart?" Rhett asks.

She releases Elliot's cock for just long enough to say, "Yes. Please."

Rhett holds onto her hips for leverage, which also keeps her from being forced closer to Elliot. As he pounds into her harder, she cries out. The sound is muffled by Elliot's dick, and he groans.

I thrust into Wren, and she screams again. "You love being used up by all of us, don't you?"

She tries to nod.

"Nothing more than a pretty cum dumpster who needs to be filled up," I add.

"Yes," she gasps as she lifts her head. "Please, please."

Elliot smiles down at her. "You want our cum, love?"

"Yes," she cries. "Ell, *please.*"

"Then you'd better suck my cock like you mean it."

With a little gasp, she gets back to work. I'm already closer than I want to be, and I have a feeling Rhett is too. I wish I could see his face. Feeling him fucking into Wren is pure heaven, but I love watching him come.

"That's it, Wren," Elliot says proudly. "You're being such a good girl tonight. Isn't she, Oliver?"

"So good," I murmur as I stroke her arm.

"Shit," Rhett chokes out. I feel him pull out, and the way he groans tells me he's probably coming all over Wren's back. "Fuck, *fuck.*"

"You hear that?" Elliot says as he holds Wren's hair. "You did that to him. You and your perfect, tight ass."

She sucks him more enthusiastically before letting out a choked whimper. Now that Rhett isn't fucking her, I've grabbed her waist, and I'm thrusting into her harder. I'm so close, *so close,* and the need for release is almost unbearable at this point.

"Princess," I groan hoarsely.

As if she knows I'm right on the edge, she releases Ell's cock and slams her lips to mine. The kiss consumes me—no, *she* consumes me—and it sends pure, fiery heat shooting through every nerve in my body. I whimper into her mouth, and she eats up the sound like she's starved for me.

"Come for me," Wren whispers as she works her hips.

The movement practically forces the orgasm out of me. I clutch her sides as it hits me so hard my vision goes blank. By the time I've resurfaced and can form a coherent thought, I realize I'm babbling. "Princess, so good, *fuckiloveyou,* I love all of you so much, you all complete me—"

With a giggle, Wren kisses me again. I groan as my body turns to jelly. As I begin moving my lips in any sort of put-together manner, Wren is pulled away from me.

"That's enough," Elliot says gruffly.

"Jealous?" Wren teases, just barely licking the tip of his cock.

"Don't test me, love. Not unless you're willing to deal with more consequences than the ones you've already earned."

With a nervous squeak, Wren tries to get off of me to let me go. But before she's moved more than an inch, I grab her hips to hold her still.

"Let me stay inside of you," I say, still out of breath. "Please."

As she smiles down at me, her fingertips ghost across my cheek. "Whatever you'd like."

As Wren finally gives all her attention back to Elliot, he groans and grabs her hair. I can tell he's having trouble holding back, but I also know he'd never do something to Wren that could scare or trigger her.

By this point, we've all realized that Wren needs to have all the control in a position like this. She's not at a point yet where she can have her air cut off, even momentarily. Hell, she may never get back to that point, and that's okay.

"Wren, *shit,*" Elliot moans. It only makes Wren work up and down his dick with more enthusiasm.

"That's it, Wren," I rasp. "Make him come in your mouth. Make me proud."

She keeps one hand on the mattress to hold herself up, and with the other, she strokes the base of Elliot's cock. I help hold her up so it's not so hard on her.

"You're doing so well, sweetheart," Rhett says. He's crawled around so he's next to us. "Focus on just the tip for a minute. Fuck, just like that. You're such a good girl, aren't you?"

Wren moans in response, but it's drowned out by Elliot gasping, "Shit, I'm coming."

Rhett grabs Elliot as he struggles to stay upright. Wren sucks him lightly one last time before popping his dick out of her mouth. With a smile, she licks her lips and sits back.

Leaning into Rhett, Elliot groans, "Goddammit, Wren. Get up here."

Slowly, she eases off of me. I roll out of the way so Elliot can embrace her without either of them having to worry about squishing me.

"I love you," he murmurs in between kisses. "God, I love all of you so much. Everything is a mess right now, but you make it bearable."

"We love you too, Ell," I say.

After that, we all start cleaning up. Wren has cum dripping down her back, and after wiping it all up, Rhett cleans in between her legs as well. Her eyelids are drooping, and by the time he's done, she slumps onto the mattress with a contented sigh.

My heart warms at the sight of her like this, so vulnerable and trusting. I take a mental snapshot of the moment so I can cherish it forever. Then I turn my attention to Rhett, who looks too exhausted to still be standing.

"Did you actually sleep this morning?" I ask.

"No," he sighs. "Not at all. I'll get to bed, but I . . . I wanted to check the bug one last time." He looks hesitant to admit it.

"I've got it." I kiss him on the cheek. "You get some rest. If there's anything important, I'll wake you and let you know."

My expectations are for him to protest, but he nods tiredly before pulling me in for a slow, deep kiss. "Thank you."

"Yeah, no pr-"

"I love you." He says it quietly against my lips, and I'm reminded of the other day, when he didn't get to say it back all the way.

Fuck. How did I forget about that? I meant to apologize, to explain myself, but I completely forgot in the aftermath.

"Rhett," I say. "I love you, too, and the other day, I didn't mean to cut you off, I—"

"We were all rushing," he says as he smooths a hand down my back. "And you're not used to me . . ." He grimaces. "Being affectionate."

"It's okay," I whisper. "I understand."

He kisses me one more time before leaving. After saying goodnight to Elliot and kissing a sleeping Wren on the forehead, I grab my laptop from the living room and get to work. I listen through a lot of silence and some mundane conversations.

I start getting sleepy just as Aubrey and Ludo start arguing. My fingers are too uncoordinated to type it all out while I'm this tired, but I listen through and make some mental notes for myself. By the time Aubrey storms off, my eyelids are drooping.

It doesn't seem terribly important, so my plan is to let Rhett sleep and just tell him in the morning. When I step into our bedroom, though, he's sitting up in bed with his laptop.

I bite my tongue to keep from scolding him. He's a grown man. I may think this is unhealthy—fuck, no, it *is* unhealthy—but I can't stop him. That decision is up to him.

"Anything?" Rhett asks.

"Not really. Ludo and Aubrey got into another fight, and Aubrey said she hates him, and Ludo said she's too loyal to her parents, and then Aubrey said he wouldn't understand because he doesn't know what it's like to love someone."

"Ouch."

"He deserves it, the bastard."

Rhett hums in agreement. "At least it's extra confirmation that Aubrey isn't working with Ludo to test us."

Which is a relief, honestly. Aubrey doesn't seem to have a malicious bone in her body—except when that maliciousness is directed toward Ludo.

"Why are you still up?" I ask.

"Couldn't sleep."

"You're not listening to the feed, are you?"

"Hacked into the resort's security camera footage."

"What—how—*why*, Rhett?"

"I'm trying to find him," he mumbles.

Fucking hell. "You can't go and see him. It's too risky. Also, he doesn't seem to like you very much."

Rhett winces, and I regret my word choice immediately.

"He doesn't seem to like *any* of us," I clarify.

"I know." He gestures to his laptop. "And if I can't see him in person, this . . . I guess this is the next best thing."

I lower myself onto the bed next to him. "You're not editing anything, are you? I thought Finn was gonna do that."

"I only have access to watch," he responds. "And I'll be honest, even that was beyond my abilities. Had to text Finn for help."

"And now you're . . . ?"

"Scanning the footage to see where Andrew's room is. But Finn already wiped him heading to the bar and leaving the penthouse, so I've been watching the common areas to see if he shows up."

That sounds ridiculously boring, but that's not what's worrying me. As I open my mouth to speak, he closes the window and shuts his laptop.

"I know," he says gruffly. "I know it's obsessive and desperate. I know I need to stop and sleep. But he's my *brother,* goddammit. What am I supposed to do? Just let him go?"

"Yeah. For now, at least."

He blows out an exasperated breath. "I hate this, O. I feel helpless."

I grab his laptop and set it on my nightstand. "That'll change soon. We won't let Ludo hurt Benny."

It's a promise we both know I shouldn't be making, but it seems to help him anyway. Sometimes he needs the reminder that we've got his back—and now his family's.

"Try to sleep," I whisper as we lay down.

He grabs my hand, intertwining our fingers, and I smile into the darkness. I love touching him. Hopefully, there'll be more of that in our future.

Chapter Eighteen

Wren

"What about this one?" Aubrey holds up a book.

"Yup."

Aubrey groans. "What *haven't* you read?"

I grin, taking the book and putting it back on the shelf. "I don't read a lot of nonfiction."

"Okay, perfect." She drags me to the history section of the bookstore. "How about . . . this one?" She pulls a particularly thick book off the shelf.

"Okay, I should've said I don't read nonfiction—*except* for history."

"You . . ." Aubrey flicks her eyes between me and the book with disbelief. "You read this whole thing? It's huge."

"Yep. Took me a whole weekend to finish it."

"Damn," she mutters under her breath. "One more try." Scanning the shelves behind us labeled Money & Finance, she slides out a book I've never seen before. It's titled *Protecting Your Investments* by Karek Brezk.

"You got me," I say with a giggle. "Too many numbers for my taste."

"Oh, I feel that." She puts the book back. "What about poetry? You said the other day you've been meaning to pick it up again."

"Yeah! I used to read it a lot when I was in college." I move toward the poetry section. "I'm not sure what to go with, but . . ." I spot a book with a light pink cover. "Hey! Don't you have this one?"

She tries to hide her smile, although I'm not sure why. "I do, yeah. I know the author, sort of."

"Sort of?"

"Really well, actually." Her grin is huge now, as if she can't hold it back. "You could say I know her better than anyone."

I laugh. "How can you *sort of* know someone while also knowing them better than anyone else?"

Aubrey shrugs, and her eyes sparkle with delight. "Some people hardly know themselves at all."

"What—*oh*." My eyes must go wide, because Aubrey throws her head back and laughs at my reaction. "You—you're—this book is a bestseller!" I point to the sign right above the shelf that indicates it.

"I know," she says, still giggling. "I have the royalties checks to prove it."

"It's under a pen name," I say, staring at the cover. "Isabella DuPont."

"I thought it sounded pretty."

"It does," I murmur, opening up the book and flipping through the pages.

"No one knows it's me," she says quietly. "You're quite literally the only person I've told. Ludo can never know."

My eyes flit to Elliot and Rhett, who're standing near the door. "I don't want to keep things from them."

"Oh, they can know." She waves her hand in dismissal. "They won't tell Ludo."

"How are you so sure you can trust us?" My voice holds a level of disbelief, but also a smidge of curiosity. Aubrey has trusted me openly since first meeting me, and I need to know if it's her personality or if it's because she knows more than she's letting on.

"A little bird told me I could." She winks at me before turning away, signaling that she's not going to give away anything else.

What's she getting at? This woman is so full of mysteries.

We browse for a little longer. Aubrey was right—they have a wonderful fantasy section, and I have to stop myself from grabbing every new book with a pretty cover on it. I end up deciding to buy two, and I take pictures of the rest so I can add them to my never-ending list of books to read.

Once we're done looking around, I go to check out, bringing Aubrey's book of poems as well. The cashier tells me my total, and I stare at my wallet. Elliot's card is nestled in the slot right above my own, but I'm not sure what to do. Will he say something if I don't use his card? Will he say something if I do?

I glance behind me, to where Elliot and Rhett are hanging out by the door. My hope is that he won't be paying attention, but I find them both watching me. Quickly, I turn around and pull out my own card. But just as I'm about to swipe it, I feel a warm, hard body press up against mine.

Elliot's hand covers my own and pulls it back from the counter. "What're you doing, love?"

"Paying for my books." My voice comes out all nervous, like a kid who just got caught with their hand in the cookie jar.

"Not with that, you're not." He plucks my card from my hand, slides it back into my wallet, and pulls out his own.

I gulp. "Ell, I can pay for them."

"So can I."

Aubrey snickers beside me, and when I give her a pleading look, she just shrugs. "Spend his money, babe."

"But these are just for fun. I don't want to waste—"

"You think something has to be practical for me to buy it for you? Oh, absolutely not, love."

"I—well, you see—" My voice falters because I don't really have a good excuse.

The cashier gives me a bewildered look. "You have someone willing to fund your reading habit, and you're saying *no?* Honey, do you know how expensive books are?" They gesture to my books on the counter. "Especially hardcovers."

My whole body feels like it's on fire. I gulp in air as I look to Elliot. "You're sure?"

Elliot places his card in between my fingers and guides my hand to the credit card reader. "Swipe it."

I'm so used to obeying whatever he says that I do it without thinking.

He places his lips right next to my ear and murmurs, "Good girl."

I swear my knees go weak. If it wasn't for the counter in front of me and Elliot behind me, I'm pretty sure I'd be a puddle on the floor right now. Thankfully, Elliot said that quietly enough that only I heard.

Rhett eases my books out of my hands and carries them for me. My head feels a little light, so when Elliot takes my hand, I let him guide me out of the store. It's not until I'm in the backseat of our rental with Aubrey that I truly process everything that happened inside.

"So you're a poet."

"Mmhmm."

"Do you not like being a lawyer?"

Aubrey wrinkles her nose in disgust. "Oh god no. It's what my parents wanted for me, and at the time I was deciding my career, I didn't know what I wanted. It took me until a year or two after I graduated to figure it out, honestly."

"But your parents don't know."

"They'll find out when the time is right."

When the time is right. There she goes again, hinting at something bigger. Something more.

"What do you mean by that?"

"It's quite simple, really," she says. "Or, I suppose, not at all. Have you ever wanted to escape your life? Start over again with a new name, new friends, new everything?"

"I used to wonder if I could. But it was more of an escapist fantasy than anything else."

"That's how it started for me, too. But then I realized I could make it my reality. At first I thought about just moving away. I've always wanted to live somewhere on the west coast, close to the ocean. I wouldn't mind the space from my parents. I love them, of course, but sometimes distance is good. Helps you grow into your own person."

"But you decided to do more?"

"She inspired me." Aubrey taps the cover of her book, which is now sitting in my lap. "The woman I found as I poured my heart out onto paper. I realized I could *actually* disappear. Being a Stallard comes with built-in enemies and a lot of social pressure to be perfect. A ruined reputation could hurt the family business. But being Isabella DuPont offers nothing but freedom and a clean slate."

"So you're going to start over?"

"Completely."

Tilting my head, I try to work through a way to make that happen. "I don't understand. How are you going to do it if you're marrying Ludo?"

"I'm going to die."

My stomach sinks. "What? Aubrey, no. Why—"

"Oh, not *literally*, silly. I'm going to fake my death."

Instantly, my chest feels a thousand times lighter. "Oh," I breathe out. "Wait. But you said you only wanted distance from your family. This is a lot more than that."

"They'll be in on it. And while I'm leaving Ludo immediately, I'm not faking my death right away. The plan is for me to go into hiding and start my new life as Isabella DuPont without anyone's knowledge. My parents and Ludo won't like it—I'm well aware—so once I'm safely out of reach, I'll contact them and update them.

"The details aren't relevant right now, but my plan is to make it look like I'm taking a year to travel—sometimes with Ludo, usually without. After that, I have a couple other ways to make our marriage look real without me actually having to be present. I already avoid existing in the public eye, so it won't be too hard to fake.

"After about a year, that's when we're going to fake my death. A car crash in a small European town, I think. The familial tie will be established enough that everyone will think of my parents as being under Ludo's protection, so they'll be safe until they're done working this case."

"And you'll be free to live as Isabella DuPont the whole time?"

She smiles. "Correct. That's the thing about this deal—as long as it *appears* that I'm happily married to Ludo, my parents still get his protection, and he still gets their network."

"But they have to be on board for it to all work, correct? Ludo and your parents?" I ask.

Aubrey nods. "They'll get detailed instructions once I know they can't find me. And trust me, they'll go along with my plans. Otherwise, everything they've been working toward will go to shit. They can keep up the ruse of our marriage without me. They all lose if they don't."

In the passenger seat, Elliot turns to look at us. "Sorry to eavesdrop, but it's impossible not to hear the two of you in here. Aubrey, I wish you the best, but how are you going to make sure Ludo can't find you? You know he'll try. This will be a huge hit to his pride, and he'll hate that you disrespected him like this."

"You haven't put the pieces together?" Her voice carries a hint of surprise.

"No," he says, frowning. "I don't have enough information."

"Who's the best at making people disappear?" Aubrey asks, prompting him in the right direction.

For a moment, Elliot stays as lost as I am. But then his eyes light up, and he smacks his forehead with his palm. "How didn't I see it before?" he groans. "Sparrow is helping you."

"Bingo," Aubrey says with a proud grin. "She'll help me get a new identity and start my new life. As long as my parents and Ludo keep up with the lie and follow my instructions, everything should work perfectly."

"When are you planning on doing this?" I ask.

"The night of the wedding."

My jaw drops. "That soon?"

"I'm not putting my future on hold for anyone," Aubrey says as we pull into a parking spot at the resort. "Not for my parents, and *definitely* not for Ludo."

We get out of the car, and Rhett takes my books again. For some reason, that simple action sets off butterflies in my stomach.

"You won't miss your friends? And your parents?" I ask as we make our way across the lot.

"Oh, of course I will. Everyone who moves across the country does. But I also have lots of friends who know me as Isabella DuPont. Now

I get to meet them and actually *be* her. And once I know my parents won't try to stop me, we'll find a way to see each other a couple times a year. Without Ludo knowing, of course."

"I guess that's a fair point."

"And doesn't it sound fun?" Aubrey's eyes are full of wonder as she stretches her arms out like she's trying to fit the whole sky between them. "Getting to start over, building your life from scratch, going on new adventures . . . ah, I can't wait."

"It does," I say quietly, glancing at the guys. "I suppose, in a way, I am doing that. Minus the whole faking my death thing."

"I'm glad," she says, and her voice is sincere. "You deserve to find who you really are, and you owe it to yourself to *be* who you really are. My only regret is that I won't be around to watch you grow personally."

"I think I'll miss you," I confess. We've known each other for a few days, but we've clicked so well.

"I'll send you post cards, or letters." She gasps. "Maybe even your own poems! But before then, we still have a couple weeks to hang out. You can even come to my wedding, if you'd like. Actually . . . I think it might benefit us all if you're actually *in* my wedding."

"Let's wait to continue this conversation," Elliot says. "Aubrey, why don't you come up to the penthouse with us. It offers the best privacy we'll find here."

As we get closer to the hotel building, I notice a familiar figure sitting on a bench. His long sleeves and pants hide his wounds, and his sunglasses obscure his face, but it's definitely Andrew. As smoothly as I can, I look away, noticing that Rhett and Elliot are already staring straight ahead.

Once we're upstairs, Oliver sweeps me into his arms and gives me a kiss hello before doing the same to Elliot and Rhett. When we left this morning, he was still sleeping. Rhett says Oliver was up late working, which had me worried, but he's his usual cheerful self.

"I see you found some gems at the bookstore," Oliver comments, picking up the pink book. "Oooh, this looks fun! It's ... ah. Poetry."

Aubrey and I both burst into laughter at his disappointment. "I'm the author," she manages to wheeze out.

Oliver's eyes widen. "Oh, shit, I'm sorry. I didn't mean—"

She waves off his concern. "No worries. I'm well aware poetry isn't for everyone. But your reaction? Whew! Priceless."

Elliot checks the time on his phone before gathering all of us around the kitchen table. Rhett has already grabbed his laptop, and he's frowning at the screen.

"Aubrey, I'm curious about the rest of your plans," Elliot says. "I'm assuming you're not telling us all this for shits and giggles."

After catching Oliver up on everything Aubrey told us in the car, she gestures to me. "Like I told you a couple days ago, Ludo has severely underestimated me." She pauses, then admits, "Okay, I gave him reason to not even consider me when it comes to business-related things. So I'm able to eavesdrop on a lot of his conversations, and I've even stolen some stuff off his computer. That's what I'm giving Sparrow in exchange for helping me disappear. Information and secrets."

Oliver perks up, and the hope in his eyes warms my heart. "So you could feed us information as well."

"Better information than you'll get from leaving a pair of sunglasses lying around."

We all stare at her in silent shock.

"H ... *how?*" Elliot asks.

Aubrey rolls her eyes. "You think I wouldn't notice a pair of sunglasses lying around that aren't mine? Besides, I saw Wren holding them, but I never saw her actually wear them. Suspicious, don't you think?"

I groan and sink into my seat. "I knew I was gonna fuck this up somehow."

"What? Oh, no, Ludo is completely unaware. You think he pays attention to what my sunglasses look like? He usually ignores me—and I do the same to him."

"Fair point," Elliot mutters.

"Here's the thing, though. If I'm going to do this, then I—"

"Wait," Rhett says. He looks up and nods to his laptop, his expression hardened. "We have a problem."

Chapter Nineteen

Elliot

"What do you mean, we have a problem?" I stand and circle the table so I can see what's on Rhett's screen. "What the . . . how did you gain access to these feeds?"

"Finn helped me. I couldn't sleep last night."

"Oh." The word is steeped in disappointment, and I clear my throat in an attempt to sound normal. "Right, okay. So what's the problem? Everything looks fine."

Rhett points to one of the resort's security camera feeds, which is currently recording two men who're standing next to the private elevators that leads to the penthouses.

"They're not guests," Rhett says. "I've looked through a decent amount of the footage, and I don't recognize them. As far as I know, no one is staying in the other penthouse, and I haven't seen them check in."

"Then how did they get a key card to the elevator?" Oliver asks.

Rhett's jaw ticks. "They stopped in the lobby to speak with Andrew before heading straight for the elevator. I didn't see him pass anything off, but it's too late to go back and check again. We need to assume the worst."

"They could just be Ludo's men on their way to pick me up," Aubrey says nervously. "Right?"

"He would've given us a heads up." Rhett gestures for her to come closer before pointing at the screen. "You recognize them?"

"No, but he has a lot of employees. They can't get in here, right?"

"I wouldn't count on that," Oliver says. He's already in motion, standing and pulling Wren from her seat. "You two, come with me. We need to get you out of the line of fire."

"Line of . . ." Wren doesn't finish the sentence. "No, but you guys—"

"This is our job, princess. We'll be just fine." He doesn't stop moving, grabbing Aubrey's wrist and pulling them into Rhett's bedroom.

Rhett grabs his laptop and follows. "They just got into the elevator," he calls. "We have thirty seconds, max."

After pulling my gun out, I crouch behind one of the couches. I'm out of view of the door, so if they come in with guns blazing, they at least won't be able to aim directly at me.

"We can't kill them," I say. "Ludo will want to question them." I glance to where Rhett is hiding just inside the doorway to his room. He's attaching his suppressor to the end of his gun.

Fuck. Mine is still in my room. "Rhett, I don't have—"

"I've got it," he says calmly. "Just stay down until I move. Oliver, the girls?"

"Locked in the bathroom," he replies as he skirts around Rhett and dashes into my room. "I'll knock over a nightstand."

When the two men walk into the penthouse, they'll pass Oliver's hiding spot pretty quickly while facing the general direction of me and Rhett. It should work well for what we've set up for—as long as we time everything perfectly.

Oliver is barely able to slip into the bedroom before we hear the *beep* of the key card reader. The door unlocks, and it swings open.

"Where are they?" one of them whispers as two sets of footsteps sound against the hard flooring. "Andrew said he just saw them come up here."

"Showering? Taking a group nap? I don't see them out on the deck."

"We just need to find her and get out of here."

The door shuts quietly, and their footsteps come closer. My pulse picks up as I keep my eyes on Rhett. Gun in hand, jaw set, and barely moving, he waits.

Seconds tick by. The footsteps get even closer.

And then we hear it—a loud *thud* from the room behind them.

The perfect distraction.

Rhett doesn't hesitate. He leaves the safety of the doorway and shoots twice. I'm up and moving before he fires the second shot.

Both men are on the ground. One has dropped his gun, but the other is simultaneously clutching his bleeding thigh while trying to aim at Rhett.

"Drop the weapon," I snap, aiming my own gun at him. Shooting it isn't the best idea since it'll be much louder, but I step forward with confidence. *"Now."*

"Shit," the man hisses before setting his gun down.

"Slide it over," Rhett demands as he steps closer. "You, too." He nods to the other guy, who's been inching toward the gun he dropped.

After they both slide them over, Rhett kicks them farther away. "Oliver?"

"Got it." Oliver steps out of the bedroom and starts searching the men. He pulls out a smaller gun and a knife and adds them to the pile.

Once we have them tied up, Rhett grabs his laptop and starts going through the security footage, no doubt making sure these two men are working alone. Oliver grabs two belts, tightening them above their gunshot wounds. Rhett hit them both in the thighs, and the last thing we want is for them to bleed out on us.

As Oliver works, I pull out my phone and call Ludo. It rings and rings, and I'm afraid it's about to go to voicemail when he finally picks up.

"Holloway."

I don't bother hiding my irritation. "Was this another one of your goddamn tests?"

"What are you talking about?"

Well, that's a relief.

"You'd better get up to the penthouse quickly. I've got two men here you're going to want to question. You're gonna need a way to get them out of here discreetly."

Ludo swears before hanging up.

"Anything?" I ask Rhett.

"So far, so good," he replies. "I don't see anyone else who looks suspicious."

"They have access to the security camera footage," one of the men groans to the other. "That's how they knew we were coming."

My heart stutters at that realization. If Rhett hadn't hacked in and been keeping an eye on things, the past couple of minutes could've gone way worse.

"Rhett," I whisper.

"Don't let your mind go there." He drops a kiss to my forehead. "Go check on the girls. Oliver and I have this handled."

In the bedroom, I knock on the bathroom door. "Hey, it's Elliot. It's safe now."

Slowly, Aubrey unlocks and opens the door. Wren is clutching one of the candles the resort provided, and she's in position to throw it at my head. When she sees I'm alone, she sets it down, and the glass jar *clangs* against the counter.

"Oh thank god." Without a moment's hesitation, Wren throws herself into my arms. I'm taken by surprise and stumble back with a grunt. "You're okay?" She pulls away and looks me over frantically.

"What? Love, of course I—"

Oh. Right.

I forget that Wren hasn't seen us in action much. She has no idea how smoothly we handled the situation out there. In fact, all she *has* seen is us failing to protect her when Jordan took her.

Reassuringly, I circle my arms around her waist and press my lips to her temple. "We're all fine. Could've taken them down in our sleep. Now come on, there's no sense in you two hiding in here anymore."

"Is there blood?" Aubrey asks weakly as she follows Wren into the bedroom. "I don't do well with blood."

"There is. If you'd prefer, you guys can stay in here. Just a heads up, Ludo is on his way."

They stay in the bedroom—understandably. Wren looks curious, but I don't think she wants to leave Aubrey alone.

We've left the two guys on the floor where they fell. No sense tracking blood anywhere else. I crouch down in front of them, ignoring the way they're squirming in pain.

Our job is to keep Aubrey safe, and we've effectively done that. Any information Ludo needs, he can pull from these men without us. But if we have an opportunity to learn more about Ludo and his enemies, we can't pass it up.

"The way I see it," I say, "you have two options. One, cooperate and tell us what you want with Ludo and Aubrey. Or two, keep your mouths shut until Ludo tortures you to within an inch of your life. He's not known for his kindness."

"We're aware," one of them snaps.

"At least tell us who you're working for. Maybe that'll placate him."

"We'll take our chances."

With a chuckle, I stand. "Sure."

When Oliver searched them, he found their wallets, too. I go through them, snapping pictures of their IDs. No doubt, they're fake, but they could lead us somewhere helpful.

"I hear Ludo lets his victims sit in pain for hours. Days, even." I drop their wallets back to the floor with their weapons. "And you two tried to come after his fiancée. I wouldn't be surprised if he's crueler with you."

"I said we'll take our chances," the same man growls.

"Suit yourself."

It's not long before my phone vibrates, so I pull it out of my pocket.

Ludo: We're here. Let us up.

Right. Grabbing one of our key cards, I say, "I'm gonna get Ludo."

I take the elevator down to where Ludo is waiting on the ground floor. One of his men is with him, dressed in a hotel uniform and pushing a laundry cart.

"You got that together quickly," I say.

"Best to always be prepared," Ludo replies, tapping his temple and smirking.

There's barely room for all three of us in the elevator, but the ride up doesn't take long. Once I've gotten us all inside the penthouse, Ludo sighs at the two men on the floor.

"Recognize them?" Rhett asks.

"No." Ludo frowns, circling them with his hands in his pockets. Then he grins. "But I'll be getting to know them *very* well soon enough." Slowly, he crouches down to look one of the men in the eye. "You look like you're planning on keeping your mouth shut."

He doesn't give him a response.

Ludo shrugs, and his grin widens. "No worries. The longer you refuse to talk, the more fun I get to have."

I turn away to hide my grimace. These two men, most likely, were going to hurt Aubrey in some way. For that, they deserve to be put through hell. But the type of hell Ludo brings . . . it's a level of agony that only the lowest scum of the earth should have to suffer through.

Ludo stands. "Where's Aubrey? And Wren?"

"Bedroom," I answer. "Didn't want to be around the blood."

"Right. I forgot about that."

Beneath his cool exterior, I imagine Ludo is seething. He's a master at keeping his emotions under wraps, but I've been watching the man for long enough to at least somewhat understand him. Coming after his fiancée like this was a major act of disrespect—one he won't take lightly.

Ludo looks over the three of us. "You've earned my trust, so I don't suspect any of you." Gesturing to the men on the ground, he adds, "Obviously."

Oliver narrows his eyes. "But?"

"Very few people knew where we'd be this week." Ludo's voice is reserved, as if he's lost in thought. "If someone knew where to find us, that means I've got a rat. And rats . . . they get the worst punishment of all."

My mind immediately goes to Andrew. Somehow, he's caught up in all of this. If he's somehow connected to the rat—or he's stupid enough to *be* the rat—then he's in deep trouble.

It can't be him. That just doesn't make sense.

I don't look at Rhett. Can't. I'm not sure how long he'll be able to keep his composure for, so the best thing I can do is keep Ludo distracted.

"Do you need us to keep an eye on Aubrey while you deal with them?" I nod to the laundry cart.

"That would be helpful." Ludo sighs. "And then we'll need to get packed up and leave. I can't deal with these two properly until I'm home, and I'm not moving forward with any business until I know who among us is a traitor."

"Of course. Just text me when you're ready for us to bring Aubrey to the condo."

Ludo uses some kind of sedative on the guys before we load them into the cart. Thankfully there are plenty of sheets already in it to cover them up with.

Once they're gone, we rush to clean up the blood. We need to finish our conversation with Aubrey before she leaves.

"We'll have to get the proper chemicals to get it completely off," I say as I scrub my hands clean. "But it'll do for now. I'm not sure how long we have until Ludo texts us."

Since the coppery smell still lingers in the air, we decide to finish talking outside. Rhett can't stop pacing.

"You said you could give us information," Rhett says to Aubrey. "Up until you leave, correct? Which you're doing the night of the wedding?"

"Correct," Aubrey replies. "But I need to know—are you planning on stripping Ludo of his power? Because if you do that . . ."

Fuck. "Then your parents won't have anyone looking out for them."

"I can't take part in this if I know it'll hurt them," she says.

"What if we protect them?" Oliver suggests. "I mean, we can't right now. Not until we're finished with Ludo. But after that, we'll have the availability, and we could keep them safe until their case is over. We don't wield the power Ludo does, but most people know not to fuck with us. And the ones who don't know usually find out pretty quickly."

"You think that'd work?" Aubrey asks, glancing between all of us.

"We'll make it work," Rhett says, his tone firm. "We need as much information on Ludo as we can get, and we need it quickly. If this is what we have to do, then so be it."

Wren perks up. "Once Ludo is dead, will you come back?"

"No," Aubrey says with an apologetic smile. "This marriage is only one of the many reasons I want to escape this life. I'm tired of it all, Wren. Like I said, being a Stallard comes with a lot of expectations. If I'm anything less than perfect, it could hurt my family's business. I want my parents to succeed—I truly do. But I want to live my life *my way.*"

"And being Isabella gives you that opportunity."

With a nod, Aubrey takes Wren's hand. "Like I said, I'll write you. But I don't want to stay in Philadelphia, and I don't want to be a Stallard anymore."

"So that's it?" Rhett finally stops pacing. "You give us information, and we keep your parents safe for the duration of their case once Ludo's dead?"

"Almost," Aubrey says. "I need one more thing."

"Go on," I say. There's little we wouldn't do to get Andrew and Benny away from Ludo faster.

"I can't sneak out of Ludo's mansion without help. Getting past his security is beyond my capabilities." Aubrey turns to Wren. "That's why

I think it makes sense to have you as a bridesmaid. You'll have a reason to be there early *and* a reason to stay late, if needed. And, you know, I like you a lot."

A single glance toward Rhett, Oliver, and Wren tells me none of them have any objections. This could be the breakthrough we've been looking for—the final piece that gives us access to everything we need to ruin Ludo.

"It's a deal," I say as my gaze returns to Aubrey. I find that the hope shining in her eyes transfers to me, too. And when I look to Oliver, he's grinning with relief.

"This is it," he says. "This is finally it."

"I can't believe it," Rhett mutters.

"What?" Wren glances between all of us.

Taking her into my arms, I kiss her. Then I pick her up and spin her around. My shoulders feel lighter than they have in years, so much so that I half wonder if I'm about to float away.

"What is it?" Wren asks again as I set her down. "What can't you believe?"

"We've finally reached it, love," I say, leaning down and kissing her again. "We've finally reached the beginning of the end."

To be continued...

Deleted Scene

If you want to read one of the deleted scenes from Wretched Corruption, go to subscribepage.io/wc-bonus and sign up to my email list.

Author's Note

Thanks so much for reading Wretched Corruption! The story will continue in Ruthless Desires 5. There will be 6 books total in the series.

A special thank you to my sensitivity and beta readers (you guys are the best), and thanks to everyone who gave me song suggestions for the playlist. It turned out *much* better than it would've if I'd been compiling it on my own.

If you'd like to stay up to date with my latest writings and adventures, you can check out my website elirafirethorn.com or follow me on Instagram, Pinterest, and TikTok @elirafirethorn.

Also By Elira Firethorn

Dark Luxuries Trilogy

Deepest Obsession
Twisted Redemption
Darkest Retribution
Dark Luxuries Epilogue

Ruthless Desires Series

Blissful Masquerade
Perfect Convergence
Undying Resilience

Standalones

Moonflower

Printed in Great Britain
by Amazon